GOBLIN SLAYER

11

©Noboru Kannatuki

©Noboru Kannatuki

"By the way, why *did* you bring your chain mail into the bath…?"

This foreign steam bath
was the perfect thing
after exhausting
themselves in the desert.

"...Ahhh...
Humans
think
of the
strangest
things..."

Contents

©Noboru Kannatuki

GOBLIN SLAYER

✦ VOLUME 11 ✦

KUMO KAGYU

Illustration by
NOBORU KANNATUKI

YEN
ON
NEW YORK

GOBLIN SLAYER

KUMO KAGYU

Translation by Kevin Steinbach ✣ Cover art by Noboru Kannatuki

GOBLIN SLAYER vol. 11
Copyright © 2019 Kumo Kagyu
Illustrations copyright © 2019 Noboru Kannatuki
All rights reserved.
Original Japanese edition published in 2019 by SB Creative Corp.
This English edition is published by arrangement with SB Creative Corp., Tokyo, in care of Tuttle-Mori Agency, Inc., Tokyo.

English translation © 2021 by Yen Press, LLC

Yen On
150 West 30th Street, 19th Floor
New York, NY 10001

Visit us at yenpress.com ✣ facebook.com/yenpress ✣ twitter.com/yenpress
yenpress.tumblr.com ✣ instagram.com/yenpress

First Yen On Edition: March 2021

Yen On is an imprint of Yen Press, LLC.
The Yen On name and logo are trademarks of Yen Press, LLC.

Library of Congress Cataloging-in-Publication Data
Names: Kagyū, Kumo, author. | Kannatuki, Noboru, illustrator.
Title: Goblin slayer / Kumo Kagyu ; illustration by Noboru Kannatuki.
Other titles: Goburin sureiyā. English
Description: New York, NY : Yen On, 2016–
Identifiers: LCCN 2016033529 | ISBN 9780316501590 (v. 1 : pbk.) | ISBN 9780316553223 (v. 2 : pbk.) |
    ISBN 9780316553230 (v. 3 : pbk.) | ISBN 9780316411882 (v. 4 : pbk.) | ISBN 9781975326487 (v. 5 : pbk.) |
    ISBN 9781975327842 (v. 6 : pbk.) | ISBN 9781975330781 (v. 7 : pbk.) | ISBN 9781975331788 (v. 8 : pbk.) |
    ISBN 9781975331801 (v. 9 : pbk.) | ISBN 9781975314033 (v. 10 : pbk.) | ISBN 9781975322526 (v. 11 : pbk.)
Subjects: LCSH: Goblins—Fiction. | GSAFD: Fantasy fiction.
Classification: LCC PL872.5.A367 G6313 2016 | DDC 895.63/6—dc23
LC record available at https://lccn.loc.gov/2016033529

ISBNs: 978-1-9753-2252-6 (paperback)
        978-1-9753-2253-3 (ebook)

10 9 8 7 6 5 4 3 2 1

LSC-C

Printed in the United States of America

GOBLIN SLAYER

❖VOLUME 11❖

GOBLIN SLAYER

† CHARACTER PROFILES

"I am to goblins what goblins are to us."

GOBLIN SLAYER

A strange adventurer active on the frontier. He is famous for reaching Silver (3rd) rank hunting only goblins.

"Protect, heal, save."
—The Three Holy Tenets of the Earth Mother

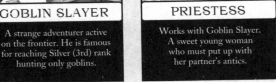

PRIESTESS

Works with Goblin Slayer. A sweet young woman who must put up with her partner's antics.

"Ignorance is bliss, for learning is the highest joy." —Elven proverb

HIGH ELF ARCHER

An elf girl who adventures with Goblin Slayer. A ranger and a skilled archer.

The only things that matter to her are the weather, the animals, the crops...and him.

COW GIRL

A girl who works on the farm where Goblin Slayer lives. The two are old friends.

"How can you go adventuring without pen and paper?"

GUILD GIRL

A girl who works at the Adventurers Guild. Goblin Slayer's preference for goblin slaying always helps her out.

"Before they're polished, jewels and precious metals all look like rocks. No dwarf would judge a thing by its appearance alone."

DWARF SHAMAN

A dwarf spell caster who adventures with Goblin Slayer.

"A naga does not run."

LIZARD PRIEST

A lizardman priest who adventures with Goblin Slayer.

"Train yourself: kill with the blade. If blood flows, let it be the enemy's."—First of the "Secrets of Steel."

HEAVY WARRIOR

A Silver-ranked adventurer associated with the Guild in the frontier town. Along with Female Knight and his other companions, his party is one of the best on the frontier.

"Only a tangled skein awaits those who carelessly spin tales about love or the universe's mysteries...not to mention a woman's beauty."

WITCH

A Silver-ranked adventurer at the frontier town's Adventurers Guild.

"I won't make friends tomorrow with an enemy I respect. I'll do it today."

SPEARMAN

A Silver-ranked adventurer at the frontier town's Adventurers Guild.

"Love does not consist in gazing at each other, but in looking outward in the same direction." —A poet

SWORD MAIDEN

Archbishop of the Supreme God in the water town. Also a Gold-ranked adventurer who once fought with the Demon Lord.

©Noboru Kannatuki

Long ago they scattered our sand like the stars,

then lay to rest on a faraway brilliant land.

Bend an ear to hear our whispered words:

a tale of the sound of the wind…

The particles of sand that leaped into the air caught the moonlight and sparkled like gems.

Was it simple escapism to entertain such thoughts when they were so inappropriate to the time and place? Regardless, it only lasted a second. The horse-drawn carriage crashed back down to earth, and I frowned as I nearly bit my tongue.

It was hard to call this conveyance a *horse*-drawn carriage anyway. It was being pulled by a kelpie with a mane of froth. And it didn't have wheels such as one might imagine on a carriage; it had runners. It was effectively a sleigh.

"GGORRRORB!"

"GBG! GGROOROGB!!"

And with the riders jabbering behind, one could be forgiven for seeking a bit of escapism, even if it was in the middle of a getaway. Maybe it wasn't even proper to call them riders, these diminutive soldiers mounted on dogs.

"Ha-ha-ha! Hell of a thing, this. How'd we get into this mess anyway?"

"I'm not sure this is a laughing matter."

I pulled my overcoat tighter around me and stole a glance at the two rogues having their jaunty conversation. A man in a military cap who looked like a spy held a crossbow at the ready, watching vigilantly out the back of the carriage. Beside him was an elf girl with red hair, her own overcoat pulled almost to her eyes; she seemed at ease despite the careering vehicle. I could hardly believe she was the same race as I. Could even a noble elf become thus if she grew accustomed enough to life in the urban sprawl?

In addition to those two, there was the young man driving, a cleric girl, and a wizard who didn't look quite right. I still mistrusted the princess's decision to put her life in the hands of such rogues.

"Can't you use the gun like you usually do?"

"Could, but it's gonna take more than one or two shots to finish this." The spy grinned, then pulled the trigger on his crossbow. There was an audible *snap* as the mechanism deployed, then several bolts went flying.

"GORGB?!"

"GGBBOOGB?!"

The little arrows pierced the riders' leather armor, and they were unhorsed—or perhaps that would be undogged—and tumbled out of sight. The spy seemed to handle the crossbow easily despite its considerable recoil; he remained alert even as he produced more ammunition. There was a click as he readied the new rounds, and he shrugged with remarkable cool for someone who had just killed several opponents.

"Besides, there's all this shaking. Could never get a solid aim with a pistol."

"Hey, are you insulting my driving?" the well-built driver demanded. He was a sprite-user who was controlling the kelpie.

The spy was unmoved. "I'm just saying none of us are used to all this sand."

"Hot during the day, cold at night, isn't it," the elf said, but she didn't sound too upset; she even smiled. "How about you? Doing okay?"

"In all honesty, I'd like to get away from this," replied a petite human girl. I thought I recognized the holy symbol bouncing at her chest as the mark of the God of Knowledge. The girl had been meditating in a corner of the carriage; she must have returned her flying spirit to her body to give this answer. She wiped the sweat from her forehead and, sounding somewhat put out, added, "…I mean the climate *and* our friends out there."

"Still more coming?" the spy grumbled.

"Yeah," the cleric replied with a nod. "They're as fired up as we are. They don't have any wizards or priests, but they do have numbers. More than ten of them, I'd guess." The girl must have used some kind of miracle, for she sounded as if she had observed them firsthand. But then she gave the spy a puzzled look. "Can't you see them with your Bat Eye?"

"Don't wanna," he said, frowning openly.

"Now, now, you have to face reality," came an unexpected voice. It belonged to a strange creature that had popped its head out from among the luggage. It looked like some wizard's familiar, and it had been the go-between that brought these rogues and us together—or so I was told. I was not, however, especially pleased to trust my destiny to this bizarre thing and some master who refused to show their face. I had no idea how these rogues could trust a wizard who got no closer to danger than length of their familiar.

"Now, I understand this may not seem like the most opportune moment, but I'd like to review the terms of the assignment." Almost as if it could read my mind, the creature glanced at me. "We were to get you out of that castle and deliver you to the nearest village. Does that sound right?"

"Indeed. We don't intend to lean on your skills beyond that."

"You know that means we can't help after this no matter what happens to you, not even if you get caught by bandits or slavers or something."

"Don't be ridiculous," I said. "Nothing so foolish would befall us." I puffed out my chest.

The elf wizard frowned, but I was only interested in having something done about the situation we were in at this moment. These people the princess had retained to aid us, people whose names we didn't even know, were at this moment, our only lifeline. My colleague—my friend—beside me grinned and whistled. This was why nobody liked rheas.

"Eek?!" I exclaimed involuntarily. An arrow tore through the curtain and buried itself not far from me. Apparently the small riders had come within bowshot. Now I could hear the rhythmic whizzing of arrows slicing through the air, more and more of them smacking into the carriage. Our vehicle looked all but defenseless. As far as I could see, we were doomed.

"A-anyway!" I shouted. "Your reward has been paid in advance, so at least earn it!" Even I knew that the best we could hope for if we were captured was to be put to forced labor in the mines.

"Don't have to shout," the spy said nonchalantly. Then he kicked a bundle of rope off the luggage rack. It bounced across the sandy ground like a ball, coming loose and wrapping itself around the legs of some of our pursuers.

"GOOOOOBG?!"

"GR?! GOGBB?!"

They were stuck in it like flies in a spider's web. As soon one of them tumbled, he got the others caught up with him. Even the sounds of the ones who were busy mocking their companion for his ineptitude soon faded behind us, and that was it for them.

"Never hurts to be prepared," the spy sniffed. Then he leaned out past the curtain, crossbow and all, and called to the driver, "Can't you get any more speed out of this thing? Might not be so lucky next time."

"Kelpie'll get ticked off and go home," the driver replied. "And you owe me for that rope."

"Be happy to compensate you for it, if you can pull your weight as our sprite-user."

"Too many wind sprites around here. If this was a coastline, I could run all the way to the edge of the board; easy."

"Oh," the elf, who had been deep in thought, said suddenly.

"What's up?" the spy replied.

"...Mm, just a thought."

I looked at the elf suspiciously. In my opinion, spell slingers were hardly different from stage magicians. The spy didn't so much as glance at her; he remained focused on aiming his crossbow. "Think we can turn this around in one fell swoop?"

"I swear on the great magus Garfield's Power Nine."

"Good by me."

That was the entirety of their conversation. He didn't ask if she could actually do it. For the spy, the brief chat appeared to be enough; he grinned and pulled the trigger of his crossbow. There was another *bap-bap-bap* of arrows flying, and more of the riders were swept away.

"GGBOORGB?!"

"GRORB! GGGBORGB!!"

That didn't eliminate all our pursuers, though. The enemy showed no sign of letting up. They weren't courageous exactly. They just believed they were different from the idiots who got shot.

"Hmph, popular guests we have…," the cleric of the God of Knowledge said in an exasperated tone. She waved a hand in the air and said quietly, *"O Guardian of the Candle, smile upon my light, which bows not before ignorance, stupidity, faithlessness, or pride."*

A bluish light darted through the air, followed the arc of her fingers, and settled directly in front of one dog's nose.

"GOOGB!!"

"GOOBGBR?!"

The riders struggled to control their quailing mounts, whereupon the crossbow sang out again. Our pursuers were in no position to dodge the bolts, which lodged in their necks and sent them tumbling to the ground. More riders leaped over them, though, howling and brandishing weapons as they surged forward. Witnessing this, the girl who served the God of Knowledge smiled coolly. "Did that help you conserve your arrows a little?"

"Don't think you have to worry about that anymore," the spy said, pulling some kind of cylinder from his hip. "Those were my last shots."

I was agog at the poor planning and the indifference, and my eyes only got wider at what happened next. There was a *thump* so great I could feel it in the pit of my stomach, and the carriage was filled with a blinding flash of light followed by equally obscuring smoke.

"GOOGBR?!"

One of the riders had actually laid a hand on the luggage rack of the carriage, but he now tumbled away, his head looking like a smashed fruit. The spy must have braced the cylinder against his bent left arm and then let loose with it.

"What a barbaric weapon…!"

Maybe I sounded more derisive than I had meant to, but the spy shrugged and produced a package wrapped in oilpaper, also at his hip. He tore it open with his teeth, emptying the fire powder and balls into the mouth of the cylinder. Then he tossed the bundle to the floor of the carriage and calmly took up position again.

Terribly frustrated—*not* frightened, I assure you—I looked at the elf. She was just muttering something with her eyes closed; I didn't think I had seen her do any actual work before this moment. I opened my mouth to speak, thinking I would give her a piece of my mind, but my rhea friend tugged on my arm, stopping me.

"What? You think I should keep out of it?" I said. I was about to remark that this was hardly the time, but I was stopped by the girl's voice, which suddenly seemed overwhelming.

"*Caelum…ego…*," she intoned with tremendous clarity. Even I, who had no propensity for magic, knew they were words of true power. The faint jangling of the gold charm around my neck proved it. Wind began to spin up at her words, and I felt the air itself tremble. She was an elf—of course she would control the wind. "*…offero!* I offer up the heavens!"

As the girl concluded her spell, a great gust sprang up. It was a damp, heavy wind.

The mounts were more sensitive than the riders. All of them stopped in their tracks to look up at the sky.

"GORGB…?" After berating their animals for a moment, even the riders noticed the change in the atmosphere and looked up as well.

Great black clouds spread across the horizon. There was a sound like the grumble of a thunder dragon. And then: *splish.* The first drop of the spell hit the earth.

Rain.

Rain slammed into the sand so hard that it blocked out all sound and sight until the world was as dark as ink.

It didn't do damage, of course. It was just rain—a monsoon. The riders realized this soon enough and began to laugh, putting the spurs to their dogs.

"KEEEEEEEEELLLLP!!"

But their confidence was misplaced. The kelpie whinnied proudly as its hooves struck the sand, and it took off at a full trot. It went faster, then faster again until it was swifter than the wind, speedier than the rising of the sun; it traveled like a storm. The foam from its mane flew even into the passenger compartment of the carriage, forcing me to blink. My rhea friend was cackling and whistling and clapping.

While I sat totally silent, my fellow elf girl let out a breath.

"Nice work," the spy said, and the girl smiled and nodded.

"Thanks," she replied. "Now we just have to run."

"Leave that to me," the driver cut in. "You've heard of running between the raindrops? Well, we *are* the raindrops!"

"I'll keep an eye out the back anyway, just in case," the cleric of the God of Knowledge said, patting the creature, which had taken up residence on her knees. "I doubt the Bat Eye works in the rain anyway."

"Spare me your sarcasm." The spy frowned, then grabbed one of the enemy arrows that had come through the curtain. He put it and the rest in his quiver—perhaps this was what passed for preparation with him. I questioned whether they would be useful, being longer than normal ammunition, but he seemed bent on using them regardless. He continued in a light tone: "Eh, if they catch up to us..."

"They won't," the driver said. "And I'm going to remember the rope."

The spy shrugged without so much as a smile and changed tack: "If anyone *new* shows up, I'll have these ready for them. You get some rest."

"I'm not that tired," the red-haired girl objected, but then she smiled shyly and nodded. "Well, I should make ready anyway... I want to maintain this rain for a while, too." With this earnest acknowledgment, she sat down in her corner of the carriage and pulled her knees up to her chin. She wasn't looking at me or my friend or even her fellow rogues but somewhere in the distant sky. Realizing now that she was a Rainmaker, I privately revised my estimation of her.

After a while, the wizard girl said, as if she found it all vaguely entertaining, "Still, that was my first time doing...that..."

"Sounds dirty," the cleric chided.

"Huh?" the girl said, but then she realized and went red up to her long ears. "I—I didn't mean it like *that*...!"

"Hoh-hoh-hoh-hoh! Well, you are getting to that age. Spring is coming!" The small creature chortled merrily from the cleric's knees. Then it turned around once and flicked its ears. "I get it, though. Runners don't often get this kind of work."

"Yeah. Never figured I'd be doing it, actually." The spy loaded his new ammunition into his crossbow, chewing over the words: "Goblin slaying. Feh!"

CHAPTER 1

A Pounding Heart

"I'm sick and tired of goblin slaying!" she announced, slamming a hand down on the round table. *She* being, of course, High Elf Archer. Her ears were thrust back as she made this proclamation; it garnered the attention of all the adventurers and servers in the tavern—but only for a second. They quickly went back to whatever they had been doing as if to say, *Oh, it's that elf again.*

All of which simply meant that the tavern at the Adventurers Guild this afternoon was having a perfectly normal day.

"Are yeh, now? Bet we could find you a nice dragon to kill instead. Or maybe you'd like to become a bounty hunter?"

"Not what I meant, short stack." High Elf Archer waved a dismissive hand at Dwarf Shaman, who was sitting across from her with his chin on his hands, and who had been drinking for the better part of the afternoon. The elf drew a circle in the air with her pointer finger, ears twitching as she muttered something about how he just didn't understand. "These days it's been nothing but goblins, goblins, goblins, goblins, goblins, right?"

"Well, he is *Goblin* Slayer...," replied a petite human cleric also sitting across from High Elf Archer. She smiled awkwardly, fiddling with the cup in her hands, then glanced to one side. Beside her, silently polishing a dagger and a sword of a strange length with an old rag, sat an adventurer. This man, who wore a cheap-looking metal helmet and grimy leather armor and had a small, round shield strapped to his arm, was called Goblin Slayer.

It wasn't clear whether he had been listening to the conversation or not, but now he grunted, "Hrm." Then he added: "I don't see any particular problem with that."

"Ha-ha-ha, no problem, but also no particular stories of adventure, valor, or daring," Lizard Priest said, taking a big bite of the wheel of cheese in his hand. He swallowed noisily, exclaiming over the flavor like the very picture of a dragon consuming a hero.

Dwarf Shaman watched this elaborate show of mastication with a grin, then reached for one of the dishes still on the table. For lunch they had ordered bread, ground pork, and vegetables—all very familiar. As he stuffed a slice of bread slathered with pork into his mouth, Dwarf Shaman pushed the plate of vegetables closer to High Elf Archer. "Watch it, Beard-cutter. Your oil'll get in the food."

"Sorry." Goblin Slayer slid back a bit from the table but didn't stop working. His sword was not a remarkable one, but a single oversight could result in a critical fumble. Heaven forbid the blade chip when he drew it out, or get stuck in its scabbard, or break in the first exchange of a fight.

Lizard Priest, who had briefly ceased his cheese consumption, reached out with a knowing grunt. "Pardon," he said as he snatched a small onion off the plate of vegetables and popped it in his mouth like candy to cleanse the palate. Priestess supposed the way he rolled his eyes in his head was because of the sharp flavor.

Beast people don't seem to eat many aromatic herbs, in my observation.

Not that she was particularly inclined to eat a great deal of the little onions, herself. It wasn't that she disliked them. She enjoyed popping them into her mouth; biting down; and feeling the delightful, vinegary flavor of the little pickled treats melting on her tongue. But a young woman, even an adventuring young woman, does start to worry about certain odors. That seemed to be why High Elf Archer was forever perfuming herself with some flowery smell of the forest. Not that Priestess was jealous of her—well, not *too* often.

"I lost count after ten goblin-slaying expeditions," High Elf Archer

said with a cute little snort, waving a hand at Lizard Priest. "I'm starting to worry being with Orcbolg is going to make me forget there *are*
other monsters."

"We did meet that vampire, and those sasquatches...," Priestess
said without much conviction. She herself wasn't especially dissatisfied
with the current situation—which was something else that seemed to
annoy High Elf Archer.

"Yeah, last winter," the elf shot back. She took a few dainty sips
of her watered-down wine, then sighed theatrically. "Did you know
when we went out to that vineyard, some of the other adventurers got
to fight demons and stuff?"

"That doesn't interest me," came a mutter from Goblin Slayer.
He must have finally been happy with the condition of his weapons
because he put his sword back in its scabbard and his throwing knife
back on his belt. High Elf Archer gave him a look: *You're literally just
going to throw them away regardless.* But he didn't seem to notice. He said,
"While the other adventurers are fighting their demons, it's my role to
take on the goblins."

"Why am I not surprised? To be fair, I guess it would be pretty weird
if you were suddenly all, 'Down with demons!'" High Elf Archer let
out a defeated breath and slumped on the table; the amazing thing
was that even that gesture looked elegant coming from her.

"Feeling a little drunk?" Priestess asked, casually glancing into her
friend's wine cup, then pouring a bit more water into it. "I do have
to admit, we've been doing a lot of perfectly ordinary goblin hunts
recently."

"There's nothing *perfectly ordinary* about doing nothing but goblin
hunts!"

"You think so?"

"I know so!"

Priestess cocked her head, still not quite convinced, and High Elf
Archer looked helplessly up at the ceiling. Even this conversation had
a familiar ring to it, and none of the others in the tavern paid them
any mind. This strange adventurer and his party were just part of life
in the frontier town now. Seeing how everyone else regarded them,

even the novices who had registered just this spring soon took them in stride. Even if more than a few privately agreed it was strange to hunt nothing but goblins...

"Ahh, but it's a pleasure havin' the long-eared lass here," said Dwarf Shaman. "I never want for fine accompaniments to my wine."

Lizard Priest picked up Dwarf Shaman's jar of fire wine and poured it liberally into the shaman's cup. "I can only apologize that you must endure a lizardman pouring for you."

"Not t'worry. I'm afraid havin' an elf wait on me might snap me out of this nice buzz. Might be funny but not much else." He drained the cup with satisfaction, droplets splashing onto his beard—but then he squinted. Perhaps it was because High Elf Archer had suddenly looked up from their drinking party, her ears twitching. Her gaze was pointed toward the entrance of the Guild. A moment later, Goblin Slayer looked as well, followed by Lizard Priest and Priestess.

Three adventurers tumbled through the door of the tavern, each with their own perspective on the situation:

"Finally, finally home..."

"Get ahold of yourself, you're embarrassing us...!"

"Ugh, I'm so hungry. I could hardly take another step!"

The group consisted of a young warrior accompanied by a cleric of the Supreme God, as well as a hunter who hailed from the harefolk. All of them were covered in mud and blood.

High Elf Archer frowned and let out a sound of dismay. Priestess, very much accustomed to this particular stench, just smiled slightly.

"M-my goodness... Was it as bad as it looks?" Guild Girl said, for once emerging from behind the reception desk. She had too much experience of adventurers to let her smile slip, something Priestess admired very much.

Calmed by Guild Girl's unflappable demeanor, the warrior nodded firmly, even though he looked like he might collapse right there in the doorway. "It was rough, but we made it somehow. Those goblins are good and slain."

"Good work," came a short murmur—from Goblin Slayer, of all people, provoking first astonishment and then a giggle from the cleric.

"Good work, sure," she said. "Great work. His club never hit anything but the air, and those sling-stones didn't do much better!"

"Eh, we pulled it out anyway," Harefolk Hunter said nonchalantly. She (they were pretty sure she was a she) had mottled brown and white fur now, which at the moment was in some disarray, with flecks of dried blood spotting her coat. Priestess got up out of her chair, moistened her handkerchief at the tap, then went over to the three adventurers. "Once you've made your report, you'll have to be sure to wash up properly, all right?"

"Ooh, thanks for this," Harefolk Hunter said as Priestess dabbed at her face and hair.

"Look at her, acting all grown-up." High Elf Archer chuckled. "I understand, though. You want to take care of people with less experience." She spoke so softly that Priestess didn't hear her. High Elf Archer wasn't actually criticizing Priestess's sweet-hearted, smile-inducing behavior.

"Whatsoever we may think of our own goblin slaying, theirs certainly constitutes valor and daring," Lizard Priest added with a laugh.

"Ha-ha-ha, you've got that right!" Dwarf Shaman said.

"Yo, tell us all about it when you have a few minutes!" Heavy Warrior called over the hubbub of the tavern. The scout boy and druid girl in his party, who were friends with the warrior and the cleric, didn't appear especially worried. But they must have been happy nonetheless to see their friends come back home. They were smiling and waving.

"You have a successful adventure, you treat everyone to a round—that's the tradition! We'll be waiting!" Female Knight added.

"I like the sound of that!" Padfoot Waitress said, clapping her hands. "That means you'll be ordering *lots* of different stuff tonight, right? Whoo-hoo!"

"H-hey, we didn't make *that* much money on it!" Amid this storm of praise and teasing and shouting, Warrior's face went red; was it embarrassment or something else? All the adventurers, even those who didn't know his name, were shouting to him. Some congratulated him on a job well done, others on his coming back alive, still others complained he had lost them a bet. "Dead pools," gambling on who would bite the dust, were not precisely in good taste, but they were one of the superstitions here. After all, if the object of the bet was lucky, they would "win" by coming home alive. And since they had won, it was a nice excuse to demand a drink from them.

And that was the Adventurers Guild: noisy but comfortable.

"Lively place, this," the harefolk girl remarked as Priestess continued to wipe her fluffy fur.

"It certainly is," Priestess said. "It's always like this." She herself had been suitably overwhelmed by the environment at first, but these days she was entirely used to it. That seemed a little sad to her sometimes, but there was unquestionably a happy side as well. And she felt genuine pride in the Steel rank tag that hung from her neck. "I'm sure those two will be happy, even if they aren't going on an adventure today."

"They're *real* adventurers. When it comes to goblin slaying, we hardly have the right to talk to the Frontier's Strongest," Cleric said with a half smile.

Priestess understood the feeling, but still pursed her lips reprovingly. "I'm sorry, but I think Goblin Slayer is the Frontier's Kindest, no? Here. Hold still."

"I think that's a bit cruel, don't you? …Oh, thank you." Cleric was palpably relieved to have some of the dirt wiped off her hair and face. On the way home from the adventure, she recalled, the warrior and the scout had been so tired, she'd had to be the one to keep an eye out—and she was in the back row.

Yes, you must be tired.

Priestess worked gently at the layer of filth, kind and comforting to this exhausted young woman.

"Oh yeah, yeah. Say, miss, may I tell you something?" Harefolk Hunter asked, her long ears twitching; she also suddenly had a piece of bread in her hand.

"Yes, what is it?" Priestess replied, not pausing in her work.

"Aw, nothin' much," Hunter said. "But over at the town gate, we ran into someone said they were lookin' for you. They're waitin' right there."

"What?" Priestess looked at the door to discover a slim figure in an all-consuming overcoat. The neat curves of this person's legs were visible under their tight-fitting leather pants. And at their hip hung a beautiful silver rapier, almost blinding in its brilliance.

This person regarded the room full of chattering adventurers with what looked like a fond smile. When she noticed she had Priestess's eye, she removed the overcoat, revealing rich locks of honey-colored hair.

"Hello, and pardon me for being away for so long," said the woman—once an adventurer, now a merchant. Priestess let out an exclamation of surprise and joy, abandoning her work on Cleric's face and hurrying over to Female Merchant. She clasped her friend's hand in her own for the first time in much too long.

"What brings you here all of a sudden? None of your letters said you were coming..."

Female Merchant didn't let her pleasure show as openly as Priestess, but it was evident nonetheless that she was happy. "Ah, it's a business matter, one that came up rather abruptly. I must be circumspect about separating my business and personal lives..."

This reunion, of course, did not escape High Elf Archer, who exclaimed, "Well, haven't seen *you* in a while! Don't just stand there chatting; come over here! Orcbolg, put away your toys."

"Oh, I couldn't... Look, you know me. Whenever anything happens, I just come crying to you..." Female Merchant sounded quite embarrassed, but she didn't act it. She let Priestess lead her over to a seat.

"Hrm," Goblin Slayer grumbled, but after he had cleaned up his tools and items, the table turned out to be quite spacious.

"This calls for one thing—more drinks! Yo-ho! Get this girl an ale!" Dwarf Shaman called out, and Lizard Priest added, "Bring some side dishes as well, whatever seems apt. And some cheese."

"I-I'm not very good with alcohol," Female Merchant said as she was ushered into her seat. "Well, all right, thank you. An ale will do." She didn't sound very sure.

Female Merchant probably knew her way around these sorts of situations. Priestess, on the other hand, had a feeling Female Merchant had spent some past life trading barbs with great merchant families or the scions of noble houses. Priestess had always been careful never to ask too much about Female Merchant's former party members, but this much she had intuited. And how fortunate and wonderful a thing it was to have a proper chance to sit down all together and have a drink.

"So what is this business you're on?" Priestess asked, offering some bread and pork.

"Yes, about that." Female Merchant nodded. The dainty nibbles she took of the bread were befitting of a noble upbringing. Unlike High Elf Archer's effortless grace, this was a studied decorum that made Priestess think of a princess. "As a matter of fact... Well, as a point of formality, I intend to go properly through the Guild."

With that little disclaimer out of the way, Female Merchant glanced around the room. The rest of the Adventurers Guild was so busy celebrating the return of some of their own that they weren't paying any attention to this table.

Female Merchant sucked in a breath, her shapely chest moving up and down, then said resolutely: "There's a quest—an adventure—that I earnestly ask all of you to participate in."

Priestess knew immediately what Goblin Slayer would ask next. So, she presumed, did everyone else at this table.

It could be only one thing...

§

"So it is goblins."

"Yes, that's the gist."

"When are you leaving? I'll come with you."

They were seated in the Guild meeting room. Goblin Slayer sat across from Female Merchant; Priestess sat next to him stiff with anxiety. The soft sofa supported her modest behind quite nicely, while her slim legs reached down to the carpet, which was thick enough to swallow her shoes. The shelves all around them were lined with the trophies of great adventurers, mementos that looked down on them.

Priestess reflected on how rarely she came in here, how disconnected she felt from this room. Almost the only times she visited were for promotion interviews.

It was different for Goblin Slayer, sitting stolidly beside her, and her other companions. They were all Silver rank, the third-highest level an adventurer could achieve and the highest rank to be out in the field. They were entrusted with weighty assignments and frequently (Priestess imagined) met with important quest givers here in this room.

But not her. She was still untried, lacking in experience. She could hardly be called a novice anymore, but she didn't believe she quite counted as fully mature yet, either. And yet here she was with Goblin Slayer, privy to the details of this quest. Her Steel rank tag left her feeling hopelessly out of place.

Especially with everyone else waiting downstairs...

The presence of Female Merchant across from them prevented Priestess from shifting uncomfortably. She wanted to sit up straight as she listened so that she at least appeared like an adventurer who knew what she was doing.

"As it happens, a large number of goblins have been sighted near the border with the country to the east."

"The east? That would be in the direction of the desert, wouldn't it?" Guild Girl solicitously placed steaming cups on the tabletop as she listened to Female Merchant's story. Guild Girl's tea was one of Priestess's little pleasures. She took a cup in both hands, blowing on it before taking a sip. The warmth filled her mouth. Female Merchant took a saucer with a practiced air, enjoying the tea with all the elegance she usually exuded.

Only Goblin Slayer didn't move. After a moment's silence, he said simply, "Is that so?"

Guild Girl, having taken a seat herself, tilted her head in puzzlement, causing her braids to bounce. "Oh?" she asked. "You don't know it?"

"I don't," he replied, crossing his arms and leaning, armor and all, back against the chair. "I've never left this country."

This was somewhat surprising—and at the same time, somewhat not. Priestess exchanged a look with Guild Girl, then her eyes met those of Female Merchant. None of them could imagine this strangest of adventurers prioritizing a trip to the border over the destruction of goblins near at hand. And most people naturally knew more about their own homes than about foreign lands, even if they had the means to find out about such places, which many didn't. Was it not enough to be familiar with the environs of one's village? Who cared what was beyond the mountains?

Nonetheless, from a Silver-ranked adventurer, it was a mildly unusual pronouncement.

"But if there are goblins, the matter is settled. What's the situation?" Goblin Slayer asked. Priestess smiled as he leaned forward in the same as he always did.

"They aren't exactly a friendly nation," Guild Girl said with a strained expression. She was cognizant that she was, first and foremost, a bureaucrat, a representative of her government. She had to choose her words carefully. "A number of different countries share our eastern border, but that particular nation…" Guild Girl admitted that there were at least roads that reached it, but then she shrugged. "It doesn't have an Adventurers Guild."

Priestess made a sound of surprise. She had heard vaguely of the nation that lay on the far side of the shifting sands, but this detail was new to her.

"They do have adventurers," Guild Girl clarified. "Or at least, people who call themselves that."

What kind of place could it be? Priestess wondered, putting her index finger to her lips. A country with adventurers but without an Adventurers Guild. Over the past two or three years, she had gained much experience and learned many things, but the world was a vast place, and there was still much she didn't know.

Didn't he say once something about there being so many people who knew more about the world than he did? Priestess nodded to herself, remembering something Goblin Slayer had previously said. But if so, one need only listen, look, remember, and learn. Hadn't she learned from her friend, so much separated from her in age, the importance of retaining one's sense of wonder at the unknown?

"But why are relations with that country so bad…?"

"We prefer the term 'not good,'" Guild Girl said pointedly, but she smiled. Diplomacy, it seemed, was tricky. "Anyway, back in the time of the last king—their last king, not ours—people used to come and go between our countries much more freely."

But when possession of the throne changed, restrictions on foreigners in the country tightened. Disquieting rumors implied that soldiers were being levied, weapons and equipment gathered, and an army assembled. During the battle with the Demon Lord, some of the king's soldiers allegedly slipped across the border into this nation, calling themselves mercenaries or a volunteer army or some such.

A group of heroes, who all just happened to be in the same place at the same time, rose up to protect the people— Yeah, sure. It was awfully convenient that so many visitors with fine weaponry, horses, and obvious military training had been around just then.

"Could it be just…" *A pretext?* Priestess was about to say, but wisely swallowed the words.

Guild Girl smiled. Or rather…she pasted on a smile. Priestess nodded. "In any event, that's the situation and the reason things aren't very good between us…"

"But the goblins are multiplying," Female Merchant interrupted in a low voice. The clacking of her teacup somehow sounded like a sword being drawn. "And they're starting to come into this country. We can't let this go on," she said before adding, "It has to be investigated." She then shut her lips tight.

Terror. Fear and hesitation. It would have been easy to see any of these things in the shaking of Female Merchant's clenched fist. But Priestess had also seen the light flare in her eyes. Pale and cold, a chill flame. She thought she recognized it; she took a breath and let it out, expelling everything that clung inside her.

Still, though…

As she breathed, her head started to clear, began to work. A country with which relations were "not good." A desert place with no Adventurers Guild. A land swirling with unsettling rumors.

Goblins entering this nation's territory. Going to investigate. Adventurers going to investigate.

Her quest is…probably something else.

It was something higher than just commerce. Probably higher even

than Sword Maiden; much, much higher. An image of the royal entou-
rage they'd met while delving the Dungeon of the Dead flickered through
Priestess's mind.

In the past, she wasn't sure, but she might have resented such a situation.
But now, curiously, she didn't. It helped that the quest giver was a cherished friend of hers. Someone who was almost—she was too embarrassed
to say this aloud—like a little sister. Priestess knew of the girl's painful past,
and so she was filled with the desire to help, even if it gained her nothing.

A big part of it was having accompanied Goblin Slayer on his negotiations with the Rogues Guild. There were things in the world best
done in the shadows. Things best handled not by the clumsy inter-
vention of a national government but by adventurers. Now that she
thought about it, her very meeting with these rare and precious companions had arisen because of such an incident.

It's a kind of destiny.

The thought made her feel a little easier. Diplomacy truly was a
tricky subject.

So when Priestess asked her question, she did it as politely as she
could, as broadly as she was able. "Wouldn't it be, ahem, the business
of Gold-ranked adventurers to handle such a case?"

Typically, it was those with the rank of Gold or above who handled
matters of national import. Typically.

"Indeed. I was simply hoping I might be able to ask you to act as my
bodyguards while I travel there on a merchant mission." Female Merchant's stiff expression softened unmistakably. Embarrassment, perhaps. Almost shyness. As if to say that she wished to adventure with
them again, even if only in the capacity of quest giver.

I would be thrilled to think that was how she felt. Priestess nodded. Female
Merchant let out a relieved breath.

Guild Girl, though, quickly rained on this parade: "I'm afraid we
certainly can't send someone of Steel rank on such a mission," she said.
Priestess gulped. Female Merchant's face was hard. Guild Girl, however, didn't stop smiling as she ostentatiously straightened the paperwork Female Merchant had given her. Priestess figured this was what
you called a difference in experience. After all, in terms of number

of quests she had been a part of, Guild Girl stood head and shoulders above the others in the room. Female Merchant was used to these situations by now, but she was still the newest member of this group. And Priestess was only slightly more experienced than her.

Priestess looked at the metal helmet beside her. Its owner grunted and said without further hesitation, "But this does involve goblins. So I'll go."

"Of course," Guild Girl replied with a gentle smile. "I'm not objecting to you, Goblin Slayer, sir."

"You don't mind passing on this quest?" he asked Priestess.

"Ahem, however, the quest giver specifically brought this quest to her," Guild Girl explained.

There was some uncomfortable hemming from Female Merchant. Priestess glanced over at her, but by then the expression was already gone from her face. Priestess wasn't exactly distracted by the brief interlude, but nonetheless it took her a second to comprehend what Guild Girl said next.

"As such, I believe this calls for a promotion interview!" She clapped her hands, grinning from ear to ear. This wasn't her pasted-on smile but a real one.

"Wha—?" Priestess blinked. "Promotion? You mean...to Sapphire?!" She jumped out of her seat before she knew what she was doing but then caught up with herself, blushed furiously, and promptly sat back down.

Promotion from the eighth rank to the seventh. This was unquestionably her first step into the middle ranks. She would no longer be "a novice with a bit of experience," but a real, established adventurer. Priestess unconsciously clutched at the rank tag at her neck. Her heart was pounding.

"That's right," Guild Girl said. "You'll be able to travel to such dangerous—" She stopped and cleared her throat. "I mean, less-than-stable areas as this quest requires."

Can I really do this? Priestess wondered. What should she do? What was the right answer? She spotted a flicker in Female Merchant's eyes. "Uh, um..."

Hoping for some kind of help, she turned to Goblin Slayer once more, but he grunted, "Hrm. In that case, I don't believe I should decide whether you accept or not."

He was clearly planning to go regardless of her choice. That was just natural for him; Priestess felt it as a *thump* in her insides. No one was asking her whether she could do this. They weren't telling her not to. Everything, all of it, was for her alone to decide.

One could come up with any number of perspectives and reasons. But then...

Protect, heal, save.

She knew what she had hoped to do by going out into the world. She bit her lip, then drew a breath and said, "I...I'll do it!"

Priestess saw Guild Girl smile happily. Female Merchant's eyes lit up. As for the expression on the face behind the visor of the helmet beside her, Priestess couldn't guess. But the fluttering in her chest was enough for her.

She knew what she wanted: to be an adventurer.

§

"So please, tell us about the desert!"

"Y-yes, sir, please..."

Geez, talk about your ambushes..., Spearman thought, scratching his head. He had only just gotten back to the Guild from an adventure. Returning a withering *what-about-it* look to the glances from other adventurers, Spearman took stock of the situation.

Standing in front of him bowing her head was the priestess from that weirdo's party. Beside her, also bowing (he noted her excellent command of manners) was a girl he didn't recognize, but who he assumed was a noble or the like.

"Heh, heh," Witch said from beside him, openly amused. This was the worst possible situation.

Only choice is to charge in, then.

For one thing, there was nothing less cool than trying to come up with an excuse to run away when a couple of girls asked you for help. And yet... Well.

"Why don'cha ask, y'know, *him*?" That question bugged Spearman. In fact, he sort of felt compelled to ask. He wouldn't be the one risking his life here, so it wasn't appropriate for him to go heedlessly giving advice to another person's party.

"Well, you see..." Priestess scratched her cheek with embarrassment, not quite able to come up with the words. "He said we should ask you two...that you had more experience of other countries than he did."

Spearman gulped. *He'd* said that? Now Spearman's back was really against the wall. *That sonuva*— But Spearman tempered his private annoyance. He could hardly call himself Silver rank if he wasn't ready to at least try to look good for a less-experienced adventurer, especially a girl. Humility was all well and good, but a man with no confidence was a man you couldn't rely on. Outward appearance and inward character, confidence and genuine ability, were two sides of the same coin. Spearman would hate to be without either of them. He was more than a little way from being called a great hero, but he had to be able to respond appropriately to this.

And so with a glance at Guild Girl to make sure the object of his affections was watching, he nodded. "Let's find somewhere to sit down. Wouldn't be a good look for me to make a couple of young ladies stand around."

Pretending it was for his own benefit gave Spearman a fine excuse to transfer them to the bench in the waiting area. Witch followed along, smiling as if she knew everything, but it was too late to worry about her. It had been too late the moment he had swallowed his pride and asked her to help him read and write and to deal with magic spells. She had probably figured him out right then.

Doesn't mean I can go lookin' lazy in front of her. In this respect, Spearman felt his thinking was different from that of the weirdo or even of Heavy Warrior. *Or maybe they'd act different with some newbies around.*

He dismissed this fruitless line of thinking. He personally never expected to take on a pupil or disciple, or to usher a novice adventurer into his party in the name of educating them. Teaching the next generation, that was something he could think about decades from now when he had retired from active adventuring. Nothing more, nothing less.

"So... The desert—that's...what you wanted to...ask, about?" With Spearman absorbed in his own thoughts, it was Witch who started the conversation. She took out her pipe with a smooth, elegant motion, then tapped the end with a finger, lighting it. The violet smoke she exhaled, slow and luxurious, wrapped itself around her voluptuous body as if she had domesticated a breeze. In contrast, the two girls stiffened and squeezed their hands on their knees.

At Spearman's inquiry, the priestess girl said she was on her way from the novice ranks into the middle ones, but...

Eh, I guess that's about how it goes. Spearman suppressed a smile. If you were always just a little concerned as you went forward, it meant you were going about the right pace.

"Yes, ma'am," Priestess replied to Witch's query. "But... Well, we really don't know anything at all, so we don't know what to ask first..."

"I've heard it's so hot that it's recommended to bring something to block out the sunlight," Female Merchant said.

"Sure enough, it'd be a rough trip without something like that. Even with it, a god of sunstroke can still get its hands on you and kill you off." Spearman said this with an intent to give them a little fright and received a gratifying "Huh?" from the girls, who looked at each other.

"Um," Priestess said hesitantly. "Do they have those there, even though there aren't mountain passes?"

Gods of sunstroke were widely believed to be a kind of demon that lived in high mountain passes. They clung, unable to be dislodged, to the backs of those who labored out in the heat. They would suck dry the spirit and vitality from the body until the victim grew faint and ultimately died. There was no agreement about what they were: the spirits of those who had died of starvation, evil ghosts from the depths of the earth, or perhaps something else entirely.

Spearman had encountered these creatures once or twice. Back when he had acquired some metal armor for the first time and put it on without really thinking it through—back when he was less experienced than he was now. When he thought back, he remembered old mercenaries at the tavern in his hometown recounting with laughter how often knights, even in the military, would simply topple from their horses and die.

"You ask me, they're probably some sort of spirit of illness," Spearman said, but then he made a motion with his hand as if to wave away the entire subject. Gods of sunstroke were no big deal if you knew how to deal with them. Eat some provisions, have a drink of water, and rest for a bit in the shade; that was all it took. Of course, there was no shade in the desert, so you had to be especially careful. "Anyway, it's more than just hot, the desert," he added. "Gets mighty cold at night."

"Cold?" Female Merchant said, blinking. She looked a little pale somehow. "You mean...as cold as the snowy mountain?"

"Yes..." Witch nodded. "About that cold, I would...say." Was Spearman the only one who noticed Female Merchant shiver at this? A bad memory, perhaps. Her fingers brushed a spot on the back of her neck. "And...so," Witch went on with a sweetheart glance in Female Merchant's direction, "you take a thin...light, cloth, you see? And cover yourself. From head...to toe."

"Not exposing any skin, that's the smart play," Spearman explained. "Nothing's out in the open, nothing gets burned." He glanced at the girls' pretty faces. It would be a true shame for such pale, fine skin to swell and redden with sun or frost.

Precious treasures ought to be protected. Spearman repeated for emphasis, "Top and bottom, remember. Have a nice, thin overgarment made. Something loose, made of hemp."

"What do you mean 'and bottom'?" Priestess asked, puzzled.

"It's for reflection," Spearman answered.

Until they saw the way the sun sparkled off the sand for themselves, they would never understand. Priestess, though, put a finger to her lips and said, "I see. It really is like going to the snowy mountain..."

Oh yeah... I guess she's been to that mountain a couple of times. Spearman remembered she had joined that warrior and his cleric friend as part of their party on a trip to the snowy mountain. *Well!* Spearman felt himself smile a little. She really was gaining some experience.

Fighting monsters wasn't the only way to accumulate experience points. Personal growth meant more than just improved abilities or new skills. People who didn't understand that had a tendency to rush ahead and wind up dead. But this girl, he saw that she was taking the true path and making a fine job of it.

Even if she may not see it herself. And who could blame her, surrounded by Silvers like she was...

"Is there anything else?" Spearman was pulled back to reality by the piercing, direct question. He realized Female Merchant was looking at him with eyes as clear as glass. As if the rapier at her hip wasn't evidence enough, this look was proof that she was no callow child. She, no less than Priestess, had acquired some real experience.

"Oh, sorry," Spearman mumbled. There was much to teach them. "First off, quicksand. The only thing quick about it is how fast it'll drag you under..."

Then there was the wind to warn them about. The monsters that lived in the desert. How to travel. How to rest. The desert towns. Whatever questions Spearman couldn't answer or whenever he forgot something, Witch would jump in with her own advice. It was all knowledge they had gained by going places they didn't know and didn't understand and simply failing again and again.

He had no intention of giving all this up without a reward. Anyone who expected him to, didn't understand the true value of this knowledge. But helping someone trying to go farther down the path, that was different. At least Spearman thought so.

Female Merchant nodded along seriously, writing in a notebook with a pencil, providing a constant, scratching background noise to their conversation. Beside her, Priestess was repeating everything Spearman said quietly, committing it to memory. The only things they really had in common were their honey-colored eyes and their gold hair, yet, to Spearman, they came to look like sisters. He pictured them returning safely from their adventure...

Yeah, I like that picture.

Witch's interest seemed suddenly piqued. She gave a motion of her pipe and exhaled some smoke. "Say. You, do you...not need to...write anything down?"

"Oh, no, ma'am," Priestess replied smoothly. "I wouldn't want the information getting into anyone else's hands. That could mean trouble."

Spearman looked up without a word. All he saw was the ceiling.

"Is something the matter?"

He didn't worry about who had voiced the question. Maybe Female Merchant, maybe Priestess. Maybe both.

"...Nah, never mind."

Well, he *did* mind, but... No, it was fine. He would just let it go. It wasn't his responsibility.

"Gygax!" Spearman cursed under his breath, then resumed telling the girls what he knew. Witch chuckled softly beside him, and it sounded to him like the laughter of some god.

§

He's working pretty late today, she thought, stilling the hand that was stirring the stew and gently stretching her arm. She looked past the canary in its cage, out the window. In the evening gloom, she could just see an orange light seeping out from the shed.

He was there. Just knowing that brought a bit of a smile to her face.

It was nothing unusual for him to come home late. He was often out on adventures, after all. Even on his days off—if they could be called that—he tended to go out, or at least help with chores around the farm. Her thought about "today" specifically was simply because he was cooped up in the shed.

He'd been there all afternoon, ever since he had come home and then announced that he had something to investigate. He'd gone into the shed with a selection of the great many books he'd received some years ago. Most of them had been donated to the Adventurers Guild; she had even helped move them, but now...

Books, huh?

She was actually impressed he could read. She herself knew her letters; she had learned by stumbling imitation. Sums, too, she could handle some of. It came in handy around the farm. But reading a real book, that was difficult. Studying was hard. One could certainly survive without learning things, but to live better, she suspected learning was crucial. Take the meeting her uncle was attending tonight. One had to understand commerce.

It's got to be tough on him, she thought, then smiled at herself for acting as if it had nothing to do with her. At the moment, it didn't. But how much longer would that be true?

Her uncle was getting on in years. She tended to picture him as he had seemed to her in her younger days, but when she took an honest look at him now...

Well, there were a lot of challenges.

She let out a sigh and smacked herself on the cheeks. Time to get her perspective back.

"All right!"

With a purpose determined, it was best to move directly into action. Fretting and dragging your feet would eventually leave you paralyzed. That's how it always was.

She nodded to herself with conviction, then clawed through the shelves until she found their camping oven. A small cast-iron object, it was literally a portable cooking device made to be used when camping. She put some of the stew from the big pot into a smaller one and closed it with the lid, then took a couple of slices of bread. She made sure to grab a spoon, wine jar, and cup, and then, with the pot of stew dangling from her other hand, she went outside.

Now, that's a summer sky. She looked up at where the twin moons floated in a sea of stars. The breath she exhaled gave no hint of fogging but joined the cool breeze that swept through the humid air. The gentle murmur of the farm was all around her. In the distance, she could hear the mooing of some restless cows. If she strained her eyes to look down the road, she could see the lights of the town in the distance.

She spent a moment drinking in the familiar scene, then pattered over to the shed. Squinting against the light that poured out from within, she pushed the door open gently to a quiet squeak of hinges.

"...Hey, I've got dinner, okay?"

"All right."

That was his entire answer. But for once, his voice didn't sound muddled.

The shelves were packed with items she couldn't identify, and he sat

at the far end of the little shed. He was turning the pages of some kind
of book by the light of a lamp.

He wasn't wearing his armor or his helmet. The sight of him quietly
but intensely engaged tugged on her heartstrings. Not wanting to dis-
turb him, she entered and closed the door behind her as quietly as she
could.

"What's that you're reading?"

"I'm researching about the desert."

The desert? It took her a second to understand the word, and she
looked at him in puzzlement. The desert. Just desserts. Justice. Des-
erts. Ahh—the desert.

She came to the end of this chain of associations—but she also came
to the proper meaning of the word. She had never expected he would
be researching anything other than goblins. Though when they had
been small, of course, he had pestered his older sister with questions
about all kinds of things.

"I've found a book that appears to include stories from that country,
but they're mixed in with stories from a variety of other places," he
said, shaking his head as he flipped the pages. Magic lamps and spirits, a girl of cinders. "It's like an old acquaintance of mine once told
me...you will never know until you go and see things with your own
eyes."

"You mean you're going to the desert country next?"

"I expect so."

"Huh..."

Wonder what kind of place it is.

She remembered hearing, long ago, that the desert was part of the
country just over the eastern border and that there they rode donkeys
with lumps on their backs or something...

When she mumbled this aloud, he mumbled back, "Seems that's
true."

I was sure it was just a story...

One thing a desert was sure to have was lots of sand. She frowned,
trying to picture sand as far as the eye could see. She had never
encountered anything of the sort, though, and the image in her mind's
eye wasn't much more detailed than a child's scribblings. Finally she

abandoned the half-formed vision. She sat down heavily, leaning against his back. She felt him, firm and warm, behind her. "Your dinner's gonna get cold."

"I know," he said and a second later added, "I'll eat it in a moment."

She thought about that for a second, then laughed; there was nothing she could do. They had known each other a long time, even if there were five years missing in the middle. She knew immediately that he was mulling something over intently.

"Is it a tough place, this desert?"

"I don't know," he said. "I've never been."

"Oh, that's right," she replied with a nod, and he responded in the affirmative.

"It's a whole other country. Your first time in another country. That's amazing." She clapped her hands, a show of innocent pleasure. She herself had never been to another country. It was really something.

He did take me to see the elf village, though.

She didn't think that was exactly the same as a foreign country. A wonderful place, the sort of place some people might never see in their entire lifetime, and a cherished memory, certainly. But actually going to another nation to do what one was going to do—what was that if not an adventure?

"You've never been there, either." His words were short. They almost sounded like a grunt, like he was squeezing them out. "I thought it might be best to ask…if you minded or not."

"Oh…"

I get it. So that was what he meant. Ages ago, she had gone to a town he had never been to. It had become a fight and the last she had seen of him for a long while.

Now their positions were reversed. And that was why he seemed a little nervous. She smiled as she connected the dots. She turned, and before he could grunt at her, she had her arms around his head.

"…What?" He sounded troubled. Somehow, she found it terribly amusing, and she mussed his hair enthusiastically. She was surprised to find he didn't resist her but took the mussing like a docile puppy.

"Hey. You want to be an adventurer, don't you?"

"…"

©Noboru Kannatuki

There was no answer. But she didn't really need to ask.

"Then you have to adventure."

She pulled his head close and whispered the words into his ear. Once again, there wasn't a response right away; she didn't expect one.

After a long moment, he asked, "…Is that so?"

"Sure is," she responded, then, nodding, added "Definitely" for emphasis. "And to help you on your adventure, I think you should eat the food I so thoughtfully made for you and then get a good night's sleep before you set out."

"…Hrm," he grunted but once again didn't resist. She pulled the stewpot over to them, opened the lid, and shared the bread and stew with him. The stew had gone a little cold, but even so it was a labor of the heart.

It always would be.

CHAPTER 2

FREEWAY WARRIOR

"Good health to you, scaled priest."

"Mm. And may you find fine battlefields, yourself."

The one-eyed woman who was the commander here said her final farewells to the adventurers, and then their carriage went racing over the border and into the Mid-world.

It had been just over a week since they set out from the frontier town. The sky was blue, the wind carried the smell of the fields, and the journey was quite pleasant overall. And best, the horses and carriages Female Merchant had acquired were of the highest quality.

When Priestess pictured a carriage, a luggage rack and curtain were the extent of the accoutrements she imagined, so she was taken aback by her current conveyance. It had silk cushions lining benches on which one could recline at ease, and it was wide enough to stretch out one's legs. And the way it hardly shook at all! There were springs under the floor, explained Female Merchant, who held the reins. Priestess's reaction to this was:

"Springs?"

That was all.

Her discomfort at having no idea what sort of mechanism was involved did not last very long. After all, to go from riding almost amid the luggage to this most luxurious of carriages made her feel like a princess.

There was that carriage the archbishop rode in, but that was made to be discreet...

This— *This* was different. It was the very best carriage the head of the Merchants Association could requisition. Priestess was enjoying this very rare opportunity.

"Hrrrm..." By contrast, High Elf Archer was puffing out her cheeks. "She seemed awfully friendly with you," she teased Lizard Priest, her long ears twitching. *"Awfully* friendly. You know her from someplace?"

"Oh, an acquaintance from long ago," Lizard Priest said with a slow shake of his head, evidently unmoved by High Elf Archer's tone. "Ahem—though when I say *long ago,* I do not mean a century or two."

"Yeah, yeah, I get what you mean," High Elf Archer replied, sticking out her modest chest. "You short-lived people think of fifty years as a long time, right?"

"Ha-ha-ha-ha-ha-ha-ha!" Lizard Priest laughed openly in earnest acknowledgment of this truth. Or perhaps he had taken High Elf Archer to be making a joke. "I might call her a former comrade in arms...or perhaps a former employer."

"So a friend of yours?"

"Indeed."

"Huh, really," High Elf Archer murmured, then lay back on her seat. That might sound somewhat uncouth, but the elf made it look downright elegant. She appeared to be quite at home, virtually of a piece, with the resplendent carriage.

And so it was not her behavior that caused Dwarf Shaman to snort but her clothing. "Yeh weren't able to do anything about that outfit, lass?"

"Huh? There's nothing wrong with my outfit," she retorted. She kicked her feet and was upright again in an instant. The clothes she had on were altogether different from those she normally wore.

They were going to a foreign nation and adventuring in a desert at that. They had each prepared their gear. Goblin Slayer wore a mantle over his usual armor to help block the sun, as well as he might. The light would heat the metal, and the best he might hope for would be to end up a little cooked; but if he wasn't careful, he could die inside that armor.

High Elf Archer, however, had really gone whole hog, as it were. She was wearing a long-sleeved, long-hemmed shirt made of a thin cloth and leg coverings of the same. There was even a cloth wrapped around her head. A belt tied around her waist kept it all together. It looked easy to move in, but…

"I knew yeh were busy buying *something* at the capital. And you wonder why you don't have any money."

"Coins are like seeds, my dear dwarf. If you just hold on to them, they'll rot. Getting them out there, that's what makes them useful."

"…I hate to admit it, but once in a while you actually say something sensible."

"It'd be weird not to let them grow," High Elf Archer muttered under her breath, and Dwarf Shaman finally threw in the towel. He shrugged, a gesture High Elf Archer took as an admission of defeat. She flicked her ears happily and poked her head out toward the driver's bench. "Thanks for getting this together," she said, holding out her arms to show off her outfit. "I figured if we were going to another country, I wanted to look like I belonged. I love it!"

"Oh, er, of course…," Female Merchant said, taken off guard by this burst of approbation. "Think nothing of it. I don't know much more about this place than you do… If you like the clothes, that's what matters." The slight flushing of her ears indicated that she wasn't entirely unhappy with High Elf Archer's compliments. Priestess smiled a little more, then decided to lend her dear friend a helping hand. She herself was very unused to praise, after all.

"I don't know much about commerce, but don't you handle a lot of things from foreign countries?"

"I handle many and see even more. But I rarely try on the wares…" Female Merchant was visibly relieved to return to a subject she had some experience in. "Even less do I…*ahem*…" She took a moment to find the words. "…go to a shop and have something made for a friend."

"It's not the same thing?"

"Not at all. I was nervous."

©Noboru Kannatuki

Priestess giggled while Female Merchant rubbed the nape of her own neck, looking down in embarrassment. There was no one here who didn't know what marked that spot. But for just that reason, she was able to be this relaxed with them, and that made her happier than anything.

"Man, I should've invited you when my big sis got married." High Elf Archer kicked her feet with some disappointment. Did the abrupt change of subject, the inability to remain focused on one thing for long, come of her being an elf or simply her being her?

A little of both, probably, Priestess thought and smiled, catching Female Merchant's eye. Female Merchant grinned back.

"Hmm?" High Elf Archer said.

"Oh, nothing. It's nothing, is it?"

"No, no. Nothing at all."

"Oh yeah? Fine, fine," the elf murmured and looked out the window, but then she suddenly clapped her hands, exclaiming "I've got it! You'll have to go to my home after this. They're right in the middle of a celebration, and I'm sure they'd be happy to see you!"

Female Merchant looked uneasy. "Er, ah… Are you quite certain?"

"Sure I am!" High Elf Archer's ears sprang up, and she drew a circle in the air with her finger. "I'll write you a letter of introduction! 'Cause I dunno if I can go with you. We can have a dress made for you and everything!"

"Th-thank you…very much."

Female Merchant bowed her head respectfully while High Elf Archer bubbled with plans. Priestess watched the two of them, thinking, *A letter of introduction. In other words, proof that she's friends with an elf princess.*

She could only imagine how that young elf king would react. At least his wife, she was sure, would be quite pleased. After all, how could they fail to love this innocent little sister?

It happened just as Priestess was having this thought.

"Wow…" Her eyes went wide as she saw the scenery outside the carriage. The green fields that had accompanied them for so much of their journey suddenly gave way to stretches of white sand. "That's incredible… I thought it would change over more gradually."

"Me too. I haven't actually seen it in person before," Female Merchant replied with a nod.

The scenery had changed totally.

We've come such a long way. Confronted by the blue sky overhead, a sky that seemed unusually low and close, Priestess couldn't resist the thought. Sticking her head out the window, she found that the air was hot and dry. Truly, she was far away now from the western frontier of her kingdom.

"...It might be about time to put the snowshoes on the wheels," a voice muttered. It was, needless to say, the one who had been silent until that moment: Goblin Slayer. High Elf Archer chided him for suddenly bursting into the conversation, but he didn't appear to care.

He stretched his arms and legs slowly, then began to cinch down the fasteners on his grimy armor and helmet. Priestess quickly followed suit, making sure her chain mail, which she had loosened for the journey, was likewise tightened down. Relaxing fastenings during moments of rest was a long-standing rule she had learned from him.

"Y-you've been awake this whole time?" Priestess asked.

He replied with a quick nod. "I've only been napping. Once we leave our nation, the chance of goblin attacks will be very real... Hey."

"Yeah, right away." It was Female Merchant who answered this time. With a motion of the reins, she got the horse to slacken its pace and then come to a halt. Behind them, the carriage bearing the luggage likewise stopped. Goblin Slayer looked out the window to make sure, then turned to Dwarf Shaman and Lizard Priest.

"What should we do?" he asked.

"Think that's obvious. Eh, Scaly?"

"Indeed, there is only one thing..."

The three men looked at one another, then promptly stuck out their fists, their hands forming various shapes.

"...Hrm."

It was Goblin Slayer who, grunting, left the carriage. It would be his task to attach the snowshoes to the carriage wheels.

§

High Elf Archer diffidently watched a bird wheeling far above her in the sky. "Snowshoes. Why do we need snowshoes?"

Quickly bored inside the stationary carriage, she had clambered out and onto the rooftop. She spent a moment or two remarking on how peaceful it was but was soon craning her neck to see what was going on with the wheels.

"I've never used them on sand before. There are no guarantees."

High Elf Archer might have been thoroughly impatient, but Goblin Slayer, for his part, appeared completely calm. He laid boards with some sort of twisty piping attached to them just in front of the carriage wheels, then signaled to Female Merchant with a wave of his hand. She nodded and edged the carriage forward, provoking a "Yipes!" from High Elf Archer on the roof.

"On the snowy mountain, carriage wheels, like one's feet, can become stuck in the snow and unable to move. It may be the same with sand."

"Yeah, that's great. You're big on hedging your bets, aren't you, Orcbolg?" As the man in his armor pulled up the edges of the boards so they grasped the wheels, High Elf Archer jumped down over his helmeted head. She didn't even kick up sand as she landed, just took a few dancing steps forward. Leaving no footprints, of course—she was a high elf, after all. "...Don't think we need them, though."

"Then we'll know more about them next time."

"Yeah, sure." High Elf Archer grinned and shrugged. The meticulous streak in this strange adventurer was hardly new.

"How's it look, Beard-cutter?" Dwarf Shaman called out the window, although he didn't seem to feel the question was really necessary. These snowshoes had been made by dwarves, you see, and he was more than confident that there would be no issues with them.

"We'll have to run them to be sure," Goblin Slayer answered with a shake of his head. "I may not have attached them the right way."

"I'm sure yeh followed the instructions, but instructions ain't always perfect."

They had used several of the luggage straps to secure the runners against the weight, but there wasn't a very obvious way to tie them. It might seem humorous if they were to fail, but the resulting cascade of luggage could all too easily tip the carriage over. If you simply laughed this off as stupidity, then you would never make progress or find ways to improve. Dwarves knew better than anyone that steel could only be tempered by heating, pounding, and then cooling it.

Dwarf Shaman leaned his stubby body out the window as far as he could to inspect the carriage wheels, then gave a nod of approval. "Be best if we could change the horseshoes, too…"

"Horseshoes," Goblin Slayer repeated softly. He had the knowledge, of course, but not the know-how. "Does one change horseshoes for the desert?"

"What I hear, sand dwellers use round shoes for their horses. Maybe to keep the horses from sinking in the sand or maybe to take the burden off the hooves."

"Hmm." Goblin Slayer grunted at this explication. If and when he got back, he would have to ask the owner of the farm about this. That person knew far more about domestic animals than he did. "For the time being, perhaps we can simply wrap their hooves in reed-woven hoof covers."

"Make sure they get water, too. And let them graze now, while they can." Then Dwarf Shaman glowered at the sun blazing above them. "And see if yeh can do it before you cook in that armor of yours."

"That's the plan."

In the distance, High Elf Archer could be heard complaining about how hot it was.

The driver of the luggage carriage behind them was making similar preparations for the desert. "Want me to take care of the horses?" High Elf Archer asked when she saw this. She was met with an indifferent "Please do" from Goblin Slayer. She bounced over to the horses and spoke a few words in a language that did not belong to people.

Goblin Slayer silently busied himself affixing the snowshoes to the second and third wheels. Each phase of the job was accompanied by the creaking of the carriage moving back and forth, and inside Priestess had a finger to her brow, striving to commit everything to memory. Someday—someday, she might come to the desert herself to fight goblins. Not that she could readily imagine it, but that didn't mean it wouldn't happen.

And if it does, I'd like to be prepared.

No amount of preparation could make one completely content—
which is to say, completely eliminate worry. But it could, nonetheless,
be helpful. Not all the time or in every situation, but she would be
happy if it sometimes helped.

"…Still, I thought it would be more…you know, like a sleigh." This
was another conundrum she wanted to resolve.

Lizard Priest rolled his eyes in his head and leaned forward, amused
by her mumbled words. Inquiries from the next generation were
always gratifying. "There is ofttimes more than one way to approach
things, that is all it means," he said.

Carriages, for example, might have two wheels or four; they might
be pulled by one animal or several. They might be designed primarily
to carry luggage or focus on speed as the owner wished. There was an
endless number of possible variations.

"The particular choices we make are not right, nor are they wrong.
Such is the way of the world."

"I see…" Priestess nodded. This made sense to her.

"What's more, sometimes a flaming stone from the heavens may
crash suddenly down upon us."

The point being that unexpected things happened in life. So saying
this, Lizard Priest took out some provisions—no, perhaps it should be
considered a light snack—consisting of a bit of cheese and started in
on it.

Priestess watched him exclaim over his food with a fond smile, then
decided to ask her next question. "I wonder how the people here live."

"Hmm… Perhaps we will discover the answer when we arrive.
Horses, for one thing, cannot live without grass." Lizard Priest twisted
his long neck in perplexity, but ultimately wrapped his tail up comfortably. "A horse's legs spring from water and grass. So perhaps these
folk have some other mode of conveyance. Let us see…"

"…I'm given to understand they have lumpy donkeys they ride,"
a small voice said from the driver's seat. Priestess looked over to see
Female Merchant fiddling with the reins. "And it seems that much as
horses cannot live here," she went on, "their donkeys cannot live in
our lands."

"Oh-ho," Lizard Priest rumbled, much intrigued. "You've dealt with these creatures before?"

"Just once," Female Merchant said. "It was unable to walk very well and quickly took ill..."

Priestess thought hard, but unable to come up with a response to her own question, she asked it out loud. "Um, these lumps, they're... on the donkeys' heads?"

"No. Their backs," Female Merchant clarified. "They form two hills, if you will."

Wow... Priestess breathed, impressed, trying to picture it. It seemed her image of unicorn-like donkeys had been rather mistaken. "You know about so many different things. It's really wonderful," she marveled.

Female Merchant didn't precisely contradict her, but her ears went red. Priestess giggled, which only seemed to embarrass her friend more.

Not long after that, Goblin Slayer climbed back into the carriage with an "I'm done." And then with a *whoosh*, the carriage set off over the sands, making a road where there was none. The only markers anywhere to be seen were half-buried statues of the Trade God and other patron saints of traveling. They had little choice but to rely on these markers, without which they might well wander into the desert and die of thirst.

In spite of this risk, Priestess—accompanied by High Elf Archer and Female Merchant, too—was enchanted by the scenery. The sun was falling lower, its light turning red and dyeing the sand a mellow pink color. The red and blue of the sky mingled into purple, and the clouds caught the last of the light, turning them a blazing white.

Meanwhile the wind brought not only a fiery heat, but a mysterious, sweet aroma from somewhere.

"That smells like...flowers," High Elf Archer said, her mind clearly elsewhere. "Like flowers that only bloom after the rain. Who knows when they bloomed last? But it's like the smell never left."

It was almost impossible to believe, but she was right: It was the aroma of flowers.

Who knew there were flowers in the desert? Priestess could smell it, too, the slightest hint of a floral scent amid the blowing sand. "That's...really something," she said.

"Yes... It really is." The whisper came from Female Merchant on the driver's bench. She looked out over the faintly crimson world, blinked a few times, then rubbed the corners of her eyes. Something glimmered on her rosy cheeks.

For some reason, this made Priestess unaccountably happy.

§

"...Huh, what do you think that is?" Female Merchant inquired suddenly as evening was closing in and all around was turning to shadow. There were no inns in the Mid-world. They would have to camp.

It was then, however, that in the darkness ahead of them they discovered a figure of some kind blocking the path.

"A goblin?" Goblin Slayer asked instantly, leaning toward the driver's bench. The silhouette, gradually becoming clearer as they approached, did indeed have a humanoid aspect.

"I don't think so..." Female Merchant, ignoring the pungent odor of the metal helmet, shook her head, sending ripples cascading through her honey-colored hair. "But I can't be sure. I can't see well enough."

"Understandable," he said. Then he called, "Hey, you!"

"Hey, *who*?" High Elf Archer growled, her ears twitching in vexation, but she traded places with him near the driver's bench. Back in the passenger compartment, Goblin Slayer quickly checked over the fasteners of his armor.

"Do you think we'll have to fight...?" Priestess wondered aloud, likewise making sure she had everything she needed. Maybe she was imagining the possibility that they would have to jump from the speeding carriage. Her movements were quick and efficient.

"Can't be sure—only sure I don't like it," Dwarf Shaman said, taking a gulp of wine and then licking the drops off his fingertips. He looked as unperturbed as ever. "Might be a man, might be a monster. 'Round here, a rank tag from the Adventurers Guild won't get you anywhere."

"Ha-ha-ha, indeed, indeed. A lawless wilderness is this..." Even

Lizard Priest acted indifferent to the situation, which made Priestess furrow her brow. This wasn't fear. Nor was it hesitation. Anxiety, perhaps.

I don't like the smell of it.

That was her thought. If she had to, she might compare it to the moment on an adventure when she stood before the entrance to a cave. It was that same weird tingling sensation that ran down her neck.

"I see armor. Shields... spears, maybe." High Elf Archer was looking hard, whispering back to the others. "Ten people. There's a carriage stopped up ahead."

"There is?"

"They're waving at us— They want us to stop, too."

"Sounds like a checkpoint," Female Merchant said with relief.

This territory didn't precisely belong to either nation, but both sent out patrols. Even here in another country, the sight of soldiers was at least somewhat reassuring. The travelers might not have the backing of the Adventurers Guild here, but Female Merchant had the patronage of her nation. She carried a travel pass bearing the seal of the king as proof of her identity. She would simply present it and explain that she was a merchant traveling with her bodyguards...

She turned to speak through the opening behind the driver's bench. "They might want a cut of what we're carrying. A few coins should do the trick." That was the way of the world. "First, we'll head for the nearest city. We might not make it tonight, but at least we can be there by tomorrow. Then we can find out more about—"

As she began to slow the carriage, though, High Elf Archer cried out, "Speed up!" Female Merchant looked at her with confusion. "Just do it!"

"What? But... But what about the checkpoint...?"

"Forget it," Goblin Slayer said pointedly from inside the carriage. "Go!"

"R-right!" Without further argument, Female Merchant cracked the reins. The sharp sound was followed by a whinny and then the clopping of hooves as the carriage picked up speed. Priestess almost tumbled over, thrown back against her seat by the sudden acceleration. She looked out the window to see the soldiers shouting something and coming after them to stop them. But the carriage was tremendously quick; Priestess couldn't even catch what the men were saying.

Strangely, even the elf and the rhea on the stopped carriage were shouting at them.

Wait... What?

Something was wrong. Priestess blinked. Did she feel funny about bursting through a checkpoint? Feel it was wrong? No, that wasn't it. Those were—

"Robbers?!"

"Thankfully, those others shouted at us to run," High Elf Archer said, sliding back into the passenger compartment and taking up her bow and arrows. "What's the plan? You want to do this?" she asked Goblin Slayer.

"Only if they come after us." He was the party leader, even if almost by default. His answer was quick. He knew full well that it was far better to act now than to come up with a brilliant plan later. "We came here to slay goblins. Not thieves."

"Hmm," High Elf Archer said, but nonetheless began stringing her great yew bow. Readiness came as easily as breathing to an elf. But not to Priestess. She worked her hands open and closed on her sounding staff uneasily. "Shouldn't we go help those people...?" she said.

"Eh, I doubt their lives're in danger," Dwarf Shaman responded, stroking his beard. "But I'll admit it ain't an easy choice," he added with a frown. "Those bandits've gone to all the trouble of dressing up like soldiers to help 'em do their thieving. Don't think they'd do anything too impulsive."

"Indeed," Lizard Priest agreed. "One might even presume that should we intervene, they might feel driven to take hostages or even start killing."

"Maybe..."

Could the others be right? Perhaps this was yet another of those things that simply depended on a roll of the dice. The words *it happens all the time* flashed through Priestess's mind. Could it really be true? She had been asking herself that question for two or three years now. And she still had no answer.

Some people said an answer found too easily was no answer at all, but...

"We do still have a problem," Female Merchant said, in a voice tinged with worry. Sweat beaded on her cheeks as she raced the carriage through the darkness. "We've been running these horses all day. And at night it's going to get quite cold...or so I've heard."

The situation was dangerous, and there was no room for error. No wonder she sounded anxious. And it was nearly nightfall. If they didn't find a decent place to camp—well, they might make it tonight, but by the next day they would die. And in the unfamiliar terrain of the desert, even tonight wasn't guaranteed...

"Gosh, you humans are so fragile and you *still* try to live in places like this," High Elf Archer remarked, her tone lighthearted in spite of the situation. She could always relieve the tension.

Priestess tried to let the remark inspire her to laugh a little. Among the things she had learned adventuring was the importance of a bit of easy banter. "The places you elf folk live in are too cramped," she said.

"We live *in* Nature, though. You humans are bent on changing it."

High Elf Archer, smile and all, looked noticeably more cheerful than she did in town. There may not have been any trees in this desert—may have been very little green at all—but it was still Nature and thus congenial to an elf.

Then, however, her expression clouded over and her ears flicked.

"What's the matter, Long-Ears?"

"Quiet." High Elf Archer closed her eyes and frowned, concentrating. "...They're coming. From up ahead."

"Ahead?"

They weren't pursuers? The party looked at one another. A separate group? But they had made too much distance on the thieves to run into a sister band.

Goblin Slayer wordlessly took out his weapon, and Lizard Priest settled into a fighting stance. Priestess found she could hear it, too: something pounding across the earth in a great hurry, like their own carriage.

Mounted soldiers?

No—she had heard this sound before. Those weren't hooves. They were paws. She heard howling voices. And Priestess could think of only one thing that rode animals like that.

"Goblins!"

Across the great, dark desert came the aura of battle.

§

"I knew it."

"Argh, my adventures with you *always* end up this way, Orcbolg!"

"It was a goblin-hunting quest, wasn't it?"

"Yeah, but still!"

Even as she complained, High Elf Archer leaned smoothly out the window and fired off an arrow. The bud-tipped bolt flew straight and true despite the darkness, disappearing across the sands accompanied by the musical twanging of the bowstring. A second later, the carriage plowed between goblin riders clutching a sundered rope. They must have been hoping to trip the horse pulling the carriage, but High Elf Archer's skill with the bow had put a stop to their nasty little plan.

"GGOOOROGB?!"

"GORBG?! GOOROGB!!"

Of course, if that was enough to get them to give up, they wouldn't be goblins. The realization of how powerful their enemies were only made them angry, and anger made them crave vengeance. Jabbering cruelly, the riders hunkered down against the necks of their wargs and gave chase.

"…!" Female Merchant bit her lip while listening to the awful shouts. It was more than simple fear that caused the hands holding the reins to shake. From inside the carriage, though, it was impossible to see how bloodless and pale her face had become.

"Change with me," Goblin Slayer said abruptly. He glanced out the window between the cabin and the driver's bench, issued these three sharp words, then opened the carriage door. Immediately, a great rush of air filled the carriage, howling like a storm. Sand still bearing the last of the day's heat entered the cabin as well, causing Priestess to cough.

"I think…," Female Merchant started, the shaking of her voice almost keeping her from getting the words out, "…I can do it."

But Goblin Slayer wasn't looking for her opinion. "No. I may need you to use spells if the moment calls for it." His voice, as ever, was non-chalant, almost mechanical. "What's more, on this quest you are the quest giver, and we your guards."

"Oh…" The voice Female Merchant heard then was the same one she had heard back on the snowy mountain: the voice of an adventurer. "Yes… Very well." She steeled herself and nodded. She tied the reins to the bench, then slid to one side. As the carriage raced along, she grabbed the railing on top and stepped onto the running board.

It would all be so simple—if the carriage weren't moving. Even at this speed, it wasn't that difficult. But the fear and anxiousness on her face had nothing to do with any chance of falling amid the whirling sand.

"GGR! GOOOGB!!"

"GORGB! GBBGOOB!"

"…Hrgh…"

She could tell the goblins were close. How easily could they catch a horse-drawn carriage on wargs? They were trying to ride up alongside, hoping to drag their foolish prey off the vehicle. She thought she could feel them breathing— No, it must just be her imagination. The howling wind whipped the monsters' noxious breath away. But still Female Merchant couldn't shake the sense that she could feel it just behind her.

She had to move quickly. She knew that. It was dangerous to stop. Of course. But her body wouldn't obey her will. Her neck burned. It hurt. It throbbed.

Her whole body tensed, and suddenly, a dagger went whizzing past her side.

"GOOROGB?!"

The goblin who had been reaching for Female Merchant went tumbling from his warg as if he had been hit with a hammer. She could hear him bounce along the ground, disappearing into a cloud of sand in the distance. Female Merchant resumed working her way along the running board until Goblin Slayer could grab her and drag her inside.

"I-I'm sorry…," she stammered.

"It doesn't matter." He passed the trembling young woman to Priestess with a quick, quiet movement.

"It's all right, we're here with you," Priestess said, puffing out her small chest. "We'll get through this together—again."

"…Yes, of course."

Priestess was relieved to see Female Merchant's expression finally soften a bit. She nodded to Goblin Slayer, who moved his helmet in response. Now it was he who grabbed the railing and leaned out, waving to High Elf Archer. "How many of them?"

"Hold on, I've got to get up top to be sure!"

"Do it."

High Elf Archer scrambled out as nimbly as a squirrel, quickly disappearing from view. Goblin Slayer moved through the darkness to the driver's bench, glaring at the oncoming goblins all the while. His armor made the transition a little safer, and while he didn't have the elegance of High Elf Archer, he still appeared practiced and certain. As soon as he reached the driver's seat, he gave a crack of the reins.

"GORGB! GRORGB!!"

Ignoring the goblins' jabbering voices, he kept the horse running. He didn't look back as he made his calculations.

Caltrops and oil are out of the question with the other carriage behind us.

He didn't even know if oil would have the intended effect when used on sand. Nor was he especially eager to find out. He would not be able to handle this alone. Well, he would simply rely on the others, then. He had a good deal of help these days.

"I think we can presume this means their nest is close… What do you think?"

"I much doubt that the little devils have the mettle to endure the desert cold," Lizard Priest said, sounding far calmer than the situation appeared to warrant. There could be few in the Four-Cornered World who knew more of battle than the lizardmen. "Nonetheless, as to whether we might scatter and destroy them… Well, I daresay the terrain is on their side."

"I want information, but they aren't the only ones we can get it from."

"The little devils are too ready to talk anyway. A quick tongue is hardly to be trusted."

"We exterminate them, then."

"We do as we always do."

The two storied warriors quickly agreed on death and destruction, and such they would pursue. The only question was how to go about it...

"Hey, they're wearing armor!" High Elf Archer told them, poking her head upside-down through the window.

"So they're well equipped...?" To Priestess, this evoked unpleasant memories of the ogre and the goblin paladin. They wouldn't go far wrong in assuming that was some greater power behind the little monsters. Some unholy alliance at work...

"I'd say about fifteen of them left," High Elf Archer added, apparently remembering what she had gone up on the roof to do in the first place, and then she disappeared again. "Correction: fourteen!"

There was another distant goblin shout. Shot through with an arrow, no question.

"GGOGB!!"

"GOORG! GOOROGBBB!!"

But the goblins, of course, would not stay quiet for this—indeed, they began screaming. There had been a frightened young woman on the driver's bench. And it was an elf girl shooting at them. They were not about to let this opportunity get away, and their tiny brains were full of fantasies of what they would do once they had their hands on the women. And such thoughts would always spark violence.

A belated moment later, there came a chorus of *fwizz, fwizz* sounds as something flew through the air. One of the things lodged in Goblin Slayer's armor with a *thwack*; he pulled it out and inspected it, discovering a slim arrow. It was light and short, like a child's toy, but it was perfectly capable of piercing and tearing flesh.

"Short bows?"

Mounted goblin archers. He grunted, unimpressed. Then he broke the arrow in half. If they had crossbows, it could be real trouble. "I'll entrust the luggage carriage to you."

"Yeah, sure. Let the elf do the dirty work!"

Goblin Slayer took the reins in hand, slowing the carriage's speed. In perfect sync, High Elf Archer danced through the moonlit sky without so much as a footfall. As she flipped through the night, she glanced down at the ground from the air. With her left hand she loosed three arrows.

"GGOROGB?!"

"GOGB?!"

"GGORGB?!?!"

The arrows rained down on the enemy, throwing goblins from their mounts and onto the earth.

"Eleven more to go... Hup!" When she landed lightly on the luggage carriage, High Elf Archer wasn't so much as breathing hard. The driver, who looked like a professional carriage wrangler, was cowering on the bench. He might have been used to bandits and thieves, but being pursued across the desert by goblins? He must have thought he was going to die.

"I should never have accepted this job, no matter how good the pay was!" he blathered.

"Guess there's all kinds of humans."

For example: desert bandits, adventurers, and weirdos who came to places like this to kill goblins.

Carriages, mounted pursuers, a running battle from one to the other—these should have been the ingredients of a fantastic adventure...

"But nothing that involves *goblins* is a real adventure!"

A high elf drawing her bow in the moonlight under a starry sky has the sort of beauty that legends are made of. Her arrows could snuff out life mercilessly, and one sent another goblin tumbling into the sand.

Ten more.

"Well! I think Long-Ears has got this under control, don't you?"

Taking on a high-elf archer on open ground was the height of foolishness. No one knew that as well as a dwarf, but Dwarf Shaman kept his tone light. He took a gratified sip of his wine as if he was simply there to enjoy the scenery, but the slingshot in his hand revealed the lie to this image. He was clearly ready to respond in a flash should anything happen...

"I'm afraid there's not much ammunition to be found inside a carriage, is there...?" Priestess, likewise armed with a slingshot, said. She looked very serious. She normally found the sling a redoubtable companion, and she still trusted it, but only so long as she had stones to feed it. One could keep a pouch of gemstones on hand, but even this had its limit. And the desert promised no easy task finding stray gravel. But then, the same was true of High Elf Archer's arrows. Supply was limited.

"The goblins do have some resources, though," Goblin Slayer said darkly. "And I don't believe these ones are simply a wandering tribe. We must strike the trunk, or batting away the branches will be pointless."

"Any hero, howsoever great, will be defeated should their lines of supply be cut off," Lizard Priest agreed with a nod.

"But we can't do it right now."

The enemy's next move had to be coming. The more so if they had a leader. It was Goblin Slayer's ceaseless vigilance that allowed them to discover it. But it came late, for he was a human and did not see well in the dark. By the time he noticed the pile of wood buried in the sand—the remains of a carriage—and pulled hard on the reins, it was too late. The horse's hooves sank into the sand, and it began to whinny noisily.

"I knew the terrain was on their side," Goblin Slayer said with a sharp click of his tongue. Even as he spoke, the horse was sinking, the carriage beginning to tilt. "It's a trap. And we were chased right into it."

"Quicksand?" Dwarf Shaman called. "Don't panic— If you don't struggle, it won't get up to your head!"

"*We* might be able to stay calm, but what about the horse...?" Female Merchant asked fearfully. Faced with this unfamiliar situation, the animal was crying wildly and shaking its head. Each time it kicked its legs or shook its body, it was sucked deeper into the sand.

"Tie a rope to the carriage behind and see if we can stop the animal." Goblin Slayer pulled on the reins, firing off instructions even as he tried to calm the horse. It might not be the best possible idea, but it was the one he had. "To let ourselves be destroyed in one fell swoop here would be idiotic."

"Understood!" came the prompt response from Lizard Priest, who had been all but left out of the battle. He jumped down from the carriage with all the power of a wild animal.

"Here, a grappling hook!" Priestess called, tossing the item cleanly to him. It was straight out of her Adventurer's Toolkit—she never left home without it.

Lizard Priest waved his tail to and fro, pushing through the sand, not even looking back as he snatched the grappling hook out of the air. On the far shore, Priestess, Dwarf Shaman, and Female Merchant worked together to tie the rope to the carriage frame.

"Hey, what's going on down there?!" High Elf Archer shouted; even as she spoke, she grabbed an arrow out of the sky as it flew at her, then put it right in her bow and fired it back. It went clean through the archer who had launched it, slinging him backward. Nine.

At this rate, though, they would soon be surrounded. They hadn't gained that much distance on their enemies. If they had to engage in hand-to-hand combat, the situation would change, again. High Elf Archer clicked her tongue, a most un-elf-like behavior.

"Oh, it's just a little trap!" Lizard Priest said from the sand, as if he were talking about a passing rain shower. Then he anchored the grappling hook on the carriage. The next step should have been to get the driver to stop the carriage, but...

"This is why I hate accompanying adventurers! This desert might as well be the entrance to hell...!"

"As hell does not exist, you may relinquish such worries," Lizard Priest told the terrified driver. "There is only the process of heaven and earth: When we die, all of us become food for the insects that live in the sand, thereby returning to the great cycle." The sermon may have seemed quite gracious, but the only response was a sort of strangled cry. Lizard Priest snorted. "Mistress ranger, I shall take the reins myself, so it will be yours to handle the attack!"

"Argh, why does it *always* end up like this...!" The carriage came to a halt, and goblins mounted on wargs approached from every side.

High Elf Archer felt around in her quiver, counting how many arrows she had left, then her lips pulled down in a frown. "Well, 'Step in a trap, break your own back,' as they say. Let's see what we can do!"

"Ha-ha-ha, words worthy of a dwarf maiden!" Lizard Priest clambered into the driver's seat with a howl, the carriage creaking in protest. High Elf Archer jumped lightly past him, an arrow ready to protect the reptilian shaman.

There were nine riders left. There might be reinforcements hiding in the darkness. And she didn't want any wargs jumping at them...

"Point is, bring down their numbers...!" High Elf Archer met the goblins with a literal rain of arrows. Goblin Slayer, meanwhile, had quickly given up trying to control the horse. The carriage creaked to a stop as it strained against the rope, but the trapped animal was in a mad panic.

"They'll get us at this rate."

Should he get down and join the battle on foot? He took the lamp hanging by the driver's bench and hung it from his hip instead. Few people underestimated goblins less than he did, but goblins on wargs were even more dangerous than usual. Nine goblin riders meant there were, in effect, eighteen enemies. Three times as many as he had in his party.

But the odds are always against us, Goblin Slayer thought as he contemplated working his way around for an attack from behind.

That was when Priestess, who had been looking at the ground in thought, raised her head again with conviction. "U-um...!" Dwarf Shaman, Female Merchant, and Goblin Slayer immediately looked at her. Priestess couldn't quite decide where to put her eyes, but still she sounded fearless as she said, "I think...there's something we can do."

We need hardly say how Goblin Slayer responded.

§

"GRROORGB!!"

"GRG! GORGB!!"

For the goblins, this must have been a most unpleasant night. The rope they had held taut, per *that person's* haughty instructions, had suddenly and mysteriously snapped. It was because of that person's assurances they had stayed up late into the "night" to set the ambush, even though they were tired.

This was why they hated listening to such people. The reason the goblins with all their resentment didn't slacken their pursuit was, of course, not loyalty. It was the terrified, weeping young woman riding in the carriage. And there, shooting at them from the roof of the second vehicle, was that not an elf female?

Yes, several of their stupider comrades had been shot to death, but the same would not happen to any of them. Look, while the elf was feeling so proud of herself shooting at them, the quarry was headed straight into the quicksand. They would need only to get close, drag her down, destroy the carriage, and do what they pleased with those inside.

Now. Now was the moment, now that the carriage was stopped. No need to hold back anymore. These people had tried to kill them. So it was only fair these people should be killed in turn...!

"O Earth Mother, abounding in mercy, please, by your revered hand, cleanse us of our corruption!"

The goblins failed to understand the words that rang out at that moment. A voice filled the air, its cool sound spreading out like a ripple and vanishing— Perhaps they didn't even hear it.

But they certainly understood when the legs of their mounts sank under them a second later.

"—?!"

"GOOROGB?!"

This was bizarre. Ridiculous. Impossible. Such was probably what these utterances meant. They shouldn't have been in the quicksand yet. They couldn't be trapped in it, not like their stupid prey could. And yet reality paid no heed to the goblins' objections. Their wargs continued to be sucked deeper and deeper into the sand.

Sucked into?

If any of the goblins had been capable of asking this simple question, he might have noticed. He might have seen the whirlpool at the center of the sand. The pure, running spring that had appeared just where their prey had been trapped.

§

"A miracle of purification…!" Goblin Slayer called out sharply, and Priestess nodded briefly in affirmation.

In the desert there was something called quicksand, sand that flowed like a river. Spearman and Witch had told Priestess about this before she left, and now her mind whirled.

They said it was bottomless, like a swamp. Exceedingly soft, a horse's hooves would sink into it. It was like a bucket of sand with water poured into it. It might look like just plain sand at first glance, but if you so much as stuck a finger into it, you couldn't get it out. Because the appearance was deceiving: You couldn't see all the water.

It's essentially a sandy spring.

And if so, there was no reason she couldn't use Purify on it.

Priestess was relieved to know her request had reached the Earth Mother. She had admonished herself never to offer another prayer that would earn a rebuff as she had before.

Naturally, she was only able to purify some of the sand. She had created a pure spring, and other sand nearby rushed into it. The mix of water and sand instantly created quicksand that would suck in anything standing in it. It was only for that one instant that someone could have seen an actual spring in the middle of it all. But she knew that *he* would take advantage of that instant. He and her friends!

"Do that thing you did with the sea serpent!"

"You got it!"

Goblin Slayer did indeed begin shouting instructions immediately, and Dwarf Shaman promptly shouted back. Then he began to intone a spell that would be salvation to the drowning horse and carriage. *"Nymphs and sylphs, together spin, earth and sea are nearly kin, so dance away—just don't fall in!"*

The horse's hooves bit into the water. Its body began to float. The sprites lifted it up, encouraged it, and helped it along the surface. Dwarf Shaman whistled to see the horse, enchanted with the Water Walk spell, trotting along. "Us spell casters do pull our weight. Beard-cutter, the least you could do is remember a spell's name."

"It was too sudden," he said from inside the metal helmet. "Cast it on the horse behind as well. We're going to fly."

"On it!" As Dwarf Shaman set about calling out to his sprites again, Priestess let out a little breath of relief.

Thank goodness it worked.

"...You're really something," Female Merchant said, looking wide-eyed at her.

"Me? Oh, no," Priestess responded with a shake of her head. "I just relied on what I'd been told. I didn't figure any of it out myself."

She was just lucky it had worked. This wasn't really a tactic to rely on in a serious fight like this. What would have happened if it had turned out to be a mistake? For all her thinking, she'd had no backup plan, and that sat uneasily with Priestess. Certainly she didn't feel she had any call to be proud of what she had done, even less so arrogant...

"No, you helped."

Why did those words, murmured from within the metal helmet, make her so happy?

Right. She nodded quickly, then looked down at the tied-off rope in hopes of hiding the flush in her cheeks. It was truly made for adventurer: Even under the weight of the other carriage, it only creaked and groaned; it never threatened to snap.

"Excuse me," Female Merchant said, finally too restless to bear it any longer. "I can keep an eye on this." Her meaning came across clearly: She wanted something to do. Priestess understood that feeling very well.

"All right." She nodded, smiling. "Let us know if there's any trouble!"

"Right!" Female Merchant exclaimed, then took the knot of the rope firmly in hand, pressing it down.

Satisfied that all was in order, Priestess slid across to the passenger seats, only to find herself looking at Dwarf Shaman. When she saw the grin on his face, she puffed her cheeks out with a "Hmph!" But that sweet show of annoyance just seemed to amuse him more. He burst out laughing, and Priestess felt—how to put it?

"I wish you'd not."

"Aw, no harm in it, lassie. I mean it in the best possible way—havin' a laugh to see you've become a real adventurer."

Could that be true?

She certainly didn't feel it herself, but she was aware of the rank tag that dangled just underneath her clothes. She was starting to become used to the weight of the steel, she thought, but there was still something that felt funny about it.

"Hey, who did all that just now?!" High Elf Archer asked, her voice like a tinkling bell as she vaulted into the carriage. The fact that her quiver was much lighter than before bespoke the fate of many of the remaining goblins. Drowning, confused, and trapped, she had picked them off one by one.

Priestess imagined the bodies of the goblins and their wargs left in the sand. She felt no sympathy or sadness for them. There was no tug on her heartstrings. There was only, in her heart, a prayer that their souls would safely reach heaven.

"It was all thanks to the little lady here," Dwarf Shaman said with a stroke of his beard and a gleam in his eye.

"What?!" High Elf Archer exclaimed. "I knew that weirdo was a bad influence. Just make sure you don't make your god angry at you, okay?"

"Er, uh, no. I mean yes. I mean… It's all right. I'm, er, I'm being careful these days." Priestess was thrown, embarrassed by this display of genuine concern.

"These days?" High Elf Archer replied, squinting suspiciously, but one could only smile. Purify was a miracle that required especially careful use.

Still…

Priestess shivered from the night air that crept into the passenger compartment of the carriage. They had just overcome one obstacle. But that was all. The desert was vast— When she thought of all the great unknown that awaited them, she realized that what had just passed was only prologue. And she was not wrong to think so. Indeed, she would see how right she was the very next day.

MUD AND STARS AND CAPTIVES

"I'm placing my hopes in each of you."

The girl had been raised, as it were, among the flowers and the butterflies. Having been brought up with the utmost care in what amounted to a cage, she knew nothing of the seamy side of the world. No one would judge her for that—human lives were so short anyway. Who could fault her parents for wanting to give her a life of silken safety?

Her father, my master—the previous king—had led a life much the same. If one attempted to shine a light into the world's gloomy corners, disruption might result, but just keep diplomacy humming and there were no problems. Let the starving starve, the sick be sick, the rich be rich, and the prosperous be prosperous, and all would go smoothly. Those who felt it incumbent upon them to change the world tended to be arrogant and cruel.

Revolutionaries felt that the status quo was wicked and that safety was of no value, and they thought nothing of trampling upon others. And why? Because they were convinced that their own actions were right and just above and beyond all others.

Thus when the young lady's cradle was brutally shattered, I took it upon myself to take her away, to help her escape. In this, I had the aid of my friend. My small, brave friend, who valued the princess more than anything in the world.

That man was cruel and violent and would no doubt use the princess for his own ends before casting her aside. The princess, I was sure, would quail before it...

But I was wrong. She was resolved to stay in the castle to the bitter end, turning upon us a gaze so stern it pierced to our very hearts.

There was no longer any hope within the castle. If there was hope, it lay outside. A knight who had once served the court was said to be leading a quiet life somewhere beyond the city. Many knights had turned to follow the prime minister, or else were under his thumb—but this man, this one knight... Perhaps...

And so, trusting our hopes to a world into which the princess had ultimately refused to flee, we ran. Us and those rogues.

§

It was all over about the time I had grown tired of trying to count the number of robbers.

Or more precisely, it felt like it was all over before I knew it.

Despite the traces of heat it still carried, the desert wind was too cold for exposed skin. My muscles cried out in pain from the uncourteous treatment I'd given them. The stars in the cloudless sky seemed oddly sideways, the light of them blindingly bright. That was what finally made me realize that I was lying on my side like a discarded doll.

My body was doused in its own fluids, sweat and spit and tears. But the smell of an elf was the aroma of flowers. The wafting stink I smelled came from the remnants of a mostly eaten banquet.

"U-urgh... This is...no way to...treat a woman," I groaned. I felt like I had something stuck in my throat, and a sharp tang of iron almost turned my stomach. I managed to make myself speak all the same because in order to maintain one's pride, one had first to excite the heart.

I grasped a cloth so sodden with dirt that it wasn't fit for a bedchamber, then crawled to my hands and knees like an unsteady newborn fawn.

What in the world did *happen to us?*

It had started almost as soon as my friend and I had parted ways with those rogues; we had promptly begun to argue about what to do next. Look for help? Out here in this desert it was like seeking one needle out of a pile of twenty million. I had urged that we should find a carriage as soon as possible, but that fool friend of mine...!

"It's a secret mission, we ought to go on foot!"

"Pfah! And pick the most difficult possible route, I see!"

From there it had quickly devolved into name-calling, and well after we parted ways, I had spotted these merchants and called out to them; but when I got aboard...

How was I supposed to know it belonged to a bunch of kidnappers—and that they'd gotten her, too?

And then my kidnappers themselves were attacked by a bunch of thieves! Just imagine.

I crawled desperately among the corpses of the brutally murdered kidnappers and the discarded dining ware. My chest and thighs scraped painfully against sand and gravel, provoking a small cry from me each time.

When the gods made our bodies, why did they have to give us so much surface area?!

But later—I had no idea how much later—I was finally able to reach what I had been aiming for: an earthenware pot, much like a chamber pot, sitting among the strewn garbage. Perhaps there was still something in it.

But when I tried to reach out to take it, I found my fingers and legs refused to obey me, their master. I didn't have the strength to stand or even to hold the pot in my grasp, and it clattered onto its side, spilling its contents onto the earth.

"Oh, for the...!"

I supposed this was my punishment for mocking the gods; it certainly was delivered quickly. I grimaced and pressed my mouth to the sand where the water was seeping into it. Trying to keep one eye on my surroundings, I lapped up the silty fluid. To be reduced to licking water from the dirt was so pathetic I could have cried, but it meant I had moisture in my throat.

"...Ergh, ugh." I tried to swish the water around my mouth, then spat out a sticky glob of saliva. Then I tried to take in a little more water. There was no flavor, no anything, but it didn't matter.

Elves lived a long time. In the blink of an eye, everyone who remembered my humiliation would be gone. And anyway, compared with the horrors taking place in that castle, this was nothing. And so—yes, that's why I'd done it.

Out of hatred for the thieves, who had been taking a cut of the kidnappers' "income," I had helped the far-away carriage escape. Or more precisely, the shrimp had helped them escape and had roped me into it. The thieves had been understandably upset, and after they had slaughtered all the kidnappers, they threatened to punish my friend severely…

"Ugh, why I'm always sticking my neck out for you is quite beyond my capacity to explain…," I muttered, but my small friend, who had shown up alongside me at some point, simply shrugged. And then, suddenly, she tossed a golden amulet on the sand in front of me. How she had managed to get back the amulet the kidnappers had taken from me, I didn't know. But she had.

"This doesn't count as a favor," I grumbled, but my friend simply grinned. Very annoying. I took the amulet delicately and hung it back around my neck.

Apparently, while I had been polishing the thieves' spears and baking bread in their oven, my friend had been negotiating with their leader. Trying to get him to sell us the moment they arrived in town tomorrow or the next day. My gods.

"I suppose they'd take some cheap price for us," I muttered angrily. "Lord, they didn't know what they had." I pulled my knees to my chest and leaned against my friend. It was too cold here in the desert to pass the night sitting alone. "If we'd been sold as water-drawing slaves in the mines, we might not have come out for a hundred years, and then what would have happened?"

My friend shook her head as if to say she didn't know. Oh, for—

If there was hope out there, where was it?

CHAPTER 3

CHOOSE YOUR OWN ADVENTURE

"Out of the frying pan, into the fire, is it…?"

Priestess almost didn't realize at first that the whispered words came from Goblin Slayer. "Wha—?" she said, glancing in his direction. He continued from just beyond the window to the driver—although he may or may not have actually been answering her. "Words my teach—my master once said."

"Well, he got the fire part right," High Elf Archer said with a shrug, then looked out the window at the blue sky. Sunlight poured down mercilessly, making even the inside of the carriage warm. Combined with the reflection off the sand, it was something like being in an oven. "If I went out there, I'd singe my ears off." Her ears twirled as if to express their displeasure at the idea.

And to think, when they had finally managed to stop for a rest the night before, it had been cold enough to chill the skin. You didn't have to be an elf to find the change in temperature jarring. It certainly didn't seem like a place for the short-lived.

Perhaps because of his people's affinity for fire, Dwarf Shaman, by contrast, seemed quite at home. It wouldn't quite be true to say he wasn't sweating a drop, but he didn't look much perturbed by it.

But then, neither of these two were human.

"…I'm profoundly sorry. This is all because I ran the horse too hard last night…," Female Merchant said in a small voice from where she was curled up in a seat. Her skin, usually white as snow, was red and beaded with sweat. Her breath came in shallow gasps. Priestess watched her chest heave painfully for a minute before helping her loosen her clothing, at which point her breathing finally calmed a little.

"Is this...heatstroke?" It would certainly be understandable. Even Priestess, who was well used to being out in the field by now, felt a touch dizzy. Female Merchant might have been an adventurer at one point, but she was still of noble birth and now spent all her time as a merchant. This couldn't be easy for her.

Priestess offered her a waterskin, and Female Merchant took it with a "Thank you" that came out dreadfully dry. She put her lips to the mouth of the canteen and drank noisily, Priestess holding the water for her. Once she had wiped away a few stray drops with a rag, she mumbled "Thank you" again.

"Now that you've had some water, have a nibble of the dried meat. It'll keep y'alive now a god of sunstroke has his hands on yeh."

Priestess nodded at Dwarf Shaman and took out some provisions, tearing off a piece with her own teeth. She held it out to Female Merchant in the palm of her hand, and the other woman took it gingerly between her fingers and started to chew the softened meat. The drink of water had put some moisture in her mouth, and she seemed to eat without too much difficulty.

Yes. Thankfully, they still had some provisions, so the situation wasn't critical. Diluted grape wine and food were both plentiful in the luggage on the carriage behind them. However, the horses' pace had slowed considerably what with the heat and only occasional brief breaks to rest and feed.

"Make sure you take it easy once in a while yourself, Beard-cutter. You and that metal helmet. Your brains'll fry before you know it."

"Right." Goblin Slayer nodded.

The situation was not critical. But neither was it particularly optimistic.

The fact that we ran into quicksand suggests we've lost the main road.

They no longer saw the statues of the Trade God, either, and the path they were seeking seemed to have vanished beneath the sands.

They might have the stars and moons at night and the sun during the day to guide them, but they still didn't know exactly where they were. When he looked out past that metal visor, all he saw was the baking sun. No mountains large enough to serve as landmarks, just sand all the way to the horizon.

Heat shimmered up off the ground, dancing in the distance.

"A mirage...?" There had been something about them in a book he'd read before he left. It said that apparitions sometimes manifested themselves in the desert and lead travelers astray...

He had been talking half to himself, but High Elf Archer, poking her head out the window, answered him. "You just take a good look, ask a few questions, and those things won't get you." She squinted, cat-like, against the hot wind and blowing sand, then shook her head and looked over. "Hey, you doing all right over there?"

"Ha-ha-ha. The lack of water concerns me somewhat, I confess, but as to the heat, I find it quite congenial," said Lizard Priest, sounding at ease. He sat on the driver's bench of the rear carriage, bathing in the sun as he held the reins.

The hired driver was hunched beside him, muttering to himself. "The desert is hell," he mumbled. "If you die here, your soul gets eaten..."

"Admittedly, it is something of a struggle against the cold of the night." Lizard Priest patted the driver gently on the back, as if his muttering was of no consequence. Indeed, he seemed to think it might be best not to speak to the man at all. "I must also say that it does concern a person to be unsure of where we are going."

"Yeah, hope we can get back to the road," High Elf Archer said, leaning against the window frame and looking downright bored as the wind ran over her ears and cheeks.

The situation was not critical, but it wasn't cheerful, either.

I've been forced to acknowledge that fact, myself. And having done so, Goblin Slayer found it was all but impossible for him to remain optimistic. So Goblin Slayer made himself join in the banter. "It's unfortunate that we were unable to recover any of the goblins' equipment."

"No kidding. Doesn't look like I'm going to be finding any more arrows around here," High Elf Archer said—perhaps aware of his need for this conversation. Perhaps not. She giggled like the sound of a ringing bell.

Then suddenly she squinted, putting her hand to her forehead to shade her eyes as she looked into the distance.

"What is it?"

"Over there. A building... Maybe? It's something anyway."

"Hrm," he grunted. There was the possibility of mistake, but no room for it. "It's settled." Tired as it was, the horse nonetheless responded promptly to Goblin Slayer's movement of the reins. Inside the carriage, a creaking and swaying communicated the change of direction.

"Careful there, Anvil. Sure you're not seeing a mirage yourself?"

"I'll show *you* a mirage," she growled, pulling her head back into the carriage. Priestess watched the argument, such a familiar scene, take shape with relief. She, too, was battling the heat. To conserve water, she would soak a hand towel, then wipe it around her cheeks and forehead. Then she would offer it to Female Merchant, whose hair was plastered to her face with sweat.

"I guess I should have trained a little harder, huh...?" She smiled weakly at Priestess, who shook her head.

"I hope we can take a rest up ahead," she replied.

Not long after, the carriage did indeed arrive at a village—but one that was altogether too quiet.

§

Shf. His outstretched foot kicked the pile of sand, naturally. As Goblin Slayer lowered the long stick that served as a brake on the carriage and jumped down from the driver's bench, he found himself thinking, *Is it normal in the desert for the sand to come up past your ankles?* His heat-roasted brain wasn't working very quickly. He gave a click of his tongue and took one gulp of water, then another. The liquid that came into his mouth, the opening of the canteen pressed up against his visor, was unpleasantly lukewarm.

"At any rate, I believe we should begin by investigating, but what do you think?"

"...Doubt we have any other choice. We have to know where we are or we won't get anywhere," Female Merchant said as she emerged, slim legs first, from the carriage. She was wearing tall boots against the sand, her cloak pulled up over her head to shield her from the sun. She gave him a hesitant nod. "But why ask me?"

"Because you're our quest giver."

She blinked at Goblin Slayer's answer, then felt her cheeks soften into a smile. It was as if some tension had been released. "Continue with the quest, then, if you would be so kind."

"Yes." Goblin Slayer nodded, then waved to his party members to proceed toward the village. As he went forward, he heard more crunching of sand behind him. The rest of them disembarking the carriage, he supposed.

Foot out, step forward. White sand glittered as he kicked it up, before it was carried away as dust on the wind. He checked the sword at his hip, careful that he could draw it at any time as he moved. Several buildings stood in the village, made either of a very white clay or sun-bleached bricks. It had been impossible to tell from a distance what this town's livelihood was, but perhaps they raised the lumpy donkeys. Or maybe it was an inn town. In any event, he hoped they could get water and information here.

"Oh man, my feet are scorched...," High Elf Archer whined, frantically kicking aside some sand. She didn't appear to actually leave any footprints, though, being an elf.

Priestess squinted against the sun that threatened to bake the party, its reflection bouncing off the sand. "I feel like it's going to burn my eyes..."

"Best plan is to not look too far up or too far down," Dwarf Shaman said. "I'm starting to think Long-Ears had the right idea with that costume."

High Elf Archer, a few steps ahead, heard him and turned around, puffing out her modest chest with no small amount of pride. "That's elf wisdom for you—real intelligence at work. You have to be in accord with Nature, with whatever environment you're going into."

"This from the people who bend the spirits of Nature to their will!"

"Better than ones who dig holes in the ground and cut down forests like dwarves do."

Their arguing voices were the only sound apart from the whipping of the wind and their footsteps in the sand. Truly, there was nothing else to be heard.

Goblins?

No, it was too *clean* for that. He shook his helmeted head as they entered the seemingly deserted village. There were so many things to think about.

"Where's the driver?"

"Hardly in any condition to follow us nor do we have the where-withal to babysit him," Lizard Priest said gaily, his eyes rolling in his head. He gestured with a slow shake of his long neck toward the curtain of the luggage carriage, behind which a man could be seen crouching. He was shielded by an overcoat, his fingers in his mouth as he muttered inaudibly to himself—as he had been doing since the night before.

The desert environment, the sudden attack and headlong escape, and now wandering aimlessly in the desert—not everyone was designed to endure such things, Goblin Slayer supposed.

"Any danger?"

"Well… I'm afraid I can't say. The behavior of those whose souls have been stolen by the desert can be impossible to foresee." Lizard Priest's jaws moved, and his tongue flicked out of his mouth. "Small as our Female Merchant may appear, she is quite…plucky. And it's not as if she cannot call out."

"Keep an ear open for her."

"As you wish."

Goblin Slayer gave the vanguard to the lizard, who shuffled forward, then he let out a breath. He had to be aware of what was around them. Had to know the status of everyone with him. As party leader, there was a great deal to think about. A great deal to do.

"What about you? How are you feeling?"

"All right," Priestess replied, smiling despite the sweat in her eyes and the harshness of her breath. "I'm okay."

"Good, then," Goblin Slayer said with a nod. "Be sure to hydrate."

"It's…concerning, isn't it?"

Hrm. Semiconsciously matching his stride to hers, he found Priestess jogging up beside him and making this unusual remark. When he tilted his helmeted head in puzzlement, though, she smiled. "I mean her."

"Ah…" Inside his helmet, he moved his gaze to survey the carriage. Female Merchant had moved to the driver's bench, using her coat to block the sun. She was looking around, on high alert. From this distance, he couldn't make out the pallor of her face. But both physically and mentally, he suspected she might be forcing herself to endure the situation. When she noticed him, however, she raised her hand and gave a broad wave. *I'm okay*, she seemed to be saying.

"After all," he mumbled, as if trying to pluck the words out of thin air, "she's our…quest giver."

"That's true," Priestess said knowingly, chuckling in the back of her throat and then picking up her walking pace. Goblin Slayer slowed his, so she could finally catch up and walk alongside him.

And so in the dizzying heat, the two of them walked side by side along the river of sand that seemed to have once been a street in this village. Barrels, farm implements: Everything outside seemed either to have been knocked over, to have been buried in the sand, or both. Nothing about the place seemed like a location people would inhabit…

"And yet, for all that…it doesn't really feel rotted out, either," Priestess said, looking around nervously, but Goblin Slayer responded with silence. He was in complete agreement with her. He didn't recognize the feeling here, but it wasn't the feeling one got in a goblin nest. He valued that intuition highly, though he wasn't the kind to let it make him hesitant.

"How about it? Find anyone?" he asked High Elf Archer.

"Yeah, but…" Her ears flicked where she stood in the doorway of a building. "It looks like they're sleeping."

"What…?" Goblin Slayer stepped over the pile of sand on the threshold and through the open door. Even just a single step inside, it felt almost cool within, perhaps because the sunlight was blocked, or perhaps it had something to do with the building materials. In any case, he headed inward through the clammy gloom, discovering what seemed to be a dining area. He could see patches of carpet under the scattering sand, but in the center of the room, rather than the round table he expected, there was a single long table. A middle-aged man was splayed out across it, asleep. Lizard Priest and Dwarf Shaman stood on either side of him.

"We checked the other rooms, and everyone is like this. Even the babes didn't make a sound," Dwarf Shaman said.

"Well now... If the other houses are all like this, and indeed, even if they are not, then this would be a most fantastical situation," Lizard Priest replied. He and High Elf Archer must have sensed the strangeness of the moment just as Goblin Slayer did.

The man lying across the table wore desert garb much like High Elf Archer had on. Otherwise, he appeared completely unremarkable, except that he was facedown, not moving.

"Um, hel—" Priestess started to call out hesitantly, but Goblin Slayer stopped her with a motion of his hand. Instead, he drew his small sword from its sheath, taking one step closer to the man, then another. Then, reaching out with his shielded left hand, he took the man's shoulder...

"Eek?!" Priestess exclaimed at the exact instant the man crumbled away without a sound. He turned to dust like a stone statue that had spent too long in the elements. The dust was a reddish color that evoked raw meat, and now all that was left of the man rested in Goblin Slayer's palm. And even that would have drained away had he not squeezed his hand shut to catch hold of it.

"What... What's going on here...?" Priestess understandably backed away. Even Dwarf Shaman and Lizard Priest blanched (though it would be hard to tell with Lizard Priest's scales).

"Hold on, now. This mean everyone in this village is...?"

"It seems to have happened in the night without their ever realizing it, and no one was spared." Goblin Slayer let out a short breath.

"That would explain the silence," Lizard Priest said with a shake of his head. "Should we presume they were attacked by some monster?"

"If so, it would have to be...Grograman, The Many Colored Death." Everyone looked at one another at this brief announcement from inside the helmet. "I have heard there are terrible things in the desert. Though I can't say I understand what they are." This thing, Goblin Slayer told them with a quick shake of his head, was supposed to be a fairy-tale creature. "But no matter—forget about it. It was simply something that came to mind."

Goblin Slayer rarely, if ever, uttered the name of any monster other than goblins. If she hadn't been so busy keeping watch, High Elf Archer might have made quite a fuss about this fact.

But at that moment, she found she had more important things to worry about. "Hey, everyone! Bad news!"

§

"E-eeyargh! I can't take this anymore! This desert is cursed...!!"

"Hey, hold it...! Where do you think you're—?!" Female Merchant grabbed the driver's arm, but he swatted her away and took the reins of the luggage vehicle. Female Merchant, falling on her behind on the sand, gave a little shout. The man didn't so much as slow down, though, as he cracked the reins and set the luggage carriage moving. Female Merchant had to roll out of the way, or her svelte, lovely body might never have been seen again.

"I'm going home! I don't wanna spend one more second in this place! I don't wanna die!!" The driver's eyes were wide and bloodshot, and foam flecked the edges of his mouth as he cracked the reins again and again. Female Merchant couldn't even manage to get to her feet before the carriage had vanished beyond the dunes. If she'd known this was going to happen, then she should have started by drawing her rapier...!

"I'm sorry. I couldn't stop him...!"

"Forget about that!" High Elf Archer shouted, bounding up to her. Kicking up sand—an elf, of all things!—as she arrived, she took stock of the situation in a glance and then helped Female Merchant to her feet. "You okay? He didn't hurt you, did he?!"

"Thank you, I'm fine," Female Merchant said, coughing. "Just a bit of sand in my mouth."

"Good." High Elf Archer sounded sincerely relieved. She gently brushed the sand from her beloved friend's hair and cheeks. She glared into the distance, giving an inelegant click of her tongue, then called out calmly but quite audibly, "Hey, everyone! Bad news!"

Her companions immediately emerged from the building. Lizard

Priest was first, balancing himself with his tail; he was followed by Goblin Slayer, who moved with remarkable agility for a man wearing so much armor. Priestess pattered after them, and finally Dwarf Shaman trundled along at the rear.

"Goodness gracious!" Lizard Priest exclaimed. "I hadn't realized that his spirit had been quite so thoroughly broken by the desert!"

Lizard Priest had thought the man had completely lost his mind, but some measure of it seemed to have come back to him. Since the despondent so often lack the motivation to do anything at all, Lizard Priest had assumed it was safe to leave the driver alone, but he had misjudged.

"What's the matter? Why didn't you shoot him?" Goblin Slayer asked, trying to ignore the impression that he could hear the sound of dice being rolled in the distance.

High Elf Archer didn't answer, but only gazed off across the sands and asked quietly, "Find anything?"

"No," he answered, shaking his head. "No one alive."

"I'd like...to give them a funeral, if we can...," Priestess said hesitantly, but she knew full well it would be dangerous to stay here for very long. Some death whose form they didn't know was on the loose. The runaway driver might prove the wisest of them. "But I guess we should go after him, quick...!"

"With a whole carriage of our own? Wouldn't be easy..." Dwarf Shaman frowned. "Might work, if I used Tail Wind..."

"I wouldn't do it if I were you, dwarf," High Elf Archer said, not bothering to hide her frown. She pointed with a graceful motion at something just over the sands. "Take a look at that."

"That" was the reason she hadn't shot the man or given chase. Yes, it was *over* the sands, quite literally. Specifically, the top layer of sand seemed to be moving. It swirled up above the horizon caught in a wild wind. Priestess mumbled distantly that it was like a great, coiled snake.

And it was coming this way. It was like a huge, dark mountain heading directly for them.

"Wha..."

Female Merchant simply stood and stared, until finally the words came.

"...t the hell is...is that?!"

"Gods, I see it now! The Many Colored Death, indeed!" Dwarf Shaman shouted, almost mockingly. "The simoon, the Wind of the Red Death! So that's what killed these villagers!"

"What is it? Some sort of monster?!" High Elf Archer hollered, looking at her diminutive companion as if she'd been struck.

"No!" Dwarf Shaman yelled back. "It's a sandstorm!"

Simoon: The name meant "poison wind." It brought blinding sand and devastating heat. Superheated stones would fly everywhere. It would mercilessly attack all in its path. Anyone caught in it would be whipped by unimaginably hot winds. They would find the sky closed off by sand and would be sucked dry until they died.

Not, of course, that all the adventurers knew these details. But being adventurers, they were acutely aware of when death was approaching. That was one thing the driver, running the carriage headlong into the storm, obviously lacked.

"Run!" Perhaps it was Goblin Slayer who issued the order. Everyone dove for the buildings.

"Ha-ha-ha-ha-ha. Now, this has become interesting!"

"This's no time to chuckle, Scaly!"

Lizard Priest, scrabbling along the ground with his claws, promptly hefted Dwarf Shaman with his long tail and placed him on his back. There was no way he could outrun the sand with his stubby legs. Right now, time mattered more than dignity.

"But you said no one was left alive inside anyway, right?!" High Elf Archer cried, sparing a glance backward as she flew along. "Don't you have those breathing rings you like so much?!"

"I have them, but I don't know if they would work in sand, and I don't wish to stake my life on finding out," Goblin Slayer replied. His breathing was still even as he worked out the best strategy in his mind. "The people here died because they didn't see it coming," he said. "We'll shut the doors and windows, barricade ourselves in."

Once a party leader has decided on a plan of action, all that's left is to carry it out to the best of one's ability. As Lizard Priest, Dwarf Shaman, and High Elf Archer went on ahead, Priestess was supporting Female Merchant on her shoulder. Still feeling the effects of a god of sunstroke, the young merchant's breath was pathetically, dangerously shallow.

"I've got you! Just hang in there…!"

"The h-horse… What about…the horse?! We can't…just leave—"

"Forget the horse."

"Yikes!"

"Eek?!"

Goblin Slayer unleashed this instruction as he sprinted between the two women. Each of them found their delicate bodies wrapped under one of his arms and hauled up like firewood. Ignoring their shouts and feeble displays of resistance, he picked up his speed.

But the darkness was faster than he was. It came closing in, relentless, even as Female Merchant continued to object: "I-I'm all right. I can… I can walk…"

"I can't help you if you fall."

Priestess burst in: "Listen to me!"

She must have decided that their best chance of survival was in Goblin Slayer's arms, even if it was a narrow chance. She twisted, looking behind her, trying to think of any way she could be of help. The oncoming rush was a proper sandstorm now, winking out any light from the sun. A dark shadow was stretching over the party, and soon it would be black as night.

Should she chant Holy Light? No, it wasn't as dark as that. Heal or Purify, then? No, not those, either.

"If we need it, I'll cast Protection!"

"Please do."

All that remained, then, was to focus her spirit completely, preparing to pray to the gods in heaven. As Priestess closed her eyes and began to murmur the words of a prayer, Female Merchant bit her lip, hard. Goblin Slayer considered saying something to her but felt his strength was best used for running.

"Orcbolg, quick!!"

Through his visor, he could see High Elf Archer up ahead. She had reached the doorway first and was shouting and waving to him. He nodded when he saw that Lizard Priest and Dwarf Shaman had dived inside already. The Wind of the Red Death was almost upon him, but he had one turn left.

"I'm going to throw you."

"Wha—?"

"Eek...?!"

Without waiting for their responses, Goblin Slayer did exactly as he had declared he would. He flung Female Merchant, followed by Priestess, toward the doorway. And then in the space of a breath, he covered the remaining distance himself. The two girls tumbled across the sandy carpet and were caught by Dwarf Shaman and Lizard Priest. As Goblin Slayer slid through the entrance, High Elf Archer slammed the door behind him.

The next second, there was an immense roar, and the house shook and groaned.

They had cut it as close as they possibly could.

§

"Close the door and barricade it!"

"As you say...!"

As he burst into the room, there came a sound like water being poured into a hot pan. If they didn't know it was bits of sand flinging against the building, they would never have imagined it.

Lizard Priest hefted the dusty table and shoved it up against the door, while Goblin Slayer grabbed the rug. The girls scrambled to get away from where they'd fallen, and he used the rug to block the window, pounding it into place with nails. Sand still trickled in through the doorframe and around the edges of the rug, but they were shielded from the worst of it.

The storm continued to pound away, but it wasn't so loud that they couldn't talk. Goblin Slayer looked through his visor at the groaning ceiling, then shook his head. "What about the other rooms?"

"I went around and secured them as best I could," High Elf Archer replied (When had she found time to do that?), batting at her hair. The motion had all the innocence of a cat grooming itself, but in an elf, it still looked exceptionally beautiful. "Ugh…I've got sand in places I didn't even know I had…" Each time she combed her fingers through her hair, a cloud of dust would poof out like pale smoke.

This alerted Priestess and Female Merchant to check their hair and clothes as well. Any way you sliced it, there was hardly a surface in the building that wasn't covered in sand. Even Goblin Slayer could feel it crunching beneath his clothes. And of course the other men could, as well.

"Maybe we should rest for a while…," Priestess suggested.

"Yeah… Not a bad idea," Female Merchant agreed with a tired smile. "On the bright side, I guess this place no longer belongs to anyone."

They had been in a state of high alert ever since they crossed the border. Mental strain led to physical strain and then to fatigue. Goblin Slayer nodded. "When you conclude the services for the dead, then rest. Nothing good can come of having our spell casters tired."

Did he have her mental state in mind? …No, not quite. It would be trouble if they stayed awake. Goblin Slayer looked around for a chair, saw there was nothing of the sort, and slumped down against the wall beside the door. He removed the sword at his hip, then kicked out one leg, leaning back.

"Even if goblins were out in this storm, I doubt they would be able to get in here." Thus it would fall to those on the front line, who were not spell casters, to stand guard. And so, as was standard operating procedure when they camped out, he and High Elf Archer would watch, while the three magic users—presently four—took rest.

When Goblin Slayer presented this plan, Dwarf Shaman stroked his beard knowingly and nodded. "Might as well pull one more little trick, then…" After all, his spells would be replenished after he rested. Perfect time to use them. Dwarf Shaman rifled through his bag of catalysts and pulled out a roll of sheepskin paper. *"Sandman, Sandman, rasp of breath, kin to th' endless sleep of death. A song we offer, so take your sand and on our dreams now place your hand."*

The paper drifted through the room, scattering dust, and abruptly disappeared into thin air. Then the sound of the storm seemed to become somewhat softer, and it seemed to them that the inside of the room was filled with a gentle warmth. Maybe that was why Priestess felt her eyelids growing heavy with sleep and why Female Merchant had to press a hand to her mouth to politely hide her yawn.

"The Sleep spell?" Goblin Slayer inquired, and Dwarf Shaman snorted. "'Tis about all I'm good for." It must have been profoundly difficult to summon the sprites with a storm like that outside. Dwarf Shaman took a swig of the wine from the jar he kept at his belt, wiping the droplets off his beard. "If you need me, I'll be off lookin' for something to eat... Ideally something not covered in sand, though my hopes aren't high."

"Allow me to accompany you. I haven't enough heat here, no, not enough heat," said High Elf Archer.

"Yeah, right," Dwarf Shaman muttered, but in any event the two of them moved into what seemed to be the kitchen.

"Okay, well, we'll...we'll just...get a little sleep...," Priestess said, her head bobbing.

"Sorry. Could you...handle things here...?" Female Merchant asked, starting to slide slowly to the floor.

"Hey, don't do that," Priestess said, offering Female Merchant her hand; she took it and they made their way to the sleeping chambers with unsteady steps. Goblin Slayer watched them for a moment, concerned lest they fall, but they made it successfully to the bedroom. There was a rattle of the sounding staff as Priestess began to pray. *"O Earth Mother, abounding in mercy, please lay your revered hand on those who have left this place, that their souls might have guidance..."* The invocation seemed to take her rather more effort than usual.

Then the two women, pushed to their very limits, collapsed into bed. Soon their breath fell into the even rhythm of sleep. They looked like sisters as they lay with their hands clasped, sleeping amid the blowing ashes that had once been people.

"..." Silently, Goblin Slayer took a waterskin out of his item bag. It was mostly empty by now; it was all too clear that he was going to have to drink sparingly and conserve what he could. Deciding that a sip was nonetheless necessary, he wet his tongue and throat with a precious mouthful, then let out a breath. He would have loved to wipe his face. His eyes stung from the sand.

"What do we do about water?" he asked.

"Good question. This storm'll probably bury the wells," High Elf Archer said, shrugging with a twitch of her ears. She took a quick glance at the barricaded window. Could her eyes see something that he, a human, couldn't? "I think there was a water jug in the kitchen, but it had a bunch of sand in it. *Probably* still drinkable, though."

"I see."

"Being all considerate, are we?" High Elf Archer scuffed some sand aside with her foot so she could sit down somewhere relatively clean. She fixed him with a broad grin.

"Hrm...," Goblin Slayer grunted. "...I don't know."

"You're not *embarrassed*, are you?"

"No." Goblin Slayer shook his head. "I truly do not understand. I don't understand this thing called a *party leader*." After that, he fell silent.

He didn't understand, but he was by no means foolish enough to suggest that a party didn't need a leader. He remembered Heavy Warrior and how he had never done anything to suggest he was less than confident in himself.

Goblin Slayer was most grateful that High Elf Archer simply said "Huh" and didn't pursue the matter any further. She did kick off her boots and turn them upside down, trying to empty out the sand that had gotten into them. *Elves might not leave footprints in the sand, but the sand could still get at their feet.* As that thought passed through Goblin Slayer's mind, he frowned at himself, at the fatigue he was feeling. Thinking pointless thoughts was proof that he was tired.

"Anyway, it's all good," High Elf Archer said. "How long you plan to be awake?"

"...Hrm."

"I want to get some real sleep, here," she added with annoyance. That was probably her way of saying that, as usual, she would take the first watch. But it was also a less than subtle way of telling him to hurry up and go to sleep.

Goblin Slayer, thinking of someone very familiar, very dear to him, felt his expression soften. He was glad he was wearing his helmet. Suddenly, he felt he wasn't sure which voice he had heard.

"Understood. I'll go to sleep."

"You better." High Elf Archer waved a dismissive hand at him, and Goblin Slayer set about loosening his armor. Then he leaned well back against the wall, took a single deep breath, and closed one eye, letting his consciousness range far and wide.

Water, food, travel, and goblins. Rest—when he woke up, he would get food from the kitchen. That and a map. And then goblins.

How did they survive in this cruel environment? It would take more than a horde. They would have to live almost like mountain bandits. In fact, the territory of the two overlapped. How was it they didn't fight? Where was the nest?

How were they getting food? And they would lack amusements, here. Their appetites were great, and forbearance was unknown to them.

They could not survive in the desert. But in that, he was the same as them.

If he could not bring his party back home alive, he could hardly call himself an adventurer. If his teacher saw him now, how disappointed would he be? How thoroughly would he mock him?

Adrift in a sea of thoughts, Goblin Slayer took another breath.

The sandstorm let up at some point, but he didn't know when.

§

It was going to be an effort to get outside. The door was bent inward, and the shutters on the windows were laden with sand.

"We are well and truly buried," Dwarf Shaman said with a look of defeat, shaking his head. No one in the party argued otherwise. After all, a dwarf was pronouncing on a matter of the earth. There could be few if any who had the knowledge or experience to contradict him.

The question, then, was what to do? Goblin Slayer mentally reviewed the cards in his hand.

"I guess digging our way out wouldn't be so easy...," Priestess ventured, peering through the gaps around the door and windows. She was no engineer, but even she could tell that they weren't going to get anywhere working by hand. If the sand flooded into the house, they would never be able to resist it. And they wouldn't know which way or how far to dig anyway.

Goblin Slayer grunted quietly. "Could you make a path using a spell?"

"Tunnel, y'mean?" Dwarf Shaman didn't look thrilled. It wasn't because he had just gotten up from a nap. "Not impossible, but if the spell were to give out while we were still moving, we'd all be buried alive, and that'd be the end of us."

"Ugh...," High Elf Archer groaned, which effectively snuffed out that idea. They might yet have to try their luck, but only after every other option had been exhausted.

"If we cannot go across, then perhaps up. The path to life and evolution may lie that way." Lizard Priest, curling his tail as he spoke, sounded like he was delivering a sermon to a congregation of the faithful.

Yes, that made some sense. The building was constructed of sundried bricks. They wouldn't need tools to smash their way through easily enough. And so long as one was not standing directly beneath the hole, they wouldn't be buried alive...probably.

There was a problem, though. High Elf Archer eyed the roof uneasily and muttered, "What if the whole thing comes down on us?"

"Then we just toss up Protection to keep it standing. Or let it roll right off our backs, as it were." Dwarf Shaman made it sound so simple.

Priestess smiled uneasily. "That miracle isn't precisely meant for that sort of thing, but...I can give it my best shot."

High Elf Archer looked distinctly nonplussed by this, but then she gazed up at the ceiling, giving a long shake of her head. No, Protection was certainly not meant for such things, but still. Still. "He really is a *bad* influence."

"...How do you mean?" Priestess asked, openly puzzled. High Elf Archer patted her on the head like a little sister. Each pat produced fresh clouds of sand, but the two of them only laughed.

"Up, then." Goblin Slayer got to his feet and looked at the ceiling, stretching to run a hand along it. He pressed gently and felt the stone press back. No buckling here. "We'll have to proceed cautiously."

"From what I remember outside, the roof looked like good, hard earth," Dwarf Shaman said, stroking his beard and then crossing his arms in thought. "No reason we shouldn't be able to get out this way, sand or no sand."

"...Don't you think we ought to eat something first?" The suggestion came from Female Merchant. Considering how nervous and exhausted she was, maybe it just slipped out. But her face was indeed dry as was her throat. And her stomach was empty.

"Good point," Goblin Slayer said, exhaling inside his helmet. "Let's do that."

The party was already mentally well prepared to borrow whatever they could from the house. It was practically an adventurer's job to procure goods from old ruins or burial sites. All the more a house where the master and everyone in it were already dead. Being respectful of the deceased, they nonetheless gathered what they could, rescuing the sand-addled water jug and pulling a piece of flatbread, long gone cold, from the oven.

They emptied out another jug and brushed the sand away. Placing a cloth over the mouth, they passed the water through it several times to get the sand out. As for the flatbread, they started a fire in the oven and heated some stones that allowed them to warm it up again. In this way, a little ingenuity helped them conserve a Purify miracle and a Kindle spell, not to mention their provisions.

"This is a good opportunity. We haven't had a chance to sit down to a proper meal in the past several days," Goblin Slayer said, tearing off a piece of bread and shoving it through his visor.

That got a tired smile from Female Merchant. "Been a few days since I had somewhere to sleep that wasn't bouncing around, too," she said.

"Just wish we could rinse ourselves off with this stuff," High Elf Archer added, tugging listlessly on her hair. Elves and filth didn't mix, and she was understandably upset.

Female Merchant looked apologetically at the elf. "Wish I'd been granted a miracle to create water."

"That'd be perfect. Start yourself up a tidy little business out here," Dwarf Shaman put in, getting a wry smile from Priestess and a significant nod from Lizard Priest, who then said, "One speaks of spending money like water, but perhaps in this place the expression is not quite so apt." Then he took a bite of bread, which looked awfully small as he put it into his huge jaws. "And speaking of water, I have heard it is possible to boil cheese in a small pot, then dip other ingredients in it. Yes?"

"Ah," Female Merchant said, squinting at him. "White wine and cheese... Yes, I've heard they do that somewhere in the mountains."

"One must say, it sounds like the food of dreams."

"Is there a demand for it?"

"Oh yes, of course," Lizard Priest insisted, nodding at Female Merchant's display of interest. "There most certainly is a demand."

They did all the cleanup with sand, whether it be washing their hands or cleaning the dishes. Having been exposed to so much sunlight, the sand was far cleaner than the rather questionable water supply.

It was a tremendously, almost incongruously, cheerful moment. It was as if everything had fallen away: The fact that there was a desert outside, that they were in the jaws of a crisis, even the goblins, appeared to have been forgotten.

The thought came to Goblin Slayer as he was contemplating goblin slaying: They had many more chances these days to sit down together and eat. Several times during the meal, he noticed Female Merchant rubbing the corners of her eyes as she laughed. But he chose not to say anything about it. Maybe the others noticed, too; and maybe they chose not to say anything, either.

None of the party members would be so crass as to tread lightly upon the feelings of the only one who was not a member of the group. Priestess, though, did treat Female Merchant solicitously, like a young child with a new baby sister. That was her choice, and if Female Merchant accepted her hospitality, then that was all well and good.

When everything was cleaned up, Goblin Slayer stood with no regrets and no attachments. "All right, let's get started."

As noted, getting outside was going to take some effort.

They positioned a chair under the roof, and since there was a question of height involved, it was Goblin Slayer who climbed onto it and began delicately removing the roof boards. Above those were the sun-dried bricks, which he broke through with equal care. To accomplish this, he used the hammer and chisel from the Adventurer's Toolkit (you know what they say about that).

With the bricks smashed, sand began flooding into the room with a *thump*. They all knew it was going to happen, yet, it was still unsettling. But the glimpse of blue sky just visible through the ceiling gladdened Priestess's heart just as much as the sand troubled it. "We'll be able to get out that way…!"

"Yep, just need t'widen that hole a little first." Dwarf Shaman held up his hands, making a little square with his fingers and peering at the gap. "Trade places with me, Beard-cutter. And Scaly, let me borrow your shoulders for a moment. Humans do the roughest work, and I can't stand it."

"Well and very well!" Lizard Priest bent over and Dwarf Shaman scrambled up on his back, literally standing on his shoulders to continue what Goblin Slayer had started. His stubby fingers wielded the hammer with utmost skill as he cracked the bricks, broke them into pieces, removed them, and cast them away. That was all the more effort that was required; after that it was only a matter of time.

And indeed, in what seemed a few blinks of an eye, the hole was wide enough for a person to climb through. Goblin Slayer was the first to go up.

"All clear," he said, tossing a rope down through the opening. Priestess scrambled up it to discover…

"Wow…"

…the horizon of the Four-Cornered World, seeming to go on forever, and a blue sky that appeared to stretch into infinity above her. She had never realized the world was such a vast place.

The clouds drifting through that distant blue were so far away she couldn't have touched them if she had reached out her arm as far as it would go. On the ground, meanwhile, all she could see was reddish sand stretching out toward every point of the compass. She squinted against the hot wind that slapped against her cheeks and held her hair in place as she felt her breathing intensify. *Huff, huff, huff.* Quick, short breaths. For some reason, the vista inspired a feeling in her like she had been thrown into the sea and was drowning.

©Noboru Kannatuki

But that was also why she—Priestess—was the first to notice. "The sand... It's moving...?"

Just small vibrations at first. Little ripples in the sand. Then it emerged: a dorsal fin like a spire.

There was a tangible *thump* as the creatures surfaced in a cloud of dust, massive fish that made her think of impossibly large capes.

At first she saw one, then more. Two. Three. One after another the great things launched into the sky, pectoral fins working, their tails trailing sprays of sand. A vast school, numerous enough to make her dizzy, emerged from the ground, nearly covering the sky, before they dove back under the sand again. The great geysers of sand they kicked up veritably rained down on the party.

"A school of sand mantas on the move...!" someone finally exclaimed in wonder. Was it Dwarf Shaman, or perhaps Lizard Priest, or even Female Merchant? But these were the last words spoken for some time, the adventurers gone mute with amazement at the overwhelming scene. It was the sort of thing one might be lucky to see just once in a lifetime—even an elf's lifetime.

"Bah... And what are we supposed to do? Jump on those sky-horses and bounce away?" They weren't, High Elf Archer muttered disconsolately, the black-clad hunters of the fairy tales. "And speaking of fairy tales, some of them mention an endless snake that seems to have actually existed way, way in the past."

"And what of it?" Lizard Priest asked with great interest, but High Elf Archer only shrugged. "The elf who encountered it back in the day is still waiting for it to pass by again." She delivered this declaration with a completely straight face, but after a short while she could no longer hide the shaking of her shoulders, and soon after that, laughter came bursting out of her. "Hah! Man, I just couldn't help myself there!" she cried, her voice like a tinkling bell, her joy reaching from the bottom of her heart up to the blue sky far away. She tossed herself back like a child at play, stretching out her arms and legs, heedless of the sand. "This is why I can't get enough of adventures."

Somebody laughed at that. It spread like a ripple, swiftly overtaking the entire party. Maybe there was nothing to do but laugh, or maybe they were all just overawed.

But none of this meant they had given up. They had no horses, no supplies, and no time, but they also had no choice except to wait for the sand mantas to pass. And once they had, the party would then have an idea which direction to begin wandering over the sand.

And despite all this, somehow—somehow—none of them felt despair, not even Female Merchant. Goblin Slayer murmured "Yes," but perhaps none of them noticed that it wasn't even necessary to say anymore that this was an adventure. And if this was an adventure, then the dice of Fate and Chance were still rolling. However the pips came out, for good or ill, it would be dramatic.

It was Female Merchant who finally saw the numbers on the dice. "A ship…," she said softly, pressing her way through the sand to the edge of the roof.

Priestess scrambled after her, wrapping an arm around her thin waist to support her. "A ship…?" she echoed, following Female Merchant's gaze. Then she blinked. There was, indeed, a ship. It sliced across the sands, great white sails full of the hot desert wind. Ship after ship, an entire fleet, triangular sails billowing—they seemed to be following the sand mantas. It was almost enough to make one forget one was standing in the middle of a desert—and then it seemed perhaps it was only an apparition.

"Well, perhaps we might hope to be rescued as victims of the storm," Lizard Priest said casually. Goblin Slayer nodded and held up his sword of a strange length. "Shout as loud as you can. And anyone with something reflective, wave it around."

"Oh, r-right!" Priestess said, raising her sounding staff.

"Perhaps this, then…!" Female Merchant added, drawing the rapier from her hip. With a clear ring of metal, there emerged a weapon seemingly forged from ruby, with a quicksilver sheen. It caught the sunlight and flashed, and this seemed finally to get the attention of the ships. The rudder of the leading vessel shifted heavily to one side, pointing the ship toward the abandoned village.

"Old sea dogs—or desert dogs, should I say? Hope they aren't trouble, at any rate." Even this foreboding murmur, though, sounded cheerful in Dwarf Shaman's mouth.

"Eh, if they are, we'll just steal the ship out from under them," High Elf Archer replied.

At length, the ship arrived beside the village in a cloud of sand, turning broadside as it came to a stop before them. Perhaps it was some kind of fishing boat. It wasn't that large—or at least, not in comparison with the sand mantas. The deck seemed to have room enough for about ten people, and upon it stood an old man with a harpoon in his hand.

"Drifters, are you?" he asked.

"Yes," Goblin Slayer replied with a reserved nod. "We're"—and there was a beat—"adventurers. We are in distress. Would it be possible to ride on your ship?"

He sounded nonchalant, and the other man likewise spoke quiet and low.

"Do as you please," said the elderly captain—a Myrmidon, his mandibles clacking as he spoke.

§

The wind as they experienced it upon the deck of the ship was different again from the breeze that blew through the desert; it was a sharp, good air. It was not due solely to the speed of the ship, but also to the Myrmidon, who had given them water and washrags. Just running a cold, wet cloth over her face was enough to provoke an exclamation of relief from Priestess. And to think, they had only been in this parched land a few days.

"Appreciate it, Master Myrmidon. Real help you're bein'," Dwarf Shaman said, but the captain met him with more nonchalance and more clacking.

"It's fine by me. My type don't need much by way of water."

Then the captain arranged his ships in an ever-shifting formation, surrounding one of the sand mantas that had been on the fringes of the school. Quite suddenly cut off from its compatriots, the giant fish was speared with one harpoon after another thrown by the Myrmidons. They could not throw as well as humans, of course, but they made up for this weakness with sheer numbers. Put crassly, if you threw a hundred harpoons at a target, one of them was bound to hit.

One harpoon, though, was hardly enough to take the life of a massive creature that lived at once in earth and sky. Perhaps it wasn't even enough to wound it; if the harpoon had a rope attached to it, it would only drag the ship along. But the Myrmidons grabbed the rope in their claws, spread the wings on their backs, and shimmied down to the manta.

Now the Myrmidons were in their element. They slammed harpoon after harpoon into the manta's back, then switched to hatchets, hacking away at it. They didn't have time to actually whittle down its health, but struck into crevices in its shell, making pinpoint slashes at its gills and fins. It wasn't long before the manta gave a mourning cry and tilted to one side, drifting lazily down through the air. Finally, it hit the ground with a great crash, spraying sand everywhere.

"If you get 'em on the ground, even the big ones die," the Myrmidon captain explained. "'S just how it works."

"A magnificent display," Lizard Priest said, rolling his eyes in his head, to which the captain replied with a clack of his mandibles, "This is how we make our living. Happens to be their mating season just about now. They form these huge schools to go find females."

It made fishing a simple matter.

With that, the Myrmidon captain turned his antennae into the wind, promptly raising his hand toward the others on the ship. In the blink of a compound eye, the sailors had adjusted the sails and turned the rudder. To Priestess it seemed like pure magic, but Female Merchant appeared to feel differently. Her face was a mélange of anxiety, concern, and excitement as she stared fixedly at the ships and the sand mantas.

"Everything all right?" Priestess asked, and Female Merchant waved a hand as if to dismiss the question. "Oh, uh, f-fine. I was just thinking it's all sort of…incredible."

"You over there," the Myrmidon captain called to Female Merchant. "You look like a merchant. I might could be had to do a little trade."

"...I would be most grateful," Female Merchant replied, looking at the deck and flushing a little upon realizing he had read her so easily.

I'm surprised, Priestess thought. She had always heard Myrmidons were colder, less-engaged creatures. But even these brief interactions didn't seem so. *I guess you never know for sure until you meet them.* Priestess diligently corrected this presupposition—perhaps it didn't go far enough to be called a bias—within herself.

Assumptions were not helpful, not when it came to the desert, or to Myrmidons, or to adventures. This much, at least, she had learned to her great distress on her very first quest.

She shot a glance at Goblin Slayer, though it wasn't clear what he took it to mean. The cheap-looking metal helmet quietly turned to the captain. "...Do you know anything about the goblins?"

Oh gosh. This again. Priestess felt a smile tug at the edges of her lips at his sheer hopelessness.

"Goblins?" the Myrmidon captain said, dipping his head in what appeared to be thought, his antennae bobbing gently. "Used to fight them and fight them pretty often back in the day, but I don't suppose you'd be interested in those stories."

"What?" High Elf Archer, her ears flicking almost like the captain's antennae, was immediately intrigued. "Don't tell me... Did you used to be an adventurer?"

"Something of the sort." The Myrmidon captain waived the subject away as if it was all too much trouble. Or wait... Could it be, Priestess wondered, that he was embarrassed? "Frankly, it all depends a bit on how much you all know—about this country, I mean."

"Well, I know diplomatic relations soured after the new king came to the throne...," Priestess said, putting a finger to her lips and trying to remember.

Female Merchant picked up the subject. "...And I've heard there have been suspicious movements on the border."

"You're not wrong, but you're not right, either," the Myrmidon captain said as he slowly took a seat. He looked dignified and self-possessed as he did so, bespeaking many years of real experience. His carapace, visible in glimpses under his robes, was streaked with a panoply of small scars. "The king hasn't changed. The old king died, that much is true. But it's the prime minister who runs this country now."

"As a tyrant?" Female Merchant asked. The Myrmidon captain shrugged, producing a clicking sound from his carapace. "There's still a princess around. Doubt she can stop him, though."

"And what, then?" Lizard Priest asked with a slow motion of his head. Lizardmen were consummate warriors. Chances were he knew the answer before he asked the question. "Those bandits we battled, who looked akin to soldiers. Were they instead...?"

"Soldiers disguised to look like bandits, most likely," the captain responded. Goblin Slayer gave a low grunt. He didn't bother to hide his intense displeasure—as if he ever did.

Priestess understood how he felt, though. This was a fact that hardly bore contemplating.

"You're suggesting the soldiers may have been working *with* the goblins?"

If those had been simple thieves or mountain bandits, it would not have been unusual for their territory to encroach on that of the goblins. But for the armed forces of the state itself to engage in such Bushwacker-esque behavior within spitting distance of goblins... Yet, it seemed the only conclusion. The goblin horde had equipment, the resources to keep wargs, and the ability to ride them. Under ordinary circumstances, no horde so large and elaborate could have survived for long within spitting distance of a national army.

The Myrmidon captain didn't respond. Instead, he clacked his mandibles. "No one knows for sure if the king died of assassination or just illness. One thing's certain: That prime minister is a clever man."

He probably means...whatever he puts his mind to. Priestess felt a rush of vertigo and suddenly felt unsteady on her feet. Humans...obeying goblins? If it were some cultist or knight-servant of the gods of Chaos, she might yet understand—but the prime minister of an entire country? What kind of plans could possibly motivate such a wretched act? Priestess hugged herself, feeling a chill despite the oppressive sun.

"Don't act so shocked. There have been humans who obeyed monsters from time immemorial." *Hrmph.* The Myrmidon expelled air from his spiracles, his antennae bobbing. "It's a mad story all around… For example, have you heard of a weapon that launches a stone using fire powder?"

"You mean the ones that look like cylinders, big and small?" Dwarf Shaman said as if this made sense to him, but Priestess had never heard of such a thing; she exchanged a puzzled look with High Elf Archer.

"You mean flintlock rifles," Female Merchant said. Priestess could only echo, "Flint lock?"

"I've heard of them," Goblin Slayer said softly. "But from what I can tell, they don't suit my purposes. I don't need them."

"Well, these people did," the captain said. "These weapons can pierce through armor. Get enough of them together, and you can sweep an enemy unit off the field. An army equipped with them could rule the day." Or at least, the captain added, it seemed that someone, at some point in this nation's history, had plotted to do such.

"And what came of it?" Goblin Slayer asked, urging the captain on.

"The opposing horseman avoided the bullets by scattering as they charged, evaded them by using Deflect Missile on contact and smashed the rifle formation."

"As well they might," Lizard Priest stated as if it were obvious, his eyes rolling in his head. "A single weapon can never rule all on the battlefield. There are too many paths to victory."

A sand-laden wind swept noisily across the deck. The Myrmidon captain looked up at the sky with his compound eyes. The sand formed a brownish haze against the blue. "All it means is…they have no idea what they look like to everyone else."

§

When the sun was just past its zenith, the ship slid to a halt with a whisper of sand. In the distance, they could see something looming like a small, dark mountain. It had several tiers of rounded minarets—a castle. It was unlike any castle Priestess had ever seen, though, and she found herself so taken with the sight that she forgot to climb down off the gunwale.

"That's the capital," the Myrmidon captain said. "We give it a wide berth. Don't want any trouble." His remark seemed to bring Priestess back to reality; she straightened up and bowed her head. "Uh, um, th-thank you very much…!" She bowed repeatedly, clasping her cap to her head. This seemed to discomfit the captain, who waved a hand.

"Don't bow and scrape. Whatever happens to you lot doesn't matter to me. I don't know how you plan to deal with the goblins, but if you want information, that's where you'll find it. Do you have any connections at all?"

"We have a safe-conduct pass and the handful of supplies we could carry…," Female Merchant said, her finely shaped eyebrows pulling into a frown. She looked something like a disappointed child. "But everything else, we lost in the sandstorm."

"The Red Wind of Death? That's a force to be reckoned with. Do you have any money?"

"Yes, some. And we have our passes… Do you think they'll really get us through the gate?"

"If they don't, the money will. And some gold and silver will enable you to do some trading in the city."

Virtually everything in this world had a price: goods, information, the right to enter a city. You could obtain them all if you could pay.

The wind rushing by told the story. The Myrmidon captain spoke as if comforting a small girl: "There are two deities in the desert. The God of Wind, and the Trade God. What the wind takes, the wind may yet return to you." Then he reached into his robes, his mandibles clacking and his feelers stretching out toward the group. "Which of you is the cartographer in your party?"

"That would be me," Lizard Priest said, raising his hand. "What of it, Captain?"

"Take this with you." With an almost casual motion, he tossed him a roll of what appeared to be papyrus paper. Lizard Priest caught it easily out of the air and unrolled it, to discover an expertly drawn diagram. "Well, well…," he said with a gasp. "A most magnificent map…"

"It depicts the area around here. Do with it as you like, so long as you don't take it out of the desert."

"Your consideration is most moving." Lizard Priest brought his hands together in a strange gesture and bowed his head deeply.

"When Scaly's right, he's right," Dwarf Shaman said from beside him. He gave his bulging item pouch a smack with his rough palm. "And we sure appreciate you sharin' your food and water."

"With all this, if we run into another storm, we might just make it!" High Elf Archer said.

"Prefer we not. Not all of us can live off mist and dew like elves, Long-Ears." High Elf Archer laughed openly at this, hopping down off the ship with an acrobatic motion. Her white robes billowed as she came to rest on the ground without disturbing a single grain of sand. Dwarf Shaman, in contrast, landed with a thump, provoking another gale of laughter from the elf. She stopped laughing when she was caught in the shower of sand kicked up by Lizard Priest's landing.

"Many pardons," he said when he saw her standing there with her hands on her hips, but then he rolled his eyes in his head as if he was not after all too concerned. Then he stretched out his long tail toward the ship so that Priestess and Female Merchant could use it like a railing as they came down.

"Now you may both disembark."

"Th-thank you."

"…Pardon me."

The girls held hands—and Lizard Priest's tail—as they worked their way hesitantly down to the sandy ground. Still perhaps perturbed by the shower of sand, High Elf Archer jabbed Lizard Priest gently in the side with her elbow. "I notice *I* didn't get a tail railing."

"I was so taken by the agility and grace you displayed that I forgot to even think of it," he said with a guffaw, and High Elf Archer puffed out her cheeks in a way most unbecoming of a high elf. It lasted for only a moment, though. By the time she was striding forth on her long legs across the sands, she was already back in good humor. "Orcbolg, hurry up!" she called, spinning and waving to him.

"Ah, elves. A cheerful people if there ever was one," the captain commented from the deck, fondness evident in his tone.

"She's always a help," Goblin Slayer said, not necessarily sure what the captain was driving at. "Me, I am not capable of behaving that way."

"You," the captain said. Goblin Slayer stopped with his hand on the gunwale. The Myrmidon captain turned his compound eyes, the emotion and expression of which were almost impossible to read, on Goblin Slayer. "You look like a man lost."

He sounded so certain.

"...No," Goblin Slayer said, but for a moment he didn't say anything further. He inhaled; considered; and finally, slowly, admitted, "Yes. I am surprised you could tell."

"It wasn't hard." The Myrmidon produced a dry clicking sound. It seemed he was laughing. "I seemed to fall in with a lot of those back in the day."

"I am their leader...," Goblin Slayer started, but then corrected himself. "Or rather, they have recognized me as such." Then the cheap-looking metal helmet swiveled from one side to the other. Through the slats of his visor, he saw his party and Female Merchant, standing on the sand and waiting for him.

"Hey, what's going on with that roof? It looks like an onion! Weird!" High Elf Archer was saying.

"Theory's simple enough, that. You pile up the stones, then add the keystone and voilà, it stands up on its own."

"There is certainly a great breadth of knowledge among the peoples of our many lands."

"I feel like I haven't stopped being surprised since we got here," Priestess commented.

"...Me too," agreed Female Merchant.

Goblin Slayer let out a breath as he watched them. He had never imagined he might come to such a place and in such company. Perhaps until this moment, he never would have thought he was even capable of it.

"I'm afraid that other than goblin slaying, I am...not good for much," he said, wondering privately what he might have been able to do about all that had happened up to this moment. Could he go forward? It would be a simple fact to say he was uncertain on this matter.

Without pomp or ceremony, though, the Myrmidon captain replied, "Any adventurer eventually has to take that step into completely unknown territory. Some die there. Some come close. Some survive. How much they fretted about it rarely comes into it."

"..."

"So I guess the only thing to do is whatever you can do."

"That's it?"

"Yes," the captain answered with a flick of his antennae. "That's the size of it."

"...I see," Goblin Slayer said after a long moment, then exhaled again.

It was not an answer. His concerns didn't suddenly vanish. It was simply a reaffirmation of fact. Gods—if his master were to see this, how he would laugh, how he would mock, how he would beat his charge mercilessly. His charge who had no smarts, no talents. All he had was guts—which meant all that was open to him was to act. It was everything he had.

Goblin Slayer squeezed his fingers on the gunwale, tensing his whole body before leaping to the sand. He landed with a *thump*, a light but powerful sound unlike that made by either Dwarf Shaman or Lizard Priest.

"May you do well, adventurer," the Myrmidon captain murmured as he watched the group depart with his compound eyes. The sun, though past the midpoint in the sky, was still bright and hot enough to burn, but soon it would soften into the crimson of evening. That would be about when those adventurers would reach the city.

The captain waved his antennae to help distract from the fact that he had come to their aid almost without thinking about it. He had left adventure behind him long ago, but every once in a long while things like this happened: The dice were inscrutable.

Perhaps this is a tailwind from the God of Travel. Or perhaps it's the doing of Fate or Chance...

"Well, personally...I'm perfectly happy either way."

And with that, the Myrmidon Monk gave a loud clack of his mandibles.

©Noboru Kannatuki

"Yoo-hoo!"

"Ugh…"

The setting was the water town—specifically a dim drinking establishment, at a booth deep inside, in what seemed like the darkest part of the room.

The people were a diminutive young lady with silver hair, who was waving gaily, and the fixer, a young man who frowned openly when she appeared.

The restaurant was impeccably furnished, not the sort of place the average citizen would have found themselves. It was only natural he should be surprised to see her there in a maid's uniform, but the girl blended in remarkably well. She was small enough to pass for a rhea—an illusion to which her arms, magically hidden, contributed.

Guess the rumors of her being back from the Dungeon of the Dead weren't just stories… Which makes her how old now, I wonder? the fixer thought insolently. As much as her appearance here surprised him, however, no good ever came of upsetting a johnson.

"And how might I help you today?" he asked the girl, looking at her. "I already reported on our progress, as I recall."

"Yeah, that's exactly what I wanted to talk about." The girl plopped herself down on a stool and waved to the bartender, ordering a very expensive drink without a second thought. Or perhaps we should say a very *strong* drink. Dwarven fire wine wasn't something the average human could handle.

A harefolk waitress brought the drink with a speed and discretion befitting the quality of this establishment, and the girl drained it in a single gulp. "One more, if you don't mind."

"I thought alcohol was strictly off-limits when one was talking about a run."

"If you can call this alcohol. More like water."

Water! If an elf drinks that stuff, it would make their head explode. The fixer gave a defeated shake of his head.

"So tell me about this progress," the girl said.

"Oh, you know. Things are…complicated."

The harefolk waitress reappeared shortly, her tail twitching and her hips swaying, and the silver-haired maid accepted another drink. This time she sipped at it delicately, savoring it even as she gave an annoyed shrug. "And this after we used the princess's demands as an excuse to request a scout."

"Your neighbor, eh?" the fixer pointed out, and the silver-haired maid nodded her agreement.

But what excuse? The fixer laughed to himself. It had all been a convenient pretext to go charging in. "This princess seems nice and calm, and that's what counts," he said. "By the grace of the Earth Mother."

It might sound as if he was being rather too direct, but that wasn't the problem. That was what this shop was for. This johnson had started it, after all.

Guess it won't do me any good, sweating the niceties…

The fixer exhaled, defeated, then called out "Miss!" to the waitress and ordered a drink. He wasn't sure how he felt about knocking back a drink while his party was out there working hard, but, well, he was in a battle of his own.

Making connections, making preparations, gathering information, cleaning up after, providing emergency support, and so on, and so forth: When it came down to it, the running itself was just the last and most conspicuous step in a long process. But just because it was so obvious, you had to be careful. Be crude when they thought you would be technical, and technical when they thought you would be crude. That was the key to longevity here.

The white animal at his feet pawed at his shoes, but he pushed it back gently with his toes.

Sorry, I know she's down with illness, but you've gotta let me off this time—I'll go see her next time.

A mage who could control several familiars was a stout ally, and thanks to *her*, they were able to maintain tight coordination.

The spy, the elf wizard, the sprite-user driver, the cleric of the God of Knowledge, the wizard who served the familiar, and himself. These six made a good party, at least in the fixer's opinion. He hoped everyone else would think so, too. That was exactly why it was his role to muster all his eloquence and volubility with every johnson, even the one in front of him now.

"And what? We cleaned up the matter of the blasphemy surrounding the consecrated wine, didn't we?"

"You cleaned up goblins. They don't count for much."

"Just send the army to the village, keep it safe that way," the fixer said, both to divert the discussion and perhaps to get a rise out of the young woman.

The silver-haired maid snorted. "If we had unlimited budget, resources, and personnel. And if every single man we had bled the royal colors," she quipped before murmuring, "Actually, I guess that wouldn't be so great." Then she looked up at him with a threatening glare. "You know we hired you to do more than kill goblins, right?"

"Naturally," the fixer replied with a laugh. "And believe me, it's been very profitable. More trouble means more business."

Cultists and vampires and demons, injustice and corruption, rebellious regional governors and pedigreed nobles. Nobody ever got rich prosecuting crimes—was it the elf who had said that? Nothing could have been truer of those who ran through the shadows cast by the great war between Chaos and Order.

"The real question is who's plumping for those goblins," the silver-haired girl said, exhaling.

Not *how*. Not *to what end*. But *who*. The fixer understood perfectly well what she meant by that. That understanding was what prompted the unpleasant feeling within him. He felt compelled to ask: "You're not going to say we should send our beloved hero in, are you?"

"Not even possible," the girl snorted. "She'd be a stupid card to try to play in a dispute between private individuals." Although there were many who thought they ought to—chiefly those with a modicum of power. The maid shrugged.

"Hold on… Are you suggesting *our* gang should bring them down?"

That would be dangerous. Immensely dangerous. But it could mean a lot of money. Some background investigation would be necessary. It was the role of a face to weigh risk and reward in the scales. Some fought with swords, some shot arrows, others fired spells; a face did battle with words.

The fixer contemplated. Which would be easier: the "demon" captain or a fight here in the water town? The familiar at his feet, sensing how things were going, had assumed a ready position with respect to the young woman. If negotiations went south and things got hot, her spells would be his lifeline. It had been the right choice to have her here.

But then the silver-haired young woman, perhaps registering the change in the fixer's demeanor, waved her hand dismissively. "No, someone else is already on it. No need for you to go stirring up the hornet's nest, too. It would be like the warrior right up front getting covered in slime."

"Oh?"

"We've got a specialist taking care of the goblins. The Lady Archbishop and her young merchant friend are handling it."

The fixer *hmm*ed with affected disinterest, even as he listened closely to what the young woman was saying. She referred respectfully to the "Lady Archbishop," but the tone of her voice was as casual as if she were speaking of a friend of her sister's. That woman was one of the Six Heroes. As for the merchant… She must mean the young noblewoman who had gone from adventuring into proper business.

All of which means there's likely to be more excitement with the next country over.

©Noboru Kannatuki

He would have to make ready. In the world of the shadows, unrest always meant potential business opportunities.

"Well, that's karma for you," the silver-haired girl said with a superficial laugh. "One good turn deserves another."

"Live by destiny, die by karma?" The fixer laughed, too. "Helpful words, if you're a child clutching her allowance."

With that, the fixer glanced at the girl. "So what are you really here for?"

"To complain." With hardly a hint of emotion, the girl swigged the rest of her drink, then called to the waitress. "There are too many venomous bugs around here. Spiders and scorpions." She sighed deeply, stretched out on the counter and let her hair splay on the bar top. The fixer wasn't interested in her age, but at the moment she looked to him like an indignant child. "Too busy with exterminating lately."

"His Majesty is?"

"The third son of an indigent noble and his little friends are." In profile, the girl almost looked amused, and the slight flush and her pale cheeks seemed due to more than just the alcohol.

What she means is, he can't let adventuring go, the fixer thought and decided to order himself another drink. It was the best stuff, the most delicious, and the strongest; it had to be. It had to be if it was to cover his friends' safe return, the prosperity of his business, the efforts of the red-haired cardinal, and a wonderful adventure besides.

"Well, you'll have to tell me all about that quest someday."

"Maybe; if there's a chance." The girl laughed, playing with the wine cup in her hand. The fixer saw just how like adventurers they were and how unlike.

"So what exactly do you want us to do?"

"Find someone and do a run, I suppose."

It was just them, their skills, the shadows, and the implacable imperative: Get the job done.

That was who they were: runners.

CHAPTER 4

THE ANASTASIS FROM GEHENNA

"...Fwoo..."

"Mmm...!"

"Phew..."

Three women together can be quite a ruckus, but at this moment the trio of young ladies was simply exhaling. The dim stone room billowed with perfumed smoke, a white mist that kept them from seeing even the face of the person next to them. The backrests of the marble benches were in fact parts of large boxes, and it was from them that the steam emerged. Dressed in only thin clothing—High Elf Archer was wearing nothing more than a towel—they relaxed and let the sweat flow. This foreign steam bath was the perfect thing after exhausting themselves in the desert.

"...Ahhh... Humans think of the strangest things...," High Elf Archer said, her ears drooping, looking as lazy as her voice sounded. It seemed a long time now since she had worried about baths as being a place where the sprites mixed. Her hair was damp with the rising steam; she looked the picture of contentment.

"It's very different from sitting in front of the fireplace, isn't it?" Priestess said.

"You know, some castles and grander mansions are heated by a fire kept in a big granite room," Female Merchant added, her tongue too lazy to form the words quite properly; she, too, looked utterly relaxed.

"It's because the stone takes heat so well. I have to say, using it for a steam bath is...unique." As she spoke, Female Merchant worked her hand along her neck muscles. Perhaps her scar was hurting her.

Priestess, holding her belongings delicately, decided to try to change the subject. "...Well, um, here we are in town. But...what do we do now?" Yes, that was the problem. Priestess closed her eyes languorously. *No*, she thought, *it's not actually a problem at all.*

Maybe her blood flow had improved. She let herself sink into the heat, so different from, more comfortable than, the burning of the desert. Even here in this country of sun and sand, steam baths were ubiquitous. She heard you could even get a massage elsewhere in the building.

But there wasn't time to get the kinks worked out of their muscles. There were things they had to do. That's right, it wasn't a problem. It was a question of how to solve the problem. Having entered the city with the Myrmidon's help, the party had found lodgings and was already onto the next thing: Rest and recuperation, that had to come first. And then they would find the information they needed to make their next move.

When you didn't know your right from your left, it was rarely advisable to charge ahead. Lizard Priest and Dwarf Shaman had said they would go find a bite to eat and check out the town while they did so. Goblin Slayer went off on his own, saying he had somewhere to go. That left the girls to themselves...

I wonder if they were being considerate.

He had left them with only the brusque command, "Rest," but they had all known one another quite a long time now. She could guess what he was thinking.

Unlike before, she very much had her choice now. She simply had to speak up. Still, Priestess had simply replied to him with "Right," and she, Female Merchant, and High Elf Archer had come to this bathhouse.

If she wasn't in good physical and mental shape, she wouldn't be able to pray to the goddess when the moment came. "This *is* enemy territory, after all."

One should relax when it was the time to relax and be on guard when it was time to do so. Priestess stretched out an arm, got some water from the basin against the wall, and washed her face. The splash of the water, the chill against her overheated skin, felt wonderful.

"I'm...," Female Merchant said diffidently, "...thinking of doing some business."

"Business?" High Elf Archer asked, her ears flicking.

"Mm-hmm," Female Merchant replied with a quick nod. "We lost our carriage, but I'm carrying some items that would be perfectly good for commerce."

Now that she mentions it..., Priestess thought. She seemed to recall Dwarf Shaman had precious gems sewn into his clothing. He'd described it to her as one way of preparing to travel, and now she saw what he meant. Luggage or cargo might get lost, but the clothes on your back tended to stay with you. Priestess pulled the cloth tighter around her and whispered, "I understand."

Female Merchant nodded. "I know a business that used to trade with our country before the usurpation of the throne. I'll ask around there."

"By yourself?" High Elf Archer narrowed her eyes. Then she leaned toward Priestess as if hoping to enlist her support. "Isn't that a bit dangerous?"

"I kind of agree," Priestess said, putting a slim finger to her lips in thought. "We don't know what's out there... And as you are our quest giver, we're technically your bodyguards." Yes, even though Female Merchant knew some magic, even though she carried a sword and knew how to use it, and even though she was a former adventurer herself, she couldn't be allowed to go off on her own in hostile territory... was what *he* would say anyway.

"I really don't think we can let you go alone," Priestess insisted.

"I see..."

Priestess blinked to see Female Merchant turn her eyes to the ground as if disappointed or depressed. Then she had to squint and force herself not to laugh. High Elf Archer must have noticed it, too, for a bell-like giggle formed deep in her throat.

It was profoundly pleasing to the two of them to have their friend act her age for once.

"Then this is two, two!" High Elf Archer said enthusiastically. She held up two lovely fingers on each hand, gesturing at Priestess and Female Merchant.

They both looked back at her blankly, as if to say: *Two?*

"Yep!" High Elf Archer said, jutting out her modest chest. "It's weird, the way Orcbolg went off on his own. It should be two by two— It's dangerous to go alone!"

That meant that Female Merchant, quest giver though she was, was being treated not as an interloper but as one of the team. There was no way to be sure whether it was really intentional, but elves' deep thinking sometimes did reveal the truth.

Female Merchant's eyes went wide for a second, and then a smile bloomed on her face like a flower. "Right! That's...fine, then," she said with a nod. *Like an obedient child*, Priestess thought. Even though their two ages weren't so far apart. Even though, indeed, Female Merchant looked the most adult among them. Priestess envied her that, just a little. But in fact, she was the more experienced; Female Merchant the less. And in that case...

"I'll be happy to—"

"I'll do 'business' or whatever with her, so you stick with Orcbolg!"

High Elf Archer had stolen a march on Priestess. The two fingers she had been holding up were now just one, pointing right at her.

"Er, uh..." Priestess blinked several times. "I was going to say I would go with her..."

"Aw, you two were practically joined at the hip all the way through that storm. We haven't seen her in ages. I wanna talk to her, too."

It sounded somehow odd to hear an elf casually use the expression "ages," and Priestess giggled in spite of herself. High Elf Archer gave her a look, apparently thinking Priestess was making fun of her. "D-don't get the wrong idea," Priestess said with a wave of her hand.

"I'm—"

She looked at Female Merchant.

"—fine with that... If you are?"

"Yes," Female Merchant said with a firm nod. "I was hoping to talk to you both a bit myself."

"That settles it, then!"

High Elf Archer was something of a strong wind herself. Priestess pursed her lips, feeling as if she had been treated just as much like a child as Female Merchant. But worrying about being treated like a child, let alone getting pouty about it—wouldn't that be the most childish thing of all?

With that in mind, Priestess nodded. "All right. I'm going to go ahead, then. I know Goblin Slayer is used to working solo, but..."

"But this isn't goblin slaying yet," High Elf Archer said with a guffaw, and even Priestess couldn't help a smile. As she was gathering up her belongings, Female Merchant looked at her curiously. "By the way, why *did* you bring your chain mail into the bath...?"

"Well, I'd hate to lose it, you know?"

High Elf Archer could only look at the ceiling without a word.

§

Priestess's nose prickled as they went outside; there was a familiar aroma of some sort in the air. It was a bit like white tea, perhaps.

Leaving the bathhouse, fresh and clean, Priestess was struck afresh by the way the town sprawled before her. It was a riot of sun-dried, lacquer-darkened brick buildings. Glass—the thin, transparent stuff was just as expensive here as it was in her home—was absent from the windows. The road was brown earth, packed hard from all the feet that passed over it. Specks of sand came riding in on the wind. The people walking along the path wore clothes she had never seen before, carried objects she didn't recognize. And over it all hung the shadow of the huge, round-roofed palace.

I know our castles back home are imposing, but this...

Castles built as defensive structures, for war, were intimidating, certainly, but this building was something different; it seemed designed to communicate how much smaller than it you were.

But this was a town, and those who lived here were people. The platinum rays of the sun as it sank in the sky were the same as anywhere. Children ran around barefoot. Elderly people played board games on tables set up at the side of the road. A woman, perhaps someone's wife, was purchasing fruit at a roadside stand.

Those are melons, if I'm not mistaken.

She had eaten one once. So this was where they came from...

Of course, it was not all bright and cheerful. Priestess knew all too well that there was more than that to the Four-Cornered World. She knew from experience that things happened all the time to upend a person's life.

She wondered sometimes if that was really acceptable.

For example, consider the people sitting in the gloomy shadows by the road, dressed in reeds, perched in front of empty bowls. And if you turned the corner just there, a seamy pleasure district might be not far beyond or perhaps an opium den. Over in the market, she was sure slaves were being sold. Perhaps some had fallen to that depth through debt, or failure to pay their taxes, or crime, or by being on the losing side in a war.

It was not a question of good or bad: It was a fact; it was the world Priestess lived in.

And then there's goblins.

Obviously, goblins weren't the only monsters threatening this world. Perhaps it was a mistake to focus on them and them alone. Ogres, giant eyeballs, dark elves, trolls, Mokele Mubenbe, greater demons, ice witches, cultists. And these were only the terrors of the world that she had seen with her own eyes. It was impossible to believe that goblins were truly the greatest danger. And yet...

That's right...

When was it they'd been in the water town? Goblin Slayer's words floated in the back of her mind.

"The air of a village that's been targeted by goblins..."

There were shadows, somehow, on the people's faces. The wind reeked, somehow. She felt an unpleasant tingling on her neck. Perhaps it was just, in a word, her imagination. But then again, intuition was essentially applied experience. Was she able to sense things she hadn't before because of her accumulated experience, or did she merely feel like it?

"..." Unable to reach a definite conclusion, Priestess grasped her sounding staff as if in supplication and hurried through the town. She saw soldiers standing guard at every crossroad: people with curved blades at their hips, watching the road vigilantly. When she thought about what had happened on the road, she decided she would have to be careful of the soldiers—careful exactly because there were soldiers present.

Thus, she tried to make her way through town as innocuously as possible, so as not to attract attention. Not moving too fast. Not looking around too much.

On their way to the inn, they had passed by the place Goblin Slayer had said he would visit. She remembered it was about...

"Um, excuse me..."

"Buh?" Priestess's inexpectant utterance sounding silly even to her own ears. She looked over to see a woman in familiar clothes—that was to say, clothing from her own country.

"Ah, I knew it!" the woman exclaimed jovially, grinning at Priestess. A long ear twitched from beneath the cloth around her head. An insignia of the Earth Mother dangled from her neck.

"An elf...?"

"Thank goodness. I knew you had to be from the same land as me. I was so scared to ask one of the locals around here." The young elf woman, still smiling, approached Priestess, who looked around in some confusion. She had certainly not envisaged this situation. "I'm actually looking for directions to the bathhouse. You wouldn't happen to know...?"

"Oh, y-yes." What exactly should she say? Priestess nodded even though she wasn't actually sure what to do. "I do, uh, know the way..."

What was this feeling, the nagging sensation that something was off? Was it because of her acquaintance with High Elf Archer and all the elves she'd met in that village? In comparison with them, this girl just seemed...

"Stop that." Priestess's harried thinking was interrupted by another unexpected voice, this one calm and clear. It came from the roadside shadows. From a red-haired girl, also with long ears.

This red-haired elf walked toward them with authority, glaring at her fellow elf with a cutting look. "You're a fake. I know it— It's obvious from the way you talk."

"Heavens, what are you talking about? I was simply asking for directions…" The scarfed elf tried to look puzzled, but her anxiety was impossible to conceal. The red-haired elf didn't say a word. Priestess looked from one to the other of them in confusion, and then she noticed something about the first elf.

Sweat beads…

"…Pardon me very much!"

"Huh?!"

When you have an idea, act immediately. That, she had learned time and time again, was the key to survival.

Priestess reached out, under the elf's scarf, running her hand along her cheek. She did feel something wet on her palm, but it turned out what she had seen gleaming was not sweat, but white face makeup. Beneath the cake of powder, she saw flashes of blue-black skin.

"A dark elf…!"

"Pfah…" The elf—or rather, dark-elf girl—gave a click of her tongue, then spun around and set off running. Priestess grabbed her sounding staff and was about to brandish it, but thought better of it. Making such obvious trouble with guards on every street corner didn't seem like the best plan…

"Good thinking. That was the right decision," the red-haired elf said with a smile.

Oh… Priestess blinked. She wasn't an expert on telling elf ages, but was this woman rather younger than she had thought…?

"…She was in cahoots with the guards. They'll be on you in a flash, claiming you were talking to a drug dealer or something… Oh look." The red-haired elf indicated a soldier coming their way with his sword in his hand and a dangerous look in his eye.

Priestess weighed the options in her mind, the best way to talk her way out of this, but the elf was already on it. Before Priestess could say whatever she had been about to come up with, the red-haired elf waved a hand in front of the soldier in a mysterious gesture.

"We haven't been talking to anyone," she said.

"…" The guard looked flummoxed for a second, but then nodded. "You haven't been talking to anyone."

"You can go about your business."

"I'll go about my business."

Priestess didn't know what she was seeing, if it was some bizarre trick or sleight of hand or something. The soldier turned unsteadily and walked back to the intersection he had been guarding a moment before.

"The effect won't last long. Now's our chance. Let's go." The red-haired elf wiped some sweat from her brow with a sigh and started walking. This time Priestess didn't see any disturbed makeup on her face. She followed the elf, still alert and careful.

"That's how it starts," the redhead said without turning around. "Then they say they need to check your belongings for contraband and they lift some of your money."

"So it's all a con?"

"Maybe not all of it—they *are* real soldiers." The red-haired elf shrugged slightly, and Priestess just bit her lip without a word.

It had been an intuition of Chaos. She didn't believe that all people everywhere had to be completely perfect at all times. Even the gods didn't desire that. But corruption and injustice were the seeds of Chaos. When they blossomed, they would put down roots, spread, and become intractable. And then they could choke the beautiful flower of a country, like an invasion of witchweed.

"Why...?" Priestess asked simply, but the red-haired elf seemed to take it in a different sense than she meant it.

"Self-satisfaction," she answered with a laugh. "Wanted to build up some karma."

Priestess could hardly speak. She had never really been the doubting type to begin with.

But to doubt everyone all the time...

One couldn't survive that way, either. She took a deep breath and let it out, her shoulders slumping. It was just like when you were in a cave. Be vigilant when it was time to be vigilant. If something happened, respond immediately. She had been saved this way. The very first thing she needed to do was evident.

Priestess stopped and bowed her head. "Um, th-thank you very much!"

The red-haired elf blinked at her, then looked a little uncomfortable—downright embarrassed, in fact—as she scratched her cheek. "It really wasn't all that serious. Uh, hey... You're an adventurer, right?"

"Yes, I am," Priestess said. "I'm trying to find a place called the Golden Mirage..."

"That's perfect, then." The red-haired elf came to a halt and gave her a smile befitting a girl of fifteen or sixteen years old. "I was on my way here, too."

Priestess looked up in sudden realization. A beautiful pavilion stood over her, as if it had just this moment appeared, like an illusion.

§

The instant she stepped inside, Priestess was, shall we say, overwhelmed. The multistory building was constructed around an open central courtyard, and the entire place was far larger than it had looked from the outside. The individual rooms were arranged in a corkscrew shape, so that they looked down on the circular center area. And everything she saw gleamed of gold—but that wasn't all.

Water. There was a waterway in the center of the building with ostentatious amounts of water in it. Real water here in the desert—enough to use for a bath!

Priestess came to a stop without really meaning to; around her, people of all races shared whispered conversations:

"Rumor has it this place is a literal illusion..."

"...Hasn't it started yet? I've been trying to get reservations for months..."

"Don't get excited. The master's chosen guards are all very skilled—"

"Hey, look at that. Isn't that the owner of that huge store?"

A woman whose lower half was that of a snake slithered along—and humming in the water tank deeper in, was that a merfolk? Some of the servers had two heads, and some of the customers had bodies completely covered with bizarre tattoos.

Priestess stared openly for a moment before she snapped back to herself, shaking her head. *No, no.* She couldn't just stand there transfixed.

She quickly followed the red-haired elf, who was heading inside as if all this was old hat to her.

Truly, everything in the building seemed astonishing. Priestess could smell the smoke wafting from pipes attached to glass bottles. Servers walked by with plates of food she had never seen before. There was a quick *thump thump* from a table where someone was stabbing a dagger between the fingers of their open hand—some kind of gambling, she guessed. Waitresses sauntered down the halls, hips swaying, dressed in clothing so revealing it was enough to make Priestess blush. The padfoot standing in front of the door deep within the establishment must be some kind of guard. He was well muscled, as might be expected, but he also appeared to be wearing armor underneath his clothing. He bulged in strange places, and then there was the piercing horn growing on his face!

"That person there… Is he a unicorn person?"

"Not sure about that." The red-haired girl laughed. "Think he's what they call a rhino man." She sat in a place at the counter from which she could see the circular courtyard, and Priestess, as if drawn along inexorably, sat down beside her. Across the counter from her, a slim employee in a mask—a woman?—waited for her order.

"Umm…" Priestess looked up at the menu hanging over her head. It was in the common tongue, sort of. She could read the names of the drinks, but she didn't actually know what any of them were. The red-haired elf laughed when she saw Priestess's distress, and held up a finger to the masked employee. "You have anything without alcohol in it?"

"We do not in fact have anything containing alcohol," the employee said with a shake of their head. "Tea or other drinks, yes. And food."

"Just bring me something sweet and cold, then, please. And a bite to eat. Chef's choice."

"Oh, uh!" Priestess squeaked. "Me too, please. I'll have the same…!"

"Very well." The masked employee bowed respectfully to Priestess, refusing to taunt her for her obvious inexperience. She—Priestess still thought they were a she—went into the back, and Priestess let out a breath. She glanced over to discover the red-haired elf relaxing, completely at ease.

Priestess's eyes settled on the elf's ears, then she mumbled, "Huh?" and blinked. Those ears were awfully short for an elf but a little long to belong to a half-elf. "You're an elf—"

She chose her words carefully.

"—adventurer, aren't you?"

The woman grinned a little and shook her head. "No, a changeling."

Priestess recalled that this was the name for the offspring of an elf born to a human mother. It wasn't clear whether such children were the product of long-dormant ancestral blood finally awakened, or if they really were a trick played by the fae...

Whatever they were, they were born different from humans. This woman must have encountered a good deal of grief in her life.

Before Priestess could apologize for her mistake, the woman went on, "And I'm not so much an adventurer as..." She seemed totally unperturbed, proof that she was already comfortably walking her own path in life. Priestess was suddenly ashamed that she had considered apologizing and glanced at the ground. "...a professional purveyor of derring-do." The red-haired changeling smiled a touch shyly. Priestess gawked at this unusual locution.

"A professional...?"

"Well, because it's my job, see. I mean, it's more than that, but..." She almost sounded like she was making an excuse.

"...Your drinks, ladies." The masked server returned, soundlessly setting down cups and plates on the table. "Peach nectar diluted with water, stewed with jujube and ice sugar, then put over milk." Continuing, the masked server indicated the plate. "And this is oil-seared skate."

"Skate?"

"The rays that fly through the sand sea."

Oh, that must be the sand mantas...

Priestess nodded, then offered her thanks to the Earth Mother and began to eat. Why not? She didn't seem to see that distinctive, cheap-looking helmet anywhere in the establishment. And that being the case, it would be against her faith to let good, warm food go cold. After she finished praying, the first thing she tried was the oil-seared—which was to say, basically, fried—fish.

"…!"

The piping-hot food crumbled into little bits in her mouth, releasing a full-bodied flavor of fish. It was like fresh-baked buttered bread, like a white bread made with refined flour. It was wonderful, but then, it was also very hot. Of course she reached for the quartz cup.

"Eep… Wow…!" The sweet, cold drink threatened to spill out from her mouth, but it was so refreshing. She swallowed noisily, and she could feel it run all the way down to her stomach, a wonderful, soothing chill.

"Mm… Yep, very good," the red-haired changeling said with a smile, smacking her lips and clearly in excellent spirits. Priestess found this a novel sight, for High Elf Archer had no interest in meat or fish.

But she couldn't spend all her time being intrigued. She wasn't here for fun. Priestess whispered probingly to the masked employee, "Um, excuse me. I think a member of my party may be here—have you seen him?"

"What manner of person do you seek?"

"Erm." Priestess held up a long pointer finger and fell into thought. How best to explain him? "He's got a helmet, leather armor, chain mail…a shortish sword and a round shield on his arm…"

…Uh-huh, that'll do. She smiled a little to realize that just the litany of his outward appearance was more than enough to make clear who she was looking for. Then Priestess noticed that the masked employee seemed a little stiff, perhaps uncomfortable. "…In that case," she (?) said, "perhaps you had best begin with a look at the person on the stage."

"Stage…?" Priestess looked up just as the lights went out, and a single large light was shone on the stage in the center of the room. The crowd fell silent, waiting expectantly for something that was clearly about to happen.

The red-haired changeling whispered in Priestess's ear, "Ooh, it's starting."

Oh boy, was it starting.

§

Long ago, they scattered our sand like the stars,
  then laid to rest on a faraway brilliant land.
  Bend an ear to hear our whispered words:
  a tale of the sound of the wind...

There was a single clear ring of a bell, and then a faint voice spread out like a ripple. Shuffling forward onto the stage came a birdwoman with tanned skin and black wings. She appeared to be young, yet, her mien was detached and chilly, and her wing fingers grasped a curved blade.

The scimitar caught the faint light of the fire burning in the brazier, glinting and glowing like a living thing. Surely this was a blade of renown.

Suddenly, *whoosh*, the sword was released into the air, and the girl took two stern steps onto the stage. She spread out her wings as if she was falling to the ground, but then with one great flap she leaped up, and the sword was in her hand again. She drew a simple yet graceful arc in the air with her body, performing a stupendous sword dance.

The girl slashed and danced in time with a melody being played behind the stage. It was an old story of heroism, an ancient tale of valor left to future generations by a woman poet. A lake deep underground in the depths of the earth. A dark dragon who ruled there. The adventurers who challenged his black fortress. They beat their way through mobs of goblins and vampires, enlisted the aid of a dark dwarf, and finally descended to the deepest depths.

Only one of them noticed the shadow on the surface of the water: a rhea scout who sounded the alarm. In an instant, the dark dragon rose up with his great, long neck, with his terrifying acid breath that scorched and seared all it touched.

A lizardman warrior interposed himself between his friends and the blast. But his scales were burned away, his flesh dissolved, and he fell to his knees. A cleric of indeterminate age immediately invoked a healing miracle, but the enemy did not wait for her to act. A warrior-witch, bearing a musical instrument on her back and the blood of devils in her veins, rushed forward to buy them some time. Her Hexblade bit into the dragon's scales, and the lizardman took advantage of the opening. He gave the beast one good smash with his great golden staff, and the monster fled back to the murky depths.

The lizardman, though, howled out the name of his ancestors and pursued the creature into the deep. *"If I can strike you down with my weapon, my deeds shall be the stuff of songs. I wish, I only wish, for women to sing of me with smitten hearts."*

And thus, he broke the monster's neck underwater with a single hammering blow...

The dancing girl communicated all this not with words, nor even a song, but simply through the way she danced with the sword. Her tanned skin took on a gentle ruddiness with exertion, beads of sweat gleaming like pearls. Some in the audience must have noticed that her expressionless eyes were staring right at a young man in the seat of honor—the owner of the establishment. This dance, utterly impassioned, utterly single-minded, was being offered to him alone.

It was a dance of love, so dedicated and unmistakable that Priestess found herself blushing to see it. "Incredible...," she whispered without quite meaning to, and the red-haired changeling, likewise a little flushed, replied, "Truly."

All the patrons gathered here in this building were transfixed by the performance. Priestess had been so taken, in fact, that she couldn't immediately snap back to reality, but found herself letting out a long breath. The applause from the crowd was scattered and sounded distant, no doubt because the rest of the audience was just as lost in their own amazement as Priestess was.

The dancing girl bowed her head deeply and disappeared into the wings, but the specter of her act remained on the stage.

"They say she's the best dancer in the country," the red-haired elf said cheerfully.

"Yes, and...dragon slaying." Priestess almost hummed the words, as if they came from a dream. She closed her eyes; it was such a nostalgic expression, dragon slaying. She had never encountered a real dragon like the kinds they spoke of in fairy stories and legends. Perhaps one day she would find herself on such an adventure. Just like the thought-less banter she had exchanged that one time.

She felt all this, even though she understood that a dragon was not a facile creature, and meeting one might not be strictly pleasant.

"Ha-ha-ha… Well, a girl can dream," the red-haired elf said, brushing her hair off her long ears. Her laughter sounded strained, though. "But you know what they say, 'Let sleeping dragons lie.'"

"Because they're so dangerous, you mean?"

"I guess so—dangerous in pretty much every way." She provided no further explanation but rolled the quartz mug around in her hand. "I guess it's up to you whether or not you believe them."

"Uh…huh." Priestess tried to make a polite sound, but she didn't really follow. The elf girl seemed to sense this immediately. "What? You've got some kind of *thing* about dragon-slaying?"

"Oh, no. I just… I had a friend who talked about it once…a long time ago."

Friend. Could she really call him that? Priestess wasn't always sure. Him, the girls. One of the girls was still alive, but Priestess didn't have the courage—rather, had yet to find the courage—to go see her. Doing so would demand, she felt sure, far more nerve than confronting any dragon.

The red-haired changeling looked down quietly, brought the cup to her lips, and drank audibly from it. "Sometimes you have friends you can't see anymore."

"Yes… You do."

Priestess didn't know anything out the changeling's past, just as the elf couldn't know what had happened to Priestess. But neither of them had to say anything to know they had each been left behind.

I'm sure it must be one of the things that keeps her going.

Just like one of the things that made Priestess continue to adventure was her companions—her friends, from her very first party.

Her thoughts were shortly interrupted, though; her memories violently dispersed. All thought of the dance on stage was cast out by a chaotic commotion that started over by the entrance.

§

"Give it back…!"

"Aw, it's right here, kid!"

"My sword… Give it back…!!"

Priestess felt herself flinch but turned and looked to discover a young man surrounded by several thugs. Well, more properly, it seemed the young man had come lurching through the entrance and flung himself at the tough guys. One of them, a lizardman with bluish scales, tauntingly held up a sword in a beautiful scabbard. The young man, meanwhile, was a mess; he had obviously been worked over pretty good. The conclusion seemed obvious: The goons had beaten him up and stolen his sword.

"I beat you fair and square, punk. You want it, come and get it."

"Dammit… Give it *back*…!!"

It was clear to all and sundry that the gang had stolen the sword from the young man. But when the victim launched himself at his persecutors, tears in his eyes but nonetheless undaunted, no one moved to help. They knitted their brows, drew their mouths, looked away, and generally refused to show interest in the commotion, so unbecoming of this elegant establishment.

Maybe getting beat up by lizardmen was just something that happened in this country, in this land?

It's too much, Priestess thought. And so she shoved back her chair and stood. The masked employee gave a soft click of the tongue, summoning the unicorn-person guard, whose full-body armor creaked and cried as he moved forward. As for the red-haired elf, she smiled a little even as she sighed.

"Hey."

Because there was someone who was quicker even than the four of them. Metal fasteners clinked on his boots in time to his steps as he approached the scuffle, his shoulders swaying. He had leather outerwear that looked military— They took him for a spy.

"I thought I was here to enjoy a little song and dance… Quietly."

"Hrngh?!" The blue-scaled lizardman turned his unusually large eyes on the spy. The spy simply held up his hands, unhurried. In fact, he looked downright relaxed. "Hey now, no need to get angry. I'm just suggesting we take this outside."

"I hear you," the lizardman said with an unpleasant hiss of amusement, his eyes rolling in his head. "Good idea. Outside it is." The lizardman stepped away from the struggling young man, heading for the door with an almost slithering motion. The spy went behind him, mindful of the lizardman's long, curling tail. The lizardman looked at him with his glassy eyes as if seeing him for the first time. "It's a hobby of mine, knocking smart shits like you off their high horses."

"Oh?" The spy smiled. "You're welcome to, if you can."

Priestess wasn't completely clear on what happened next. It looked to her like the spy smashed a fist into the back of the lizardman's head with uncanny speed. There was an instant, though, when she was completely befuddled as to what had happened. She only heard a *thump* as she saw the lizardman collapse, and she spotted a silver flash arc out from his palm. The flash grazed the spy's hat, then buried itself in the wall of the building. It was steel wire attached to some kind of sharp spike the lizardman had launched from his hand.

"I thought I said *outside*." The spy, all but expressionless, broke the steel wire with his bare hands, then picked up the lizardman and flung him casually through the door.

And then it was all over.

The lizardman's posse spared the spy a quick, withering glare before they charged out after their leader. The other customers, along with the guard and the masked employee, saw that the matter had been resolved. Everyone turned pointedly back to their own business, and the hubbub of the bar promptly resumed. Much of the talk seemed to be about the dance; it was as if the fight just now hadn't even happened.

"Sorry about the mess." The spy pulled a gold coin from his pocket and flipped it to the masked employee, who snatched it out of the air. Priestess suddenly realized the employee had a blade in her hand, one so sharp it looked like a poisoned needle. When had she drawn that? The server put her weapon and the gold coin away calmly , and nodded once. It appeared to be directed at the wings of the stage, and Priestess could just spot the dancing girl hovering in the shadows, not backstage as she had expected. She had her hand on her sword, but she looked relieved now, and with a nod in the direction of the owner's seat, she retreated back inside.

I had no idea. Priestess blinked. She hadn't even seen them all move.

"Let's see here…" Quite indifferent to the scene around him, the spy was picking up the sword that had fallen from the lizardman's hand. Even Priestess could tell it was a beautiful saber, housed in an ornate scabbard. The spy looked at it critically, then tossed it to the young man standing unsteadily on his feet.

"Y-yikes…!" He grabbed it and hugged it to himself, looking at the spy in confusion. The spy flicked up the brim of his hat and seemed to smile, although his mouth was hidden by his overcoat. "You're a lucky guy."

"…!" The young man hugged the sword even tighter and, overcome, fled the building without even saying thank you. The spy watched him go, then turned lazily back in Priestess's direction. He raised a bashful hand. "Hey."

"For crying out loud," the red-haired elf said, but her wry smile suggested there wasn't much she could do about any of it. "Are you finished?"

"Eh, guess so," the spy replied with a glance at the doorway through which the young man had departed. "Just now."

"Hmm."

"Just one thing left. Link up with the others and have a little *run.*"

The conversation seemed downright intimate. Priestess was getting a good idea of the relationship between them just listening to it. She was stiff with nervousness, but she forced herself to press her petite bottom back into the seat. "Is he a…friend of yours?"

"Mm-hmm," the red-haired elf said with an awkward scratch of her cheek. "Handles scouting duties."

"Who's the girl?" This time it was the spy's turn to ask, but the red-haired girl got out of her seat saying, "Listen, I thought we weren't supposed to draw attention to ourselves."

"Hey," the spy grumbled, "he shot first."

"You just wanted to look good," the red-haired girl teased with a giggle. "That swagger—what's going on there?"

The spy looked properly abashed, mumbled something, but then said "Yeah, you're right," with a defeated nod. "But where's the harm? I was just having some fun."

"No harm done." The red-haired elf shook her head, smiling affably, and jogged over to him. She was probably happy to see the spy had done something much like she had. Priestess understood the feeling, if only intuitively.

"Ahem." Priestess tried to pick her words carefully. "Well... Take care." It was a platitude, but it conveyed what she truly felt. It was more than enough to convey her good wishes to this person whom she had known so briefly.

"Yeah, you too." The red-haired elf smiled gently, then took a gold coin out of her purse and slid it across the counter. The masked employee collected it without even glancing down at it, then gave an elegant nod of the head. "We hope to see you again."

"Thanks." The red-haired elf waved genially, then went trundling off after the spy like a girl on her way out for the night. They were each a different height, yet walking side by side, the ease between them communicated how long they had known each other. Years and years. Priestess idly watched them go, then let out a small sigh. She didn't understand what she felt was envy.

§

The unusual pair emerged from their unusual conference shortly thereafter.

"Yeesh, I knew you looked strange, but you ask strange questions, too. Pain in my behind."

"I believe I provided sufficient compensation."

"Of course you did. I know that! Sorry, just complaining. There's been more work than I can shake a stick at ever since my underling set up that shop." The young woman snorted— Was she a rhea? No, perhaps a dwarf. She had no beard, but the profuse hair gave her away, as did her footsteps, which bespoke rippling muscle despite her slim frame. Her luxurious clothing and the long boots in which she stomped across the floor spoke to a significant reputation.

Even as she grumbled, the young dwarf shot a glare toward the owner's seat. Someone in a cheap-looking helmet followed after her, a man in grimy leather armor, carrying a bottle full of some liquid and with a scroll stuffed in his item pouch.

"And if a person dares complain to *him*, his *raqsa*, the dancing girl, either gets all upset or whips out that sword. Gods…"

Not that anyone could really complain. Whether the birdwoman was in a good mood or not, her dancing brought in good money.

The wizard who could control black sand; the dancing girl who had come up from a slave; the masked assassin; the padfoot warrior—despite her continual muttering about her subordinates who had stepped back from frontline service, the dwarf woman sounded basically pleased.

Her former subordinates had gone their own ways. That was why she didn't have enough hands. But those subordinates had started shops that were making money. No denying reality. For practical people such as her, bemoaning the state of things seemed to be a sort of sport. Goblin Slayer had never expected a proper answer anyway, so this was all just fine.

"Y'know, I used to know someone like you," the dwarf said suddenly with a leering glance at the cheap-looking metal helmet as she worked her way industriously along. "Had a thief who couldn't tackle a tower for the fear of it. A dumb country whelp who just needed to find some spine and climb up the outside."

"I've done that," Goblin Slayer said nonchalantly. "How did it go for him?"

"Oh, he did it," the dwarf said, equally unconcerned. "Real scary barbarian, that one." She was silent for a second, then frowned and whispered, "It ain't like me, but…for once, I can't find anything else to say. O Barrel-Rider's disciple." She straightened up and held her small hands out toward the adventurer and his cheap armor. "Good luck and good courage to you."

"…I've never trusted to my own luck," Goblin Slayer replied, clasping the dwarf's small hands in his own gloved one. "But I will make best use of what I've been given."

"You do that."

This and the handshake seemed to be enough for the two of them. The dwarf woman nodded to the masked employee and the horned guard, then happily put the building behind her. Goblin Slayer looked slowly around the room, then started walking disinterestedly along. Priestess resolved not to make a peep until he arrived where she was sitting at the counter. She had just had an object lesson in the complicated procedures and etiquette demanded in a place like this. It would do no one any good if she interfered with what he was doing.

"Sorry, it seems I kept you waiting." This was the first thing out of his mouth, clear and certain. "In addition to getting information, I had to do some shopping. It all took longer than I expected."

"Not at all," Priestess said with a courageous smile and a gentle shake of her head. "It's all right."

"Is that so?" His tone was nonchalant, almost mechanical, but Priestess perceived the slightest change in him.

Is something…different?

He didn't hesitate to… Well, he never hesitated. But even so, she couldn't resist the thought.

And compared with him…

How was she? She had felt nothing but lost ever since they'd arrived in this country; she didn't rate her own performance very highly. She felt so inexperienced, like a freshly minted novice who hardly knew her left from her right. She certainly didn't feel like someone who deserved a promotion. Jealousy would be beyond the pale. She wasn't even in a position to feel such a thing.

I do get so tired of this lack of self-confidence.

"What's the matter?"

"Er, ah…!" When she realized that she was being watched from inside the helmet, Priestess hurriedly waved her hand. "N-nothing, it's nothing! Just…" Her voice was cracking. She swallowed. She could still taste the faint sweetness of the drink from earlier. "I just feel bad… making you do everything…"

Yes, that was what it came down to. She hadn't accomplished anything. Hadn't been of any help. She was just…here.

She hadn't contributed in the battle. Or when they were moving. Or when there was trouble. Or now, when there was information to be gathered. She hadn't been able to do anything about the thief in this foreign town, or stop the fight at this bar. Even if she had come to the Golden Mirage with Goblin Slayer from the start, what good would she have done? She could only have stood to the side, listening to his conversations. When Priestess thought about all this, she felt keenly that she was and always would be inexperienced.

But…

Even as she had these thoughts, she couldn't help thinking that maybe, just maybe, she had done what she could. For example, she had made sure to have on hand whatever was necessary (like the all-important Adventurer's Toolkit!) and to provide it when it was needed. She kept her eyes up during battle, using her sling to support her allies as best she could. During rests between adventures, she tried to take care of everyone, handing out food and water and so on.

And then there were the miracles that she alone in the party knew. Of course, Lizard Priest was far, far beyond her as a cleric. And it wasn't as if she was the best user of miracles the world had ever seen. She sometimes screwed up. But still.

I wasn't even rebuked this last time…!

She still had some bad memories about the Purified miracle, but this time she had succeeded. The thought brought her a little bit of happiness. Even the gods had acknowledged her. Almost as soon as she had the thought, she had another one: *That was going a bit far.* She admonished herself to remain humble.

But at the same time, she let the thoughts flow. The battle with the ogre, the fight beneath the water town, her dance at the harvest festival, the attack on the fortress and the training ground. Sure, she had failed at the elf village, but then she had challenged the Dungeon of the Dead, and had managed to play a small part at the snowy mountain as well. The events surrounding the wine for the offering had made her feel inexperienced, sure, but… When she actually counted out her activities like this, she started to think: Could it be that she was working harder than she realized? If she wasn't, why would they talk of promoting her?

She was never going to be able to do everything by herself. Even the Great Hero, even the archbishop of the water town, had worked with their own parties to save the world.

Heh, no, no. Maybe it was a certain kind of evidence of her growth that she was even willing to compare herself to august groups like those. It said in the Scriptures: "The moment one thinks one is enlightened, one is not enlightened. Such a one is still deluded." In the end, Priestess's thoughts kept swirling around the same place. She understood her lack of self-confidence was one of her failings, but she had no good way to measure her growth, either. It was a question with no sure answer, and it left her feeling like she was chasing her own tail.

"No." For this very reason, it was a great joy to her to see him shake his head. "The more cards one has to play at the crucial moment, the greater a help it is."

As ever, he said a little less than she would have liked.

"…" Priestess pursed her lips in a pout but soon giggled at her own childishness. The laughter helped buoy her spirits, and she smiled and said, "Listen." She put up a finger to emphasize her words. "I don't think that's really a compliment."

"Hrk…"

"What you're really saying is that I'm just there, but I don't do anything."

This provoked a quiet grunt from inside Goblin Slayer's helmet. Priestess placed a gold coin on the counter with no small conviction, then began to shuffle away. When she reached the door of the building, she turned, her golden hair rippling. On her face was a broad smile. "So I'm going to help her for real—you'll see!"

It was a statement of her intentions, as well as a sort of vow. If she didn't manage to do it, then she would not accept promotion even if it were offered to her. And just the ability to say this made her feel more confident, even if she had no special basis for it.

"…" The unusual adventurer in the cheap-looking metal helmet was silent for a while, then simply said what he always said: "Is that so?"

So Priestess, too, answered as she always did: "It certainly is."

He brushed past her and out of the building. Priestess pattered after him. Behind them, the masked employee was giving a bow of the head. "We await your next visit."

"Of course," Priestess said with new certainty, turning back to offer a brief bow of her own.

Next time— Next time she would make sure she could come here with full confidence, even if she was alone. That was her goal, what she wanted to become. Like the red-haired elf. Like Witch. Like the archbishop. Or perhaps, like a Silver-ranked adventurer.

"I've decided on our destination."

"Don't tell me…the castle?"

"No."

They went through the door as they had this conversation. There was no sign now of the lizardman who had been tossed out nor of the spy or his red-haired friend. Priestess didn't think she had been in the building all that long, but it suddenly seemed like ages since she had felt the outdoor air on her skin. And at last she realized what it was she was smelling, the faint, familiar aroma.

Huh, so that's it…

The air here might seem different, but the smell of rain, it seemed, was the same everywhere. For reasons she didn't understand, the thought made Priestess very happy.

PRINCESS OF PERSIA

The princess despised the prime minister. Just as much as she despised the captain of the guard she had been confronting moments before.

Of course, this wasn't because she simply hated everyone. Nothing of the sort. This was not a favorable night for a ride on a sand ship like the one that now cut its way through the rain-washed air.

"Well now, Princess. I must say you're not looking in the finest spirits." Even the wind that blew across the deck couldn't carry off the obnoxious, pestering note in the voice.

If looks could kill, the princess would have murdered him with the eyes she had on him now. "How could I be? How could anyone be, after what I saw—after what you made me watch?" She spat the words with a vehemence unusual for a woman of such high birth. The words mingled with the sand and whipped away.

The prime minister put his hand on the curved saber at his hip and considered the silhouetted skyline of the capital. He offered only a dismissive snort. He didn't hide the sunbaked, blue-black skin that revealed him to be of dark elf blood. "I admit, it was not the most delicate thing to do. Consider it a reflection of our dear captain's persona."

"Unbelievable…" The princess bit her lip. "If my father were alive, he would never allow this."

"Indeed, in his passing we lost a truly fine man." The prime minister shook his head. He spoke the words, but he didn't believe them.

"I assure you, it breaks my heart. To imagine I had someone in my employ who would resort to such underhanded methods!"

This much, it seemed, was the truth. The prime minister knit his brow with sorrow, and he truly did seem to feel regret. It was the same expression he had produced for the princess at the scene of the crime. Perhaps it was all he could do; to look pleased about such a thing would have condemned one as no better than a goblin.

"He didn't understand what he was doing. He simply followed his idea through to its natural conclusion."

"Well your uncomprehending captain and you, who allowed him to do what he did, are neither of you better than goblins."

This barb seemed to touch the prime minister's pride especially deeply. His eyes opened wide, a fire burning within them, and he all but grabbed the princess. "You truly believe Order alone can preserve a country?"

"That's why ours was destroyed," the princess said, quelling her instant of fear, instead drawing a deep, measured breath into her ample chest. "But those who rely entirely on Chaos meet the same fate."

"You speak as if you knew anything about it."

"I do. Do you have any idea what you look like right now?" *Shallow, manipulative, foolish, and prideful—and beyond salvation.* "You have no knowledge nor courage. Only a filthy, haughty power."

The princess let out a breath, forced her knees to stop shaking, and stared resolutely ahead.

The prime minister didn't intend to kill her immediately, but there was still fright. He had usurped the kingship. If the princess was not recognized as the legitimate heir, there would most likely be a rebellion among the people. It would be possible to put it down by sheer force, but that would be a great deal of extra trouble... Thus, the prime minister had shown the princess what he had shown her. Perhaps he had hoped to break her spirit, but his hope had been in vain.

There was just one small thing she could cling to in this moment. By sending out a quest via her pet rat, she had been able to help her faithful ladies-in-waiting to escape. They would bring help, she was sure.

Someone or something to cast the darkness out of this nation. They had to.

"Ah yes," the prime minister said, not looking at her. "If you are thinking of your friends, let me inform you right now that they cannot help you."

"…!"

"You should know full well, Princess, how skilled our nation's soldiers are. I expect to receive their severed heads shortly."

The princess opened her mouth to retort, but this time nothing would come out.

"You haven't much time left. I advise you to think carefully."

And with that, the prime minister seemed to lose interest in the princess. She resisted the urge to collapse as she thought of the magical hourglass to which her life was connected. When all the sand had fallen through it, her life and her soul would be forfeit, plaything of the djnni for all eternity.

The prime minister, she felt sure, would not especially mind this outcome. Whether because it saved him the trouble of turning her into a mindless puppet or simply out of the cruelty that so often seemed endemic to dark elves…

The princess could only speculate as to why she had been given this reprieve. Her hands were not bound, her feet were not chained, but she was unquestionably a prisoner at this moment. And when they got back to the castle, she would certainly not be allowed out of her chambers. But still—indeed, for this very reason—there was no cause to treat her as though she were their captive.

I should at least keep my head raised. I would rather look up at the stars than down at the mud.

Even if those stars were presently concealed by dark clouds.

CHAPTER 5

GOBLIN SLAYER IN THE COUNTRY OF SAND

"Are they gone?"

"Looks like."

At this assurance from High Elf Archer, Goblin Slayer sat up on the rock shelf. Slick with the recent rain (the first in a long time, he assumed), the wet rock and sand combined to create a noticeable chill. And night was coming. It would be cold tonight, he was sure.

As clear as the air might be, though, catching sight of the sand ship far in the distance was no easy task. Even at high noon, with the leather-and-crystal telescope he had gotten, it would have been impossible for Goblin Slayer. But the eyes of a high elf could perceive such things easily. The fact seemed to be lost on High Elf Archer, who stood with her ears flicking as if this were just another task.

Goblin Slayer and the others had escaped the city under the cover of twilight and proceeded west, into the sand. A qanat, an underground tunnel, directed irrigation water to the surface, where it flowed like a river, mirrorlike; they simply had to follow it back to its source.

And when they arrived there, the party discovered the stronghold castle rising as a great dark silhouette against the night. It stood magisterial upon a cliff of bedrock that rose above the river. At any other time it might have been beautiful, but at this moment it looked wicked and vile.

"This whole area's a hamada, all rocks, so we won't want for hiding places," Dwarf Shaman said, taking a delicate sip of his dwindling fire wine supply. Now that the sand ship was past, they had a moment to breathe. "Personally, I don't know from desert ships, but that one certainly looked fancy enough for a king."

"Meaning our information was not mistaken." Lizard Priest slowly unfurled himself from where he had been hunched in the shadows of the rocks, his huge form straightening up. "It seems our dear prime minister is most interested in this fortress and that he has been purchasing many a slave.

"Or perhaps not," he added in a murmur, drinking from a waterskin that seemed inordinately heavy for something that should have been filled with simple liquid. But it was only natural: Inside was a thick cheese made of water-buffalo milk. Lizard Priest all but squeezed it down his throat, smacking his lips and announcing, "Sweet nectar!" His eyes rolled in his head as he savored the treat, and then he glanced at Female Merchant.

She had her hand on the silver sword at her hip and was crouched in a low stance; she looked very much like she had something she wanted to say. "And how, if I may ask, did things go for you?" Lizard Priest inquired.

Female Merchant blinked, then said with some satisfaction, "...I heard the same thing. They've been taking more of everything into that stronghold—resources, weapons, provisions, slaves. But..."

"Yes?"

"But even in the city, no one seemed to think they had actually taken on more soldiers," Female Merchant continued with a look of disquiet, and everyone fell silent.

There were many possible explanations. For example, maybe it was not soldiers but slaves who would be doing the fighting. If the only intention was to give them spears and send a crowd of them rushing at the enemy, there was little difference between slaves and conscripted civilians. But Priestess had the distinct impression that there was more than this at work. When she looked at the dark, looming structure, she got that familiar prickle down her neck.

She didn't know whether it was a sort of revelation or simply a compulsive idea. But...

"...The point is, they're expanding operations in there." She murmured just those few words, and the damp wind seemed to carry them away with the sand.

"Yes," Goblin Slayer said with a nod. "That at least seems to be the likely conclusion."

Gathering information wasn't the only thing they had done after they'd split into three groups in the city. Every clue they had acquired since coming to this country pointed to this stronghold. The soldiers pretending to be bandits. The fact that those same soldiers appeared to be allied with a goblin horde. Goblins who had resources enough to support mounts and equipment for many fighters. It was a large-scale force.

But death swirled in the desert. The sandstorms. The sand mantas. The baking sun. And then there was the lack of food and water.

The Myrmidons would not overlook the goblins, either, most likely.

The map they had received from the Myrmidon captain was remarkably detailed, and one look at it revealed all. There was nowhere in this area for such a large group of goblins to hide. Even bandits or a force of Chaos would have found it difficult. All the more so a group of impatient, undisciplined goblins.

So where *was* their nest?

"Thus one supposes that the key to the secret of the goblins must be somewhere in that fortress," Lizard Priest said.

"It is impossible to be certain. We won't know until we get in there," Goblin Slayer replied, then pulled the scroll of papyrus from his bag. High Elf Archer looked at it with keen interest as he unrolled it. "Whazzat?"

"Plans," he answered. He looked them over, and then, completely ignoring High Elf Archer's exclamation of "Oh!," he tore the paper into pieces and threw them away. The wind promptly caught the shreds of paper and carried them off.

"Hey, I was still looking at that!" High Elf Archer whined.

"I promised that I would show it to no one else and that after I had read it, I would destroy it."

High Elf Archer had no rebuttal, instead settling on a snort of displeasure. A second later, though, her ears stood on end and she stuck out her flat chest just as much as she could. "That's fine! I memorized it in just that one glance!"

"I see." Goblin Slayer's response was as mild as ever, provoking High Elf Archer to puff out her cheeks with a "Grr!"

"Now, now," Priestess said placatingly, even as she smiled a little. She found herself reflecting on how accustomed she had become to this sort of banter. On that first quest together, and indeed for some time after, she'd had a tendency to panic when Dwarf Shaman and High Elf Archer took jabs at each other.

But it's really a good sign. It means they're not too nervous.

Nervousness made the body tense up. You lost the ability to make instantaneous judgments.

"Mm," Priestess said to herself. Then she asked, "But how are we going to get in? Do we go right at it from the front?"

"With my safe-conduct pass, I might be able to get them to admit me as a merchant...," Female Merchant offered, but she didn't look sure. She furrowed her well-formed eyebrows, her thumb resting against her lip as she worried at the nail.

Lizard Priest continued the idea. "One cannot expect them to give outsiders, how shall we say, a guided tour of their facility. Especially outsiders from a hostile state."

Yes, there was the rub. This was different from simply marching into a goblin hole. This nest was tightly guarded.

Goblin Slayer thought silently for a moment, then the metal helmet turned toward Lizard Priest. "What do you think?"

"If we consider the annals of legendary heroes, we encounter a story in which some passed themselves off as members of the enemy army."

"And they were able to get in?"

"It would seem they succeeded," Lizard Priest said. "They fabricated a situation, then pretended to be in desperate circumstances in order to get important information to their comrades."

"Whatever we pretend to be, guests or soldiers or what have you, 'twon't be easy to reach the keep, I should think," Dwarf Shaman interjected, stroking his beard.

"Indeed, indeed. And the worse for us, for the keep is not our objective..." Lizard Priest seemed even more serious than before. What they needed now were plans, ideas, and cards to play. They had to hope that these would emerge from the discussion. Lizard Priest understood that when a group was brainstorming, the worst thing one could do was to shoot down another's idea.

"What if we were to sneak in?" Goblin Slayer asked with a grunt. "Assuming we can."

"That would be ideal," Lizard Priest said, rolling his eyes. "But it is a matter of how strict the guard is." He thumped his tail against the ground, causing little puffs of sand to jump into the air. "That good, hard rain may prove a gift from heaven."

"Yes, you're right...," Priestess said and looked up at the sky. Until shortly before, it had been pouring such rain that one would never have believed this was a desert. Behind the curtain of precipitation, a person would have been nearly invisible no matter where they went.

"Besides, I can't imagine any goblin guards will be taking their work very seriously...," Priestess added. She sounded hesitant but more engaged than usual.

Yes, if this had been a goblin nest they had been talking about, it would all have been so simple. But a stronghold? ...A fortress? In Priestess's mind, she wasn't sure what the difference was. She'd fought her way into more than one such place in her time, but...

Fire, maybe...?

No, no. She shook her head. There might be captives in there. They would have to be sure before they could consider using fire. Back to square one.

"What sort of soldiers do you suppose are in there?" Priestess asked.

"The ones we ran into at the border didn't seem like much more than thieves or bandits, did they?" High Elf Archer said, waving a hand dismissively. She saw no reason to be overly concerned about people like that, but there were no guarantees that all the soldiers in that stronghold were so lax. One bad apple—or two or three—didn't mean the whole bunch was rotten.

"Right, then." Dwarf Shaman, who had put on his thinking face, finally stopped fiddling with his wine jar and turned to High Elf Archer. Her ears sat back as she registered the nasty grin on his face.

"We're *not* pretending to be slaves again, Orcbolg! It's not happening!" She pointed a lovely finger at him emphatically as she got to her feet. She was clearly trying to cover for Priestess and Female Merchant as well, but Dwarf Shaman merely shrugged.

"Er, if it's really necessary, then I could...," Priestess began.

"...Me too...," Female Merchant added.

But the high elf snapped, "No, you couldn't! I know we talk about winning by any means necessary, but it's better if we can win without resorting to *any* means!" Then, she added under her breath: "Besides, if we left Orcbolg to his own devices, he would come up with the worst stuff."

That, at least, Priestess understood in her bones. "Well, you're not wrong...," she said as evasively as she could.

Even confronted with such orders and demands, though, Goblin Slayer only said what he always did: "Is that so?" He didn't mind having to rethink his ideas, which was part of why everyone had taken him for their leader. There was no hierarchy in the party, but the ability to glance around at everyone and then render a decision was an important quality. Parties that simply nodded along to whatever their leader said and never questioned them, though, those parties didn't last long.

When, at length, he finally said what they had all been waiting for—"I have a plan"—they listened intently. Then they turned to see what the cheap-looking metal helmet was looking at.

"...?" Female Merchant looked downright perplexed. Behind her was everything she had brought to do business with and all the party's belongings, all on a herd of lumpy donkeys.

§

"Heeeeeey! Open up! Open the gaaaaate!"

The clear, insistent voice startled the dozing guard on the other side of the castle gate into wakefulness. He had become so transfixed by the unusual sight of the pouring rain that he must have drifted off.

Crap. If anyone found out... He'd lose his head. In fact, that might be the best he could hope for.

The soldier quickly picked up his spear, peeking out an arrow port in the side of the stronghold. He looked in the direction of the little bridge in front of the main gate—and then he thought he might choke. For standing there was a refined, beautiful young woman in some foreign outfit in a style he had never seen before. She was leading several camels, and a silver sword shone at her hip. It was as though she had walked out of a story.

"Can't you hear me? Open the gate!" the young woman repeated in her commanding voice.

The guard was thoroughly intimidated, but he shouted back in a voice he hoped was just as threatening: "Wh-who or what are you?!"

"Who or *what*?! That's the rudest greeting I've ever heard my life!"

The guard found that this rebuke stung more than being dressed down by his commanding officer. The young woman spread her arms as if she couldn't believe she had to do this, but in her hand she pointedly displayed a safe-conduct pass. "I've come from the next country over to do business. I've also been granted permission to study your land. Don't tell me you haven't heard?"

Before the soldier could focus his eyes in the darkness well enough to be sure of what she was holding, the woman put the pass away. Her neatly fitted clothing that emphasized her generous chest drew the guard's gaze. He swallowed hard.

Then the guard heard the voice of his commanding officer behind him. "What's going on? Is something the matter?" He froze. He was surprised to realize, though, that this man, who had felt like a thorn in his side a moment before, suddenly seemed such a reassuring presence.

"Yes, sir—I mean, no sir—I mean..." The guard maintained an obedient attitude, while attempting to foist all the responsibility on the officer. "There's a foreign merchant woman outside, or so she claims, and I...I need orders, sir!"

"Say what?" The officer had not been expecting this at all.

Gods, if it isn't one thing, it's another!

His subordinates were idiots, and his own superior officer, the captain, was forever getting these ideas into his head. Change stations. Change sleeping quarters. Change the patrol routes. And now there was a visitor, and he hadn't deigned to tell anyone. It was trouble from hell to breakfast, and if it hadn't been for his perquisites (which was how the man thought of the thieving he did on the side), he didn't know how he would have coped.

The officer had the guard move out of the way and looked out the arrow port himself. When he saw the lovely young woman standing there, he realized he could let out some of his frustrations on her. Nobody could complain if he did his job—so he would do his job *to the letter*. It was no affair of his what might happen because of it. If the imperious-looking young woman was inconvenienced by it, if that reprehensible commander found his plans stymied because of it, well, wouldn't that be grand.

"No, we haven't heard," the officer said. "You'll just have to wait there until we can verify it."

"I see you up there!" the young noblewoman called out. It seemed she had seen clear through his little plan. Her voice was as sharp as an arrow as she said, "You think you can get out of this by feigning ignorance? This is a question of responsibility. You, what's your name?"

"Ahem, er, I— Hrm?"

"I'll have no choice but to report that I had to wait because *you* were too lazy to stay up to date on the latest communications." Quite in contrast to the increasingly troubled officer, the young woman sounded calmer and calmer. Her voice was like a storm. And like a storm, just because it had calmed didn't mean it was over. "Go ahead—verify with your superiors, send a post horse to the city, do whatever you like."

But do it knowing what's likely to happen to your head as a result, eh?

The officer could see the young woman smirking even through the curtain of night. He swallowed heavily. He glanced at the man who had been on guard, but he only stood up straighter and tried to look subordinate. Whatever happened, this guard was as likely as that girl to finger the officer as the one in charge.

Damn them both to—

In his heart, the officer roundly cursed the gods and the wind and the dice. But curse them as he might, it wouldn't make things any better.

To open the gate and let her through or not. The young woman was growing visibly more irate the longer she waited. There was no way to check who she was. The officer gritted his teeth.

"What's taking so long? Make up your mind," the young woman demanded, scuffing the earth irritably with the toe of her boots. On closer inspection, the officer could see a tall, large-bodied man standing beside the young woman. A padfoot—no, the jaws that protruded from the scarf over his head were unmistakably those of a lizardman.

She wasn't alone. Of course not. Had she been by herself, they might have been able to handle her somehow.

The officer hated trouble like this. He hated having to take time and effort to deal with things. And most of all, he hated having responsibility dumped on him. And then there was another consideration...

At least if they just cut off my head, it'll be over. But please don't let me wind up in there*!*

At last thinking purely of self-preservation, the officer shouted, "Open the gate!"

"Yes sir, opening the gate!" his subordinate said gladly and began working a pulley to raise the double portcullises.

Ahh, the hell with it!

If push came to shove, he would just run for it, the officer thought, letting out a breath.

§

"Thank you," the female merchant said, smiling, as she led her camels through the now-open gate. As for the officer of the guard who stood there to usher her in, his face was frozen in a look of profound displeasure. So she slipped a golden coin into his hand as she walked past. She knew how business was done here.

The officer blinked in momentary surprise, but his gaze softened a little, almost in spite of himself. Humans were driven by emotion, but not without occasional reference to the motivation of profit. If a person served for ages someplace where he could expect no benefits and no gain, of course he would become resentful.

...I know that *from experience.* Female Merchant felt a bitter taste on the back of her tongue, but her noble upbringing helped her prevent it

from showing on her face. If this place had been closer to the city—if it had been properly secret—things might have been different. Or had it been more thoroughly on the side of Chaos, ironically, discipline might have been tighter. But this man was still confident he could get away from the wrath of his superiors. So he was soft.

Anyway...

It was Female Merchant's experiences in the palaces and noble places of the world that had allowed her to make these calculations. If she had only ever experienced life as an adventurer, this probably wouldn't have gone so smoothly.

"A-ahem, allow me to show you to your room, then...," the officer said reluctantly, but Female Merchant stopped him.

"That won't be necessary. As I said, inspection is part of my mandate— If I simply spend all my time in my room, I won't know if I'm getting my money's worth on this investment." Then she gave him a little smile. *I know what I want*, it said. *I may be your ally, but I'm not your friend.*

Then there was... The officer looked up. There was the massive lizardman standing behind the young woman.

Except it wasn't. It was a Dragontooth Warrior, summoned with a deeply heartfelt prayer. Covered with a cloak and given a weapon to hold, it did a convincing impression of a brutish mercenary. Which was funny, considering that in the bedtime stories she'd heard as a girl, such creatures were only ever the surprisingly fragile servants of evil wizards.

Strange, then, how doughty it appears to me now.

She would never have been able to take on this "battle" alone. Forcing her hands and her voice not to shake, she said firmly, "Hence, perhaps you could show me to the garrison instead? I'm sure you must have requests regarding bedding, clothing, and food."

"M-ma'am. It's...not a pretty place..."

"As a sign of goodwill, I've brought tea and snacks for all the soldiers, if you know what I mean." The woman glanced pointedly at the load on the camels. That would give the poor officer the convenient idea that whatever it was would be of benefit to him.

"Er, ah, we—we're very thankful, I'm sure... Ma'am?"

"First, I'll need somewhere to tie up these lumpy donkeys. Do you have a storehouse? Or perhaps a corral? Is it over here?"

Even as she voiced the question, Female Merchant started walking on her slim legs.

She appeared to be some kind of foreign noble. An investor in the stronghold, no less. This was getting better. And "tea and snacks"? The scales in the officer's mind tipped crazily between the fear of the impertinent way he had treated her and the potential good she was offering him.

The effect on him—to say nothing of his subordinate—was obvious as the officer hurried after her. People speak of "good guards" and "bad guards," but things were simpler than that.

Just convince them they have to make an important decision here and now. It was the oldest trick in the book.

"You'll have to forgive me, but it seems I'll need your help a little longer yet," Female Merchant said to the pitiful soldiers, then offered them her most ravishing smile.

§

As the soldiers above were scrambling to give Female Merchant the reception she appeared to deserve, ripples were appearing on the river that ran, seemingly as wide as a sea, past the base of the bedrock on which the stronghold was built. The rain had stirred up the river and made it cloudy with mud, while night added its inky black touch. Nobody noticed the ripples or the hand that reached up and grabbed the rock face.

A beautiful young elf woman emerged. Even if anyone had seen her, they wouldn't have believed their eyes. Still less when she gave a kick and then flipped up onto the rocks, standing there proudly. "...It's clear. I don't sense anyone else around," she said with a flick of her long ears. "Come on up."

There was a bit more splashing, and now some adventurers appeared. They didn't seem wet at all despite the fact that they had just been underwater; nor did they seem to be gasping for breath. High Elf Archer reached down and helped up first Goblin Slayer, then

Dwarf Shaman, then Priestess. Finally Lizard Priest emerged with the largest ripple of all, saying "Pardon me" as he dug his claws into the rock and scrambled up.

"My oh my, never woulda believed a desert could *flood*." Dwarf Shaman shook himself off like a great big dog and settled heavily on the rocks, curling up. The power of Breath, as established, kept them dry, but perhaps he still didn't *feel* dry.

"It might be smart to keep one of these around…" Priestess, for her part, was deep in thought. She liked to think she wasn't too concerned about money, but still. *If I really want to be the best adventurer I can be… Well, maybe a magic item or two wouldn't go amiss.* Perhaps once she reached Sapphire, the seventh rank.

"Just so we're clear, this weirdo's choice of equipment is *not* typical."

"Er," Priestess hiccupped at her surprise that High Elf Archer seemed to know what she was thinking. The elf was frowning openly, which bothered Priestess a little bit. She thought this ring had come in awfully handy more than once.

"I mean it," the high elf repeated, then turned to Goblin Slayer. "So what next?"

"We sneak in."

"The question remains: How?" Goblin Slayer seemed so sure about this, but High Elf Archer only fixed him with a glare. He grunted under that helmet, then felt around in the dark, moving along the rock face. "I initially considered going in from wherever the toilets let out."

"Urgh," High Elf Archer groaned, clearly hoping to be spared this fate. Maybe she was looking up at the boards supporting the fortress where it jutted out above their heads.

"But it would prove foolish if the passage narrowed partway and we got stuck."

"Well, least Long-Ears doesn't need to worry about that. Being an anvil as she is," Dwarf Shaman said, then had to stifle his own laugh.

High Elf Archer growled at him, and Priestess looked down red-faced at her own modest frame.

"Speak for yourself, dwarf!" High Elf Archer snapped. "I might make it, but you'd be guaranteed to get stuck, being a barrel and all!"

"Not to mention, y'never know when there might be scavengers in a toilet area," Dwarf Shaman said, roundly ignoring High Elf Archer. He smiled nastily and looked up at High Elf Archer. "Wouldn't open up that door if I were you, Long-Ears. Never know if there might be a giant corpse-eatin' slug in there."

"You'd end up squishing it if you went in there yourself. *Hmph.*" High Elf Archer snorted but looked more or less satisfied, and this was the last of her objections.

Priestess couldn't see what Goblin Slayer was looking for, but everyone else seemed to be able to. "Here it is," he said, his gloved hand grasping a gate set into the rock. Priestess leaned over carefully to see it; she discovered what looked like the door of a jail cell. It had a neat lock and clean hinges, suggesting it was meant to open and close instead of remaining fixed in place. Just one thing bothered her: The lock had no keyhole, at least not on the outside.

"This isn't...quite a normal door, is it?" Priestess said. "It leads right out onto the water anyway."

"Normal? Yes and no. One could conceivably use such a word to describe it...," Lizard Priest whispered jovially, rolling his eyes in amusement. He stuck out his tongue and placed a clawed hand on the lock. "In any event, I do believe this is our mistress ranger's moment to shine."

"Yeah, sure. But this isn't my main class, okay? Outta the way." High Elf Archer slid forward, and the others slid back into the space she had just occupied. She worked one slim arm between the bars, bent her wrist, and inserted a needle-thin twig into the keyhole. "Argh, man, what a pain," she grumbled.

"Quit whinin'," Dwarf Shaman scolded her. "If y'have too much trouble, we'll just bust it open. So relax, relax!"

"You sound a little *too* relaxed!" High Elf Archer replied with a very un-high-elf-like puff of her cheeks, but after another moment's work she nodded. "There. Got it. Let's do this." The lock released with a click, and she caught it in midair, happily pushing the barred door open.

One step inside, and it was already like a gloomy cave. The floor had been smoothed and carved almost like flagstones, but it was clear that this tunnel had been bored out above the bedrock. Big stones stuck out here and there, and Dwarf Shaman sniffed at them with indignity. Dwarves would never have done such rough work. "Though it ain't bad for some humans, I guess. I admire the effort, but—"

"Urgh…" He was interrupted by a groan from High Elf Archer, who had taken point.

Here in the tunnel, the fresh breeze that had blown off the river was replaced by a fetid stench. It seemed to be the odor of someone rotting away while they still lived, mixed with all kinds of filth. It almost seemed the reek of death itself.

"Can't expect much better of a prison, I s'pose," Dwarf Shaman said. "Not meant to be a happy place."

There was a clatter, and Priestess realized the heavy thing that had just brushed against her ankles was a set of chains and manacles. She recoiled, only to find herself hemmed in by a protruding rock. She had no choice but to stand stock-still and make herself as small as possible while she waited for her eyes to adjust to the darkness.

Dwarf Shaman spoke again: "Looks like it only goes one way. Makes sense, I guess."

"Yes," Goblin Slayer replied briefly, then he produced a torch from his item pouch and struck a flint to it. There was a *fwoosh* and a glow of orange light, and they discovered that they were indeed inside a prison carved out of the stone. Stakes were pounded into the walls, chains attached to them. But what really drew Priestess's attention was a space set high above everything else that looked like a shelf.

It was the landing of a staircase carved in the rock, which extended up from the prison. But it didn't go anywhere; it led instead to several wooden beams. Beyond the beams—below them—was empty space, except for some dangling straw ropes…

"Oh…," Priestess said, putting the pieces together. "They hung the prisoners from these bars…?!" *And then threw away the bodies.* She couldn't quite bring herself to say this last part; she felt her throat close up.

"Any castle will have something like this. The more so if it be by a lake or river." Lizard Priest was trying to comfort her. He brought his hands together in a strange gesture. A beat later, Priestess clasped her own hands with some uncertainty and offered a short prayer. To

Lizard Priest, perhaps it seemed a fitting burial that the bodies should be washed away to be eaten by the fish. Priestess couldn't quite reconcile herself to the idea, but in any event they were alike in praying for the repose of the departed.

While the two clerics interceded for the peace of the dead with their respective faiths, Goblin Slayer examined the floor. Piles of excrement, eating utensils, all dry: If the prisoners hadn't been starved to death, the utensils certainly showed no sign of having been used.

"I don't think this place has been occupied for some time," Goblin Slayer said.

"Well, there sure isn't anyone here now," High Elf Archer replied. "Humans are so cruel. You hardly live for a century, but you'll lock people up for most of that time."

"It's punishment," Goblin Slayer said softly from under his visor, shaking his head. "But what's happening now is not a punishment—it's a death sentence."

In any event, he had counted on there being no prisoners. That meant there would be no guards. They had waited long enough that Female Merchant probably had most of the soldiers in the palm of her hand. But she would only be able to keep them that way for so long.

Goblin Slayer stood in front of the heavy iron door that separated the prison from the castle proper and said, "What do you think?"

High Elf Archer, to whom he had been speaking, took a glance at the door and then clicked her tongue so elegantly it was almost a work of art. "Not happening, I don't think. Even if I could manage, it would take a lot of time."

Yes, of course. Goblin Slayer nodded, then patted the door seals with his gloved hand. "How about the hinges, then?"

"That's dwarf business," Dwarf Shaman said, coming over and spitting on his palms. "A moment, if you please."

"A moment" turned out to be hardly more than two minutes, and the door was off. This sort of thing would have been ridiculous to attempt in a dungeon or some old ruins, but that's not where they were. There is a time and place for every idea, with all their various advantages and disadvantages. As removing the door was, in this case, better than picking the lock, the adventurers didn't hesitate.

"…"

Then a great dark opening yawned before them. Priestess couldn't stop thinking that it looked like a goblin den.

§

"Hoh. There's another one down," Female Merchant muttered to herself as another of the guards in the guardhouse crumpled to the ground, unconscious. She felt a trickle of cold sweat running down her cheek.

I've made a mistake.

She couldn't escape the thought. Especially not with the soldier glaring intimidatingly at her from where he sat across from her.

"…What's the matter? It's your turn."

"…Don't you think I know that?!" Puckering his face, the man grabbed the dagger lodged in the tabletop. He spread his hand on the table, then took a deep breath. "Twenty times before the sand in the glass runs out."

"Understood."

"Good! …H-hrah!" And he immediately began stabbing the knife up and down between his fingers. One slight misjudgment could have cost him a digit, but he couldn't hesitate. A moment's reluctance meant defeat. This game, mumbly peg, was all about speed and how many times you could stab the knife. It was better than stronghold roulette—in which you had six daggers, five of which were toys and one of which was real, and players stabbed at one another with them—but not by much.

I've made a huge, huge mistake.

Female Merchant struggled to keep her regret and anxiety off her face. She had only let the expression show once since she'd arrived at the stronghold. It wasn't when she had given the tea and snacks to the soldiers at the guardhouse. It wasn't when the soldiers had piled in for the goods, jostling and shoving to be first with all the enthusiasm of men who were perennially constrained by discipline.

No, it was only the moment when one of the soldiers reached out and touched her by way of a prank. "Eek!" she had exclaimed like a little girl and slapped his hand away. That was the only time.

By the time she regretted the lapse, it was already too late. Nobody enjoys hearing someone else be upset with them. The soldiers had been in high spirits, enjoying sweet treats such as they so rarely got and the lovely (if she might think it of herself as such) foreign lady.

But the atmosphere changed instantly, and Female Merchant found herself the subject of many a suspicious stare. Maybe she shouldn't have taken that step back at that moment, either. However…

They just looked so much like goblins.

She had suddenly found her ears full of whistling wind, much like a blizzard gale. The wind that intimated this was back where she had been earlier in the night. The friends, the further adventures, everything she had done up to this moment, had been nothing but a pleasant fantasy. She started to think maybe she was still trapped in that snowy waste…

"_____"

Shf. She felt the Dragontooth Warrior shift behind her. She glanced in its direction, realizing her breath was coming fast and shallow. The Warrior, of course, was just a skeleton covered by a scarf and coat; there was no expression on its face. It had no will of its own, but simply obeyed its master's command to protect this young woman. The steel sword it carried was just something she had scared up in town, a common weapon. But *back then*, she could never have imagined having someone to protect her.

And since she had been rescued, her friends did much more than simply protect her.

She took a deep breath.

"Everything's all right," she said with a brave smile, gesturing the Dragontooth Warrior back. Then she said, "Let's go about this like civilized folk," and removed her overcoat. She was aware that the sweat made her shirt stick to her skin. She ignored the soldiers who stared at her (whether it be from shock or excitement, she didn't care). With her right hand she drew an aluminum dagger; she spread her left on the table and then, with a smile like a blossoming flower, said,

"How about a round of mumbly peg? Surely strong warriors like your-selves aren't afraid, are you?"

There was a clatter of gold and silver coins piling up on the table, and, well, you know the rest.

Driven by intoxication and excitement, the soldiers didn't start small but went right for this most dangerous game. A nerve-racking gamble. The onlooking soldiers swallowed heavily each time they stood up their knives. When one man stepped down, too afraid to go any farther, there would be a crowd shoving and exclaiming, "Outta the way, I'm next!"

But gradually, their movements became less sure. Some grazed their fingers. One stabbed his palm. An odor of iron drifted through the room. And then finally, the soldiers began to drop away one by one, as if fainting with fatigue. Did the rest of the men notice the distur-bance, fixated as they were on the opponents before them? She dearly hoped they wouldn't—and she had to keep up the act to make sure they didn't. After all, the perfume soaked into her clothes only invited drunkenness. In food, the medicinal taste might give it away—but who knew what a foreign woman's perfume smelled like? They didn't give it a second thought. Especially not when they were busy being delighted by an entertainment (and an appetite) they weren't likely to encounter again anytime soon. The stimulation would get the drug into their systems quicker as well.

"You're next, li'l lady!"

"Of course. Twenty times you went, yes?" Female Merchant stroked the rings with the spikes inside to stimulate her fingers, then focused her concentration. She pulled a handful of gold coins from her purse and tossed them on the table, then flipped the sandglass over. "I'll do thirty times, then."

"Hngh...!"

There was no way to be sure you would win at mumbly peg. The closest thing to a guarantee was to focus on three factors: coolheaded-ness, accuracy, and precision. Then you could only wait for an over-taxed opponent to lose a finger or cave under the pressure.

Bah, what is it to me?

If she lost a finger, so what? It was nothing compared with having a brand burned into the flesh of her neck.

"Here I go."

Female Merchant licked her rose-colored lips with a pink tongue, then brought the dagger down.

§

"Gods… Haven't they ever heard of finishing what they started?" Dwarf Shaman complained, working his stubby arms and legs as he scrambled up the wooden tower that hugged the cliffside. "Cave" turned out to be very much the right word for the path that had been carved out of the bedrock; it contained several natural rents in the stone. Maybe it wasn't so surprising that guards didn't come down here. Priestess was taller and had longer arms than Dwarf Shaman, and even she found the path difficult to navigate. For a soldier in full armor, even one with training and stamina, to have to come here every day…

"I can't…say," she remarked, forcing her breath to remain steady, "that they…seem to have been thinking of…people coming through here."

For the umpteenth time, she jumped for the scaffolding above, clung to it desperately, then dragged herself up. No one attacked them, even when she was seized by the need to crouch down and breathe. The air underground was relatively cool without the scorching heat of the desert, a small blessing. If hot air had whipped up another sandstorm down here, they could never have gone on.

"Perhaps it was never their intention that people should do so," Lizard Priest said, not sounding unduly overtaxed. He had a large body and much strength, as well as claws on his hands and feet. He was able to grasp handholds easily, climbing up as readily as a gecko.

"What do you mean?" Priestess asked, and Lizard Priest replied, "Just as I said," scratching his long nose with a claw. "Perhaps they wished to seal something away down here. Something they desired should not be seen or touched."

"I don't care why they did it. It's a pain in the neck," High Elf Archer groused. Despite her open frustration, she worked her way up the wall with light, easy movements. *Pa-pa-pa.* She found footholds on the boards as easily as a stone skipping over water, putting a hand on her hip and bending at the waist. "I feel like I'm going to lose track of where we are." She gave an annoyed flick of her ears. "It's so hard to tell underground. And there's that sound in the distance, like a banshee."

Priestess had noticed the same thing from the time they had come down here. Maybe it was just the wind passing through the crevices of the cave. But to her it sounded something like the rattle of a creature approaching death...

I'm sure that's the noise the wind must make when it blows through a person's skeleton...

It wasn't a helpful thought, but she couldn't resist it. Priestess shook her head.

"Very well, but concentrate," Goblin Slayer said, his precise, one-limb-at-a-time movements in direct contrast to High Elf Archer's lightness of foot. He wore the heaviest equipment of anyone in the party, yet, he moved easily in it; a testament to his abilities as a scout. He would only fall if he was truly unlucky—or if High Elf Archer kicked him. Diligently avoiding the slim legs that danced just above his eyeline, he pulled himself up to the scaffolding. "There are traps."

"I know." High Elf Archer sounded calm enough, but what spread out before her was no longer cave but practically a maze. For a while now—did the number increase as they moved upward?—they had been seeing artificial partitions. Walls reinforced with building stone, floors covered in paving stones. But something felt off about them. Some of the paving stones weren't quite flush; others rattled when they were stepped on.

"Here, let the dwarf have a look."

"Nah, don't worry," High Elf Archer said, full of caution. "Quicker to go around it than to have to disarm it." She tapped her toes against the stone, and a flash of silver light jumped out of the floor. It was an array of long, sharp silver spikes, intended to skewer any careless passers-by. Obviously, anyone who rushed through here too care-lessly would find themselves greeted only by a brutal death. High

Elf Archer, drawing on all the grace of her people, slipped smoothly between the spikes. "...Huh!" she exclaimed with genuine pleasure. "All good. Let's take it slow."

Now all they needed to do was trust her judgment, going exactly where she went to avoid the spikes. And indeed, no member of the party would doubt what High Elf Archer said. How could you adventure together if you didn't trust one another? And even if she made a mistake, it wouldn't be her fault. If a scout messed up, it would be just as much the failure of the one who chose to leave matters in the scout's hands. If a scout's job was to open treasure chests, it was the duty of the front row to deal with any monsters. And while they were doing that, the party's spell casters might be just standing around, not chanting any spells, but their moment would come.

Therefore, the best adventuring parties had no hierarchy of roles. The party lived and died together.

"These things look like they would tear my dress if I so much as touched them..." Even so, it was especially difficult to get past the traps wearing a cleric's vestments. It was so easy to say *just slip past them*, but if her dress caught on something and she fell, it would be as good as jumping into the trap.

High Elf Archer giggled to see Priestess looking so serious as she worked her way along. "Don't worry. You've got it way better than that bumbling barrel."

"And a barrel is better than an anvil! It's called being well-muscled...!"

If that was how it was, then it seemed the hardest time would be had by the one with the biggest body and longest tail...

Eh, guess I'd better keep that to myself. Priestess smiled in spite of herself, looking down to hide the expression. She focused on moving delicately instead.

The order was just as always. High Elf Archer and Goblin Slayer were on point, Priestess and Lizard Priest in the middle, with Dwarf Shaman bringing up the rear. That was why Priestess was so intent on not being the weak link, but as she worked her way through the forest of spikes...

"...Is something wrong?"

She saw that Goblin Slayer and High Elf Archer had both stopped and were crouching low. Priestess was not so inexperienced as to fail to understand what this signified. She quickly grasped her sounding staff with both hands, looking for a good place to stand as she prepared for whatever was coming. She steadied her breath, focused her concentration, preparing to pray whatever prayer might be required at any time. Dwarf Shaman and Lizard Priest likewise made ready; the whole party was set. The sword of a strange length gleamed, the yew-wood bow was pulled taut, the bag of catalysts was open, claws and tail were ready.

"Watch the rear. There may be spikes back there, but we don't want them getting around behind us."

Dwarf Shaman and Lizard Priest nodded and took up positions at the back, gazing out into the cave that opened behind the party. Priestess found herself in the middle of the group; she tried to position herself so she would be prepared no matter which direction the attack came from.

"Can we deal with them here?" Goblin Slayer asked.

"It seems unlikely," Lizard Priest replied. "Spikes behind us. A single tunnel ahead. And too many of us. We can only hope their numbers are not too great."

"So we push our way through."

In that brief exchange, the party's strategy was set. And then, in the darkness ahead, they saw them. They had hoped they wouldn't encounter them. But had known they probably would.

Small as children. Equipment that made them look like hideous caricatures of soldiers. And green skin.

"Goblins?!"

"GOORG?!"

Neither side had expected or desired this random encounter. But the adventurers, ever anticipating battle, were just a step ahead of the goblins with their spears and helmets.

"Let's do it!" Goblin Slayer said, and then he dove in among them still crouching, even as High Elf Archer's arrows began to fly. A bud-tipped bolt rocketed through space, passing by the metal helmet, heading directly for a goblin's eyeball.

"GOGGB?!?!"

The arrow passed through the eye and into the brain, ending the creature's life, but Goblin Slayer maintained his momentum. That was the first goblin, but it would certainly not be the last.

"GOOROGB!!"

"GOBBG! GRRBG!!"

Goblins' strength lay in their numbers. The awful squadron of soldiers with their motley collection of weapons poured out of the darkness. Without a moment's hesitation, Goblin Slayer raised the sword in his right hand and flung it.

"GGBGOOROG?!"

It was downright slow compared with High Elf Archer's arrows, but it was more than enough to kill a goblin. The blade lodged itself in the throat of the creature who'd had the overconfidence to try to lead the assault, sending him spinning backward. As the other goblins trod mercilessly upon the body, Goblin Slayer's free hand was already picking up a spear from the ground. He raised the shield on his left arm, using the torch in that hand to dazzle the monsters, then struck upward with the spear.

"GOBB?! BGR?!"

Stab a monster through the neck and even if it didn't die immediately, it would be out of the fight. He was reduced to coughing and choking. Goblin Slayer kicked aside the blood-frothing goblin, letting go of his spear and instead pulling his sword out of the body of the second goblin. "That makes three...," he murmured inside his helmet, quickly appraising the number of his opponents. He could hear more footsteps down the hall. The number...

Ten, maybe?

Not that many of them that he could see, but if more came up behind there could be trouble. Getting through and out of here had to be their first priority.

"Light!"

"Yes, sir!" Priestess immediately assessed the strategic situation, and then, still facing forward, retreated several steps.

"All clear in the back!"

"Do what you will!"

With Dwarf Shaman and Lizard Priest behind her, she focused on the two figures ahead of her on the front row, then let out her prayer in a rush of breath: *"O Earth Mother, abounding in mercy, grant your sacred light to we who are lost in darkness!"*

A blinding flash illuminated the disgusting tunnel beneath the stronghold.

"GBBOGOB?!"

"GOG?! GGRGB?!"

The goblins screeched and covered their eyes, stumbling back from the sacred light. Something a little farther ahead appeared to be slowing them down, and they found themselves caught in a bottleneck before they could get behind the partitions. Goblin Slayer closed the distance to them in a breath, kicking the nearest monster as hard as he could. The goblin sprawled on the ground, then bumped into something and lay prone.

"GOORGB?!"

The next instant, merciless blades sprang up from above and below, almost literally biting into the creature. The goblin's death spasms sent its newly exposed blood and viscera spattering all over. It was such a brutal trap that Priestess flinched involuntarily. Was this what the goblins had been struggling to get past?

For Goblin Slayer, though, it could hardly have been more helpful. "Four. There are traps."

"I think I made it clear that *I knew that already*!"

"We'll push forward."

"Arrrgh!" High Elf Archer added something elegant but unchari- table in the elvish language, then drew another arrow from her quiver. She gave it a kiss, and the bud blossomed, then wilted away, leaving a nut. She fired the nut-tipped arrow at a goblin, causing him to reel under the impact.

"GOG?! GORGB?!"

"GGOBB?!"

As the nut-tipped arrow whirred past the goblin, it split open, spray- ing seeds. They struck the other goblins, who forgot what they were supposed to be doing and went running for cover. They might have had armor, but they were still just goblins. They didn't welcome a challenge.

"GOOBGB?!"

Naturally, some of these thoroughly distracted creatures shortly found themselves cleaved in two by a sword. Goblin Slayer could not have cared less about how a goblin died. He was substantially more concerned about the pool of blood spreading across the stones, threatening his footing.

"Six… Seven!" He was in among the goblins now, wielding weapons in both hands, striking out in every direction. The goblins' eyes were scorched where seeds had battered them; there were traps behind them and enemies ahead.

Their strength was in their numbers. They were no more intelligent or strong than cruel children. They wanted to hurt, they wanted to kill, but that was all they had. So now that they were stuck in a tunnel where they couldn't make use of their only virtue…

"This makes thirteen." So he had underestimated by a few—it didn't matter. They were the weakest monsters in the Four-Cornered World. Goblin Slayer slammed the sputtering torch into the final creature, ending its life. "Fool." He uttered a single word of admonishment as he tossed the torch aside. To Priestess, it sounded like he was talking to someone who wasn't present.

"…I guess we got past them, at least." For now, the main thing was to keep going forward. Priestess got her breathing under control, giving a rattle of her sounding staff. She offered a brief, private prayer for the repose of their souls, that the departed goblins might not lose their way after death.

Death was the end. Best not hope for more than that. Even if they were goblins.

"I sort of expected more of them…," Priestess said.

"I'd say there were plenty," High Elf Archer replied with a frown. "What do we do with all these bodies? There's too many to hide." She had the decency to look somewhat abashed, but it didn't stop her from going around plucking her arrows out of the corpses. Elves and elves alone could wield the bud-tipped shots. It would be one more thing to give them away—if the shouting and fighting hadn't been enough.

"I don't think we'll need to hide them," Goblin Slayer said resentfully, gazing into the darkness beyond. He produced a fresh torch from his pouch, lighting it on the last embers of the one that lay on the floor. "We're going straight ahead."

"Hmm…" Lizard Priest put a hand to his jaw thoughtfully, then rolled his eyes in his head as he figured it out. "I see. You have a nasty little plan of your own, haven't you, milord Goblin Slayer?"

"Nasty is nothing new for Orcbolg," High Elf Archer said with a sigh of what might have been fatigue or perhaps just exasperation. She glanced back, sending a ripple through her hair. "How you doing back there? Think it was pretty quiet behind us, right?"

"Yes, right!" Priestess nodded quickly. "I'm okay."

"Me too," Dwarf Shaman said, putting away the battle-ax he had drawn Priestess knew not when. If the front line had been pressed too far back, it would have been their own back row that would have been pushed into the spikes.

"Okay," High Elf Archer replied easily but as if she recognized this responsibility.

Dwarf Shaman narrowed his eyes and looked at the blood staining his boots. "They might be in cahoots with Chaos, but still… Is this what you normally find in a national fortress?"

"It's just the sort of thing they would come up with…thinking they were smarter than they are." Goblin Slayer wasn't exactly answering the question; in fact, he seemed to be talking to himself. Uncommonly for him—uncommonly indeed—he sounded profoundly irritated. "Using goblins as soldiers."

Goblin Slayer stuffed goblin viscera into the moving parts of the blade trap, disabling it. It was necessary in order to continue forward, but it didn't look very pleasant.

But the underground tunnel through which the party proceeded had something far more terrible in store for them. For the abyss in these depths was itself the very source of the death-rattle voice they had heard.

"It means they think no more deeply than a goblin themselves."

§

What was happening in the dark underbelly of this stronghold? Perhaps the details were best left undisclosed. It was the typical image of a goblin nest's inner sanctum. But in truth, it was even worse than that, for the young women chained there had been captured by human hands; bought and brought into this place. The hunks of meat that probably passed for food around here had all been dropped in by human hands. Some of the girls had had hamstrings or arm tendons cut; others had spikes driven through their ankles.

But then there were those with unblemished skin and no injuries, who were missing only the light from their eyes. They were being husbanded. Not by goblins, obviously. This was a stone-hewed goblin breeding ground, made by human hands.

"_____"

When the party kicked down the door and burst in, words failed Priestess. Her face didn't reflect the cruelty of the scene, didn't show revulsion— Instead, her expression seemed to ask, "Why?" The room was filled with cries of pain, supplication, despair—and the hopeless rattle of enervated souls that had echoed through the stronghold.

The girls chained up here would soon be dead. Either their bodies would succumb or their spirits would. What could one possibly say in the face of this? What was there to say?

"O Earth Mother, abounding in mercy, grant us peace to accept all things."

"Drink deep, sing loud, let the spirits lead you. Sing loud, step quick, and when to sleep they see you, may a jar of fire wine be in your dreams to greet you."

When Priestess opened her mouth, though, it was the words of a prayer that came out, followed shortly by Dwarf Shaman summoning his sprites. By the time the goblins looked up in surprise from their awful meals and more awful deeds, it was too late. They exclaimed in voices that were not voices, then started to stumble around as if sleepy before collapsing to the ground.

Then Goblin Slayer and Lizard Priest made their entrance in one swift move. In a confined space like this, arrows would not be as effective as a sword or claws and fangs and tail.

The two of them went after their prey with gusto, and made short work of the helpless monsters. It reminded Priestess of the chamber in some ruins long ago. The difference, if there was one, was that although the goblins were voiceless and stupefied, no one felt any sympathy for them this time.

No wonder the goblins earlier had not seemed at the top of their game: They had still been enjoying the afterglow of their visit to this place. Priestess watched *him* with one eye as she continued to pray. His manner with his grimy leather armor was nonchalant; he would slash a throat in a businesslike manner, hold down the woken monster, switch his sword to his other hand. She had witnessed similar scenes many times over the course of her adventures with Goblin Slayer.

And I'm afraid I'm almost...used to it, she thought suddenly. A chill ran through her at the notion. That would never do. She couldn't quite say why, but she felt she must never get used to it. Yes, this was something that happened regularly. But that didn't mean she should start to treat it as normal.

"......!" Priestess bit her lip harder than usual and clung to her sounding staff. Then she knelt in the muck and embraced the imprisoned girls. Some of them had certainly been "used" just recently, but Priestess had no hesitation at all. Heedless of the filth that stained her vestments, she embraced each one of them, all of them, cleansing their bodies.

As we know, Priestess had been granted the Purify miracle. One use, and it might have seen the entire task done in an instant. But that was not what miracles were for. They were meaningful only because Priestess herself wanted to do something to help these girls, brought them what comfort she could. Despite the vicious, bloody scene unfolding not far away, now as in the past, the silence was gentle and kind. Those who had survived this horrific breeding ground were now half in a trance rescued from their living hell.

"...Sometimes I can't believe the way humans behave." The first thing to be heard in the room was a cold comment from High Elf Archer. She had her collar pulled up over her nose, perhaps to help block the smell, and Priestess couldn't see her expression.

Priestess opened her mouth at first, then closed it. Dwarf Shaman, for his part, heaved a sigh. "And what, Long-Ears? Y'mean humans are flat evil, so they should all just go down to destruction?"

"I'm not saying that." High Elf Archer put her ears back at the suspicious look he leveled at her; it wasn't something an elf could speak to.

"Just to be clear, this isn't considered acceptable in this country, either."

"I didn't say it!" she shot back. Soon they were arguing, but at least the tension had relaxed. But then, maybe there hadn't been any tension to begin with. Priestess had just been fretting. Not about world peace or anything as lofty as that but just this simple thing: She wanted all to be well with her friends.

"Good..." She hadn't really meant to let the word out, but it seemed to reach High Elf Archer's long ears. She awkwardly scratched a reddened cheek and said, as if in excuse: "Only humans talk in those sorts of absolutes anyway, right? Whoever did this, they're the bad guy, right?"

"It is, of course, natural to see responsibility on the battlefield as belonging not to the infantry, but to their commanders." Lizard Priest spat some gore out of his mouth and onto the floor. He valued the opportunity to eat the heart of a powerful opponent—but goblins were no such adversaries. "I do agree it seems likely that some leader in league with the forces of Chaos stands over these."

"And yet, even that...what was it?" Goblin Slayer turned his head as if he might find the word floating in the air. "...That ogre thing, even he was better."

"Huh, you actually remembered it," High Elf Archer said as she bit back a laugh, most likely intentionally. Goblin Slayer ignored her completely, instead grunting softly, "Whoever it is, they're like the ones we faced at the harvest festival last year—amateurs who don't understand how to handle goblins."

"Oh... You mean that dark elf." Priestess found her thoughts darting back to the dark elf she'd encountered in town. She didn't want to be prejudiced, but she also recognized that many dark elves were aligned with Chaos and would lash out against the Order in the world. She'd even heard rumors that it had been dark elves pulling the strings in the incident with the offertory wine.

If it were to be the same thing here…

…well, that wouldn't be very good, she thought. Though she was sure it wasn't the case.

"Now we have to help these people…" No, not now. Priestess kept her thoughts moving. They were on enemy ground. She had to think. "It's a question of *how* to help them, isn't it?"

"First, we link up with our quest giver." Goblin Slayer threw away his sword, blunted with blood and gore, and picked up a goblin's spear instead. He put it across his back and supplemented it with a gently curved saber that he put into the sheath at his hip. "We'll be moving a lot of people, which is why we had to create a diversion."

"And if the girl doesn't come out of this safe, we fail our quest." Dwarf Shaman took a swig of wine seemingly as a palate cleanser, wiping the stray droplets from his beard with his arm. "We haven't exactly been subtle, so the fact that we haven't had any company seems like a good sign."

"My Dragontooth Warrior remains in fine health, so worry not," Lizard Priest said as he picked up the young women easily, now only formerly captives but still asleep. Apparently, Priestess surmised, there was some sort of spiritual connection between a caster and their familiar. That would be so for a cleric who summoned a divine messenger, and Lizard Priest seemed to have the same connection to his Warrior.

"Can you guide us along and carry the women at the same time?"

"I won't be able to look up the fine details of wherever we find ourselves, but if we need only a basic understanding, then I believe it should be possible." If nothing else, he wasn't going to be able to fight with all these women riding on his back. He rolled his eyes in his head, knowing he didn't have to say that out loud.

"That will be enough," Goblin Slayer replied with a slight nod of his helmeted head, then he set out at a bold pace. His nonchalant stride was the same as ever, and elicited a helpless shrug and a shake of the head from High Elf Archer. "You need to *scout* ahead. I know you know how to do it, Orcbolg." She accompanied him over to the door, the one opposite the entrance they'd come in by, and started inspecting it.

It looked like they had a ways to go yet. Priestess thought she understood why the soldiers above had been so eager to seal this place away, peppering it with traps, hiding it deep underground. It would be hard to live a normal life knowing such a terrible place lay just beneath your feet. And worse, to live with the understanding that your actions were part of what enabled those goblins to do what they were doing. When a soldier had to come down here, the screams and cries of the women, the captives, would torment him—even if they were a direct result of what he had done, something he implicitly endorsed.

I can't imagine they wouldn't feel that. If they didn't…

Then they were practically Non-Prayer Characters already.

Priestess went around behind Lizard Priest, trying not to think about it as she helped settle the women on his back. "…Dragontooth Warrriors are pretty helpful, aren't they?" She almost whispered the words. It was just idle chatter. There was no breeze down here to carry off the stagnant air. So they tried to talk and laugh to lighten the mood as best they could.

"Ah, the good and bad of them depends on the caster. With enough talent, one's strength can be as wide as the sky, as deep as the ocean, as endless as the earth." Lizard Priest rolled his eyes in his head, receiving a relieved exhalation from Priestess.

"I hope it will be given to me one day to have a messenger from the Earth Mother," she said.

"If your faith does not waver, then that day will come."

Priestess felt someone press on her back. Dwarf Shaman smiled at her as if to say *Don't worry about it.* She turned her eyes forward to discover Goblin Slayer and High Elf Archer already had the door open and were waiting for the rest of them.

My faith…

She wondered, even still, if that was the right word for what she felt inside. That question had been with her ever since she had returned alive from her first adventure. But at the same time, there was this thought: *Perhaps wondering is my faith.*

The things she had learned from the more experienced members of the temple, and all things she had been through so far, made her think so. She jogged after Goblin Slayer, to whom she felt just a little closer than before. She prayed for the repose of the dead, for the healing and ultimate happiness of the wounded women, and for the safety of her companions and friends.

§

When he opened the door to the guardroom, it looked as if it was strewn with corpses. Guards were slumped on the ground, all of them asleep, although these weren't healthful naps. Then there was the fact that they had been tied up with a rope. Only two people were still standing: Female Merchant, her shirt dark with sweat, and the Dragon-tooth Warrior in its long cloak.

Goblin Slayer took all this in with a glance, then asked softly, "Are you all right?"

"...Yes." Female Merchant wiped some sweat away, then pulled on her jacket, which was hanging over the back of a chair. "Somehow."

That prompted a relieved exhalation of breath from Priestess. High Elf Archer smiled, too. This in turn caused Female Merchant to blush, almost as if she were embarrassed. "I'm sorry. It took me longer than I expected..." She sounded uncomfortable; she started absentmindedly adjusting her jacket to cover for herself.

"Taking out an entire room full of guards all by yourself? Yeah, that'd take a while." High Elf Archer let out a giggle.

"Stop that," Female Merchant objected meekly. "I was hardly by myself, and I didn't really fight them..."

"To win without fighting—isn't that even better?" Priestess responded immediately. "Isn't it?" she inquired of her companions before Female Merchant could argue again.

"Hmm...," Female Merchant said, defeated by this uncharacteristic tweak from Priestess.

Dwarf Shaman wasn't about to let her get away that easily. "They have the right of it, lass. Y'couldn't have done better."

"Hoo-hoo, it seems my Dragontooth Warrior acquitted itself well also. Very good, very good."

Suddenly Dwarf Shaman and Lizard Priest, two Silver-ranked adventurers, were showering her with praise.

True to his character, Goblin Slayer offered a much more subdued compliment…

"It seems the effect of the perfume worked as intended," he said as he inspected the soldiers' bonds. That was endorsement enough, coming from him.

"So, ahem," Female Merchant said, glancing around aimlessly to hide her embarrassment. "What about you guys…?"

"We're safe, too," Priestess added with a nod. Then she glanced in the direction of Lizard Priest. "Now we have to get them out…"

The question is how to do it.

It appeared Female Merchant had let the Dragontooth Warrior do the tying, but there was no way the soldiers in this room represented all the guards in the station. And then there were the goblins. They were being kept deep underground, but there was no guarantee they wouldn't find their way to the surface.

Most pressing of all, they were now carrying several prisoners. Escape was not going to be an easy task in these conditions. They would not be able to simply cart the women away as they had done in another fortress on a snowy mountain. They were in enemy territory this time and couldn't expect to duck into a nearby town when they were out of the stronghold.

Priestess looked like a student who had been given an especially challenging problem to solve. She could be heard muttering to herself under her breath.

One answer came from High Elf Archer, as if it were the most obvious thing in the world: "Can't we just grab a sand ship from the docks?"

"There are docks?"

"I remember them from the blueprint. I'm sure they're there." High Elf Archer put her hands on her hips and puffed out her chest proudly, then glanced in Goblin Slayer's direction. "I assume that was your plan all along, right, Orcbolg?"

"As far as it went." There was a single nod of the cheap-looking metal helmet.

Priestess was privately dumbstruck; she heaved a mental sigh. *I guess I shouldn't be surprised by now if he doesn't let the rest of us in on his strategy.*

He was really, truly hopeless.

And he would probably have to learn to realize it on his own, without her saying anything.

"The women," Goblin Slayer said with a nod at the rescued girls. "We'll give them to the Dragontooth Warrior. Can you steer a ship?"

Lizard Priest gave a thoughtful stroke of his chin and a roll of his eyes. "I should think so. When we were on the Master Myrmidon's vessel, I observed the process. And what will our destination be?"

"Show me the map the Myrmidon gave us."

"Of course. As you wish." Lizard Priest produced the papyrus from his pack and unfurled it. This time everyone was able to take a look at it, including High Elf Archer. Even though none of them were cartographers, they could tell what an excellent map it was. Goblin Slayer noticed a place not far from the stronghold. "Are these ruins?"

It was marked with an X and depicted what appeared to be a circle of stone pillars. The river passed right by it; it seemed to promise a place where they could rest. Old ruins being what they were, they would have to consider the possibility of running into monsters—but for a group of adventurers, that was just an occupational hazard.

It looks like a good guidepost to head for amid all this confusion.

"Then it is settled," Lizard Priest said. "The Dragontooth Warrior shall find and prepare us a ship at the docks."

"We'll head upstairs in the meantime." Goblin Slayer rolled up the map and tossed it to Lizard Priest, who plucked it out of midair with his long claws. "Then we'll escape, link up with the Warrior, and head for the ruins."

"Well then, time's a-wastin'. Wouldn't want them to get the drop on us because we were dawdling." Dwarf Shaman was counting his remaining spells on his stubby fingers. "Let's see, magic. I've only used Stupor the once, so I have three spells left."

"And I only summoned one Dragontooth Warrior," Lizard Priest said. "I likewise have three left."

"I've used Holy Light and Silence, so I've just got one...," Priestess said, and then stole a glance at Female Merchant. For a moment she didn't understand why she was being looked at, but then she blinked and said, "…I haven't used any spells. I have two left."

"Boy, this party has serious resources." High Elf Archer giggled. Thirteen spells altogether, nine left right now. "Hey, you sure I can't adopt you? You can handle the front row *and* use magic, it's great."

Female Merchant, suddenly finding herself embraced and having her hair mussed by a high elf, said awkwardly, "Er, uh. I don't think… I could. I don't…" Her face turned beet red, and she looked down at the ground bashfully. "I mean, there's a lot I have to do. In the capital." One wasn't sure whether to look at them like two friends separated by just a few years (well, they *were* separated by some years) or like a pair of very close sisters.

With Priestess's interjection of "She said she couldn't, okay?" the amusing trio was complete. Their banter seemed downright incongruous amid the crowd of collapsed guards in this evil stronghold.

Dwarf Shaman squinted as if he were looking at something particularly bright and said, "C'mon, Long-Ears." But there was a touch of affection in his voice. "Scaly and I can probably both hack it on the front row if we need to. Anyway, Beard-cutter, what do we do about the goblins?"

"The nest is below us," Goblin Slayer observed bluntly. He pulled a waterskin out of his pouch and poured the contents through his visor, drinking deep before continuing. "It would take too long to find and destroy every individual. We need to eliminate them all in one fell swoop."

In other words, he was going to do just what he always did. He was Goblin Slayer. And he was going to slay goblins.

"And that's why we're going up…," Female Merchant said, finally free of her brief wrestle with High Elf Archer. She could feel a gaze on her from behind the visor of the helmet, and she nodded.

"Just to be clear, what is the status of your quest?"

"The prime minister of this country has allied himself with Chaos and is specifically working to increase the number of goblins in his lands. I've seen it with my own eyes," Female Merchant replied. She knew what was happening. Chaos was budding here and preparing to burst forth. "My quest is complete. All that's left is for me to report what I've seen."

"Then I will accompany you." Goblin Slayer shoved the half-drained canteen back into his pouch. His voice became even more brusque, mechanical, and nonchalant as he said: "It's good for our party to have 'serious resources.'"

Right. Female Merchant's cheeks softened toward a smile. She was happy to hear him say that.

Brief discussions followed, plans were laid, and preparations were promptly made. It was a council of war that doubled as a very short rest.

Priestess realized she didn't know how long it had been since they'd entered the fortress. It felt so long and yet so short at the same time. But in any event, time inexorably passed, and it was probably after midnight by now.

Fatigue and excitement were equally dangerous. If you weren't careful, you could miss the fact that you were tired at all. So after their conference, they drank some water, took some provisions, and spent some of their precious time in laughter.

At length, Goblin Slayer said, "Let's go," and the *five* other adventurers got to their feet. Their destination: the uppermost floor of the stronghold. What might be waiting for them there, they didn't know. Why didn't they know? Because this was an adventure.

"Oh, hang on just one second," Female Merchant said as they were about to leave the guardroom. She jogged back from the door over to the Dragontooth Warrior carrying the rescued women. "I never thanked you for your help…"

She took hold of the hood covering the Warrior's head, pulling him down toward her, and stood on tiptoe; then her face disappeared into the hood. High Elf Archer let out a sound of surprise. Just for an instant, the silhouettes of Female Merchant and the Dragontooth Warrior overlapped.

"…Sorry for the wait," she said, returning to the party at the same quick jog. Her cheeks were flushed the slightest red. Priestess, who had witnessed a moment of the denouement, likewise felt her face burn a little.

"Ha-ha-ha, that Dragontooth Warrior is a lucky fellow." Lizard Priest let out a belly laugh, and Female Merchant's face got even redder. "L-let's get going!" she said pointedly and headed for the door, out into the hallways of the stronghold.

The party followed her, still grinning until Dwarf Shaman whispered, "Just asking, but you're not planning to kill the general or whoever it is that runs this place, are yeh?"

"I don't know who it is, but I doubt it will be necessary," Goblin Slayer said, his words mercilessly cold. "If they are loyal to goblins, then we can expect only a fool."

§

They were given food. They were given a place to sleep. They were even given women. And yet, all this only increased their dissatisfaction. Here they were, forced to live in this grimy hole, while everyone else enjoyed themselves upstairs. That lot probably had much better food and far greater luxuries. They were probably sleeping away the hours, whether during the damnably hot "night" or the freezing "day."

In fact, the ones upstairs had taken away everything the goblins had fought so hard to win. Even the women. They were given the women, told they could do what they liked with them—but when they did, the ones upstairs shouted and whipped them. It was their right to do as they pleased with what was theirs!

But what enraged them most of all was how the ones upstairs thought this was all enough to get the goblins to obey. They would make their pretty little arguments and strut and preen, when inside they were hardly different from the ones who lived down here. Strutting and preening were really the only talents they had.

And they had been in such an uproar about a missing piece of paper! What did they *do* up there?

To think, they looked down on the ones who lived here! *Do this, do that*, they said, and then when it was done they complained. If they were that desperate, they should do it themselves.

And it all led to...this.

The stables were empty. The bodies of his compatriots were strewn everywhere, the stench leading upstairs. The goblin howled with rage, quite ignoring the fact that he himself had escaped the carnage only because he had been shirking his duties. If any had been there who had understood the goblin tongue, they would certainly have winced at the sheer vulgarity of his language.

They've angered us for the last time!

Goblins were always angry, always lashing out. But as so often, this one was convinced that his anger was justified. He and the others had been wrongly tormented, which was why they had every right to rise up and take back what was theirs.

They were the ones who had worked hardest in this stronghold, so they were the ones should stand atop the hierarchy. Not *they*, in fact, but *him*, this goblin thought as his shouting echoed away into the cavern. Those born and raised here, those brought in from outside—all of them should and would be enraged, should and would take up arms. They would overrun the stronghold overhead and the city nearby, all of it, taking it all and making it theirs.

The dancing girl the soldiers had been raving about, and this princess or whoever she was—the goblins would take them. The soldiers were fools not to take them, but the goblins were different.

And I should be on top of it all.

Why? Because he would be the commander of this battle, of course. The others would be his loyal servants, like his hands and feet; they would go to die instead of him. No. In fact, unlike the fools who had been killed here, he wouldn't make the same mistake. He would survive. He was sure of it.

With a vile grin on his face, his loins stirred by this simple fantasy, the goblin gave a flourish of his sword—

"GGOOOGOOGORRBB!!"

—and the next instant, his brains were spattered by an iron chain that calmly caught him across the head, and his life ended. Someone stepped on his body as it collapsed, twitching: another, larger goblin. Being the biggest goblin down here, he knew it was *he* who should stand at the top, and he howled out his conviction.

None of the other goblins objected. They were all united in their belief that they could use this big brute to their own ends.

"GOOROGG!! GOORGGBBG!!"

And thus the goblins poured out toward the surface. They ran through the underground passageways, disregarding those of their comrades stupid enough to be caught and killed by the traps—upward, ever upward.

The guards in the guardhouse were the first of the victims. And the luckiest. They were tied up and asleep, so they were eviscerated by the enraged goblins without ever really knowing what was happening.

"GORGB!! GOORGBB!!"

Bah, humans aren't so tough.

No, look. They were eating something we've never seen. What is it, crap?

There's a smell. It smells like a female. A good smell. A new one. And it smells like our breeding slaves.

Up. They've gone up. The bastards. We'll drag them back down, beat them to bloody pulps.

"GOORGBB!!"

The goblins stripped the soldiers of their equipment, then, soaked with blood, let out a terrifying battle cry and surged forward.

They would kill the humans, get the women back, and take what was rightfully theirs.

Once they had started, they would not stop until they were dead: This was the way of goblins.

§

"Wh-what the…?!"

"It's the goblins! Goblins are pouring up from the underground!"

"Who was it who had the bright idea to use goblins anyway?!"

Angry voices rang out, soon accompanied by the crash of swords, screaming and shouting, the sound of rending flesh, and the gibbering of monsters.

There was no order; everyone simply rushed in with their swords. Some soldiers were still in civilian clothes, while others hurried to pull on their armor, and a few tried to get away in just their undergarments.

Many of the death rattles that could be heard were obviously not human, but there were a few cries from the men, too. They had lived

above a goblin nest without so much as posting a guard. This was the
obvious outcome.

In other words, it was sheer, unrelenting chaos.

"Wh-who the hell are you?! Identify your squadron and—"

"The goblins will soon attack from underground."

"Wh-what…?!"

The accusatory question—issued by a man who did not yet understand the situation he was in—was met with a calm response from
Goblin Slayer, who then hurried ahead with his party. They pushed
through the corridors, past soldiers who ran by in desperate disarray, past others who tried to stop them—upward, ever upward. They
stepped aside for only one group of people: soldiers who ran through
shouting "We're transporting the wounded! Everyone out of the way!"

Priestess's eyes were briefly drawn to the wounded man on the
stretcher as they went by, but she quickly looked forward again and
kept running. Whether they went to do battle or to escape, most of the
soldiers were heading downward; she and her party were fighting the
tide.

Most of them ignored the grimy man with his diverse party and its
motley assortment of equipment. If anyone had tried to talk to them, it
probably would simply have been someone like before, someone who
didn't really understand what was going on.

The soldiers would serve as a distraction for the goblins, while the
goblins served as a distraction for the soldiers. Even though they were
numerous and had held the advantage of surprise, the goblins were
still just goblins. When the soldiers got their heads about them again,
there was no way they could lose; this confusion would be cleared up
soon enough. But it was more than enough to buy them a little time.

"…I knew you were an expert on goblins," Dwarf Shaman said,
chuckling as they jogged along, "but you do come up with the nastiest
ideas, Beard-cutter."

"It was not my knowledge that led to this idea," Goblin Slayer
replied, leaning against a wall to peek around a corner. Satisfied there
was no trouble ahead, he waved to the others, and the party resumed
running.

The stronghold might have been devised to confuse invading

enemies—but the people who worked there still had to do their jobs. What's more, Goblin Slayer and his party were adventurers. Caverns, ruins, and mazes were their bread and butter. If one memorized the map before diving in, one simply would not get lost. "When surrounded by enemies, one need only turn oneself into a friend bringing them information, no?"

Lizard Priest rolled his eyes merrily and thumped his tail on the ground. "I see, I see. My own suggestion has borne fruit, and it is a great victory for my allies." With his great, twisting tail and the claws of his feet that beat into the paving stones, Lizard Priest looked, to put it modestly, like a true monster. The glare he fixed on the soldiers who went by was in fact one of amusement—but they didn't know that.

"Gotta say...I can't help thinkin' we must look a little odd for friends of theirs."

"I told you you should all have changed your clothes like I did," High Elf Archer insisted, breezing past them. In the end, she was the least conspicuous of the lot of them. Was that because of her clothes? Or because her other party members included someone in grimy armor and a gigantic lizardman?

"I think that would have made getting in here a lot easier all along," she went on.

"I thought you didn't like disguises," Goblin Slayer replied pointedly.

"I don't like being disguised as a *slave!*" She sounded genuinely annoyed.

She does *stand out, though*, Priestess thought, huffing and puffing along at the rear of the party, where she had a perfect view of High Elf Archer's beauty. High elves had an otherworldly quality to their appearance that no change of clothing could disguise.

Priestess thought for a second, then on an impulse said: "Now, now, mustn't have over-strong preferences."

"Hrgh?!" High Elf Archer, clearly not expecting this from Priestess, choked a little bit.

"Hoh!" Dwarf Shaman's eyes widened, impressed that she had gotten to the riposte before he had. "The lass's right. You'll be an anvil forever at this rate."

"Unbelievable…! My sweet, innocent girl is being corrupted by Orcbolg *and* his friends!" It was hard to tell if High Elf Archer was serious or not. She looked up at the ceiling dramatically.

"I-I'm not being corrupted!" Priestess said, but no one engaged her further on the subject.

If they wanted to get to the top floor, they would have to take the stairs. In front of them was a steep, tight spiral staircase. One wrong move could see them tumble off the side, and there was always the possibility that enemies—soldiers or goblins—could press them from above. Goblin Slayer and High Elf Archer on the front row were palpably prepared for combat, and Lizard Priest followed their lead.

"Grr," Priestess grumbled, puffing out her cheeks as they ran along. But there was nothing to be done. She gave up objecting further.

"—…?" Priestess glanced over at Female Merchant, who was running as fast as she could, red-faced and short of breath but determined not to slow down the party. Priestess had been politely matching Female Merchant's speed, but now her eyes were wide. *I wasn't paying close enough attention.*

When she thought about what Female Merchant had been through in her life, she could conclude only that the yammering of goblins must be a terrible thing for her. And as they ran through the stronghold, even at this moment the clangor of battle was all around, and so was the yelling of goblins.

"Are you all right?" she asked her friend.

"Er, ah—" Female Merchant looked around, not quite sure what to say. Then she steadied her breathing a bit and said simply and with what might have been a touch of envy, "You're just…incredible."

"Um… You think so?"

Priestess wasn't so sure. It felt like all she could do just to follow the people ahead of her. And yet…

If I'm incredible, I'm certainly not the only one.

"I think that's true of all of us," she said.

Including you.

She took the hand of a woman who had become a first-rate merchant, making her way in a field Priestess could hardly imagine being a part of. Just as during the fight on the snowy mountain, her grip was gentle but firm. In return, she felt a hesitant interlacing of fingers and a squeeze, and it made her very happy.

"Well, let's keep pushing, then!"

"Right!"

And they went to head up the stairs giggling like girls, a sound most out of place here.

The stairs twisted upward. It suggested that they were in one of the towers they had seen from the outside. When they finally reached the top of the staircase, they found themselves in a large chamber with windows on every side. A watchtower, perhaps. Goblin Slayer stuck his head out one of the windows and looked around.

Wait... No, Priestess thought. Goblin Slayer seemed to be looking not so much *around* as *up.*

"You're thinking of going up there?" she asked.

"Yes, on top of the roof," Goblin Slayer said with a nod. "But the roof is at a very steep angle. How does the ceiling look?"

"A bit high up there," Dwarf Shaman grunted. "But if we *could* get to it, we could probably tease out a few stones and get outside."

"It's settled, then... Go."

"Yes, sir." Priestess promptly produced the Adventurer's Toolkit from her bag, offering him that old standby, the grappling hook.

Never leave home without it...! She'd picked up the Toolkit on a recommendation, and there had never been a time when she'd regretted having it.

Goblin Slayer took the grappling hook, grasped the rope firmly, and spun the hook end before flinging it upward. It lodged between the rafters, and Goblin Slayer gave the dangling rope a tug or two to make sure it was secure. Now they just had to climb.

Female Merchant was very new at this and, understandably, had some difficulty, but with the other five to pull her up together, there was no real trouble. Once in the rafters, Dwarf Shaman expertly pried loose a few of the ceiling boards, allowing them access to the roof proper. They found themselves in a perfectly arched vault of stone.

"So y'want out, do you?"

"Yes. At the highest point possible." Goblin Slayer stared up at the stones at the very top of the arch. "There's something called a key-stone, isn't there?"

"Hold on, Orcbolg!" High Elf Archer cried. She had a bad feeling about this. Priestess likewise frowned. "You don't mean to bring this whole stronghold down, do you?"

"No," Goblin Slayer replied with no apparent concern. He gave a slow shake of his helmeted head. "*I* won't be the one to bring it down."

He was looking instead at Lizard Priest.

§

Woooooooooooooooom...

There was a howling as of a great assembly of spirits, an agonized wail trailing off.

It was unlikely that most who heard the sound understood what it was. The goblins certainly couldn't. And most of the soldiers probably didn't.

No, those who simply heard the sound wouldn't have recognized what was happening—but those who saw it did. As well as those who felt the ensuing quake.

The desert was moving. The sand whirled in the distant wastes like a cloud being born right on the ground.

And it was coming closer. Ever closer. It drew nearer even as the maelstrom got larger and larger.

Most people were too caught up in the maelstrom of goblins to notice the storm of sand, but all present felt an unmistakable vibration. Faint at first, it caused the particles of sand on the flagstones to jump up and down. Then the eating utensils on tables, cast-off weapons, and even furniture started to shake audibly, to fall and crash to the floor.

Soldiers, whether fleeing from the goblins or still trying to resist them, stopped in their tracks. The thoughtless goblins were likewise stymied; they began to look around and gibber anxiously.

And then the moment came. A great wave of sand crashed against the stronghold like a tempest. A massive dorsal fin, as tall as a tower, could be seen to protrude from within the spray.

"It's— It's the sand mantaaaas!" someone shouted, but the sound was quickly swallowed by the advancing monsters. The school of huge fish, with outer shells like armor, ignored both humans and goblins and even the stronghold itself; none of it meant anything to them.

First one, then another and another, crashed into the stronghold. It was simple: sand mantas worried about nothing, but simply went straight over or through anything in their path.

It was only a matter of moments until the stronghold—famous and infamous in equal measure in this land—was reduced to ruins.

§

"Eeeeeek!" Female Merchant couldn't restrain a shout at all the shaking. Priestess held her tight. It was as if not just the guardhouse, but the entire fortress, was crying out in agony.

"O Mapusaurus, ruler of the earth. Permit me to join your pack, howsoever briefly." Lizard Priest concluded his invocation of the Communicate prayer, then shook his head almost in disbelief. "My goodness. Scales they may have, but to find myself whispering sweet nothings to a bunch of fish! One never dreamed it."

"Hrmph... I feel like that could describe a lot of things on this trip," High Elf Archer grumbled. "Like the fact that their leader isn't even here..." She opened her mouth as if to say more, but there was another great shaking, and a piece of roof came tumbling down from overhead. She swallowed her complaint to Lizard Priest and instead fired off at Goblin Slayer: "Hey, Orcbolg, what do you think you're doing?!"

"Going outside," he said, kicking aside part of the demolished roof. An open space yawned before him, and suddenly, a cutting wind whipped through the area. Priestess squeezed her eyes shut with a little yelp, and when the wind subsided, she made another little sound.

It's crimson...

It was daybreak in the desert. An indigo-blue sky was settling in the horizon. But beyond the dark sands came a red-tinged light. It spread gradually, like a flower blooming over the earth, turning everything scarlet. And indeed, a floral aroma came to them on the last gust of the rain-cleansed night wind. Priestess had seen countless dawns in her ten years and change, but never one so beautiful.

No…

That wasn't quite right. Not quite true. She thought every daybreak must be beautiful. But people so rarely noticed them. So few took the time to really look…

"Oops, yipes…"

The feeling vanished as quickly as it had come. There was another great noise, and the tower gave another violent shake. They didn't have much time now.

She'd grabbed hold of Female Merchant when the shaking started; now she said, "Can you stand?" and helped her to her feet.

"Orcbolg, just *wait a minute*!"

"What is it?" He had one hand on the crumbling roof and one foot poised to step outside, but instead he looked in High Elf Archer's direction.

The elf, her ears about as far back as they could possibly go, marched toward him, heedless of the shaking. "What do you think you're doing going out there?! Even if you made it down, this place is a mess, you'd just—"

"What?" Goblin Slayer sounded genuinely shocked. He spoke in the same nonchalant tone as always, and yet, the response was surprising. The rest of the party found they couldn't speak. They just looked straight at the cheap-looking metal helmet. "You said it yourself," Goblin Slayer went on, still sounding perplexed, almost as if he couldn't believe he had to explain this. "We'll cross over the top of them."

Now it was High Elf Archer who seemed unbelieving, but she could hardly get the words out. "Wha—? We'll *wha*—?" Her mouth worked open and shut, but Priestess remembered something High Elf Archer had said back in the tunnels. A little chatter about a hero who had done something of the sort. She seemed to remember that the hero had a name, very short and yet impressive, something one would remember their whole life.

And he hadn't forgotten this tiny detail.

"…Gods," Dwarf Shaman said finally. "The one thing I can always be sure of—life with you is never boring."

"Is that so?"

"Falling Control, am I right? I'll get it ready to go, just hold on."

"Thank you."

Dwarf Shaman took a swig of his wine to get himself fired up, then clapped his hands together to summon the earth sprites. The desert was a place of sunlight, moonlight, sand, and earth sprites, and gods of fire and wind. They would surely be willing to help this adventurer.

"Come out, you gnomes, and let it go! Here it comes, but take it slow! Turn those buckets upside-down—set us gently on the ground!"

Priestess thought she could hear faint laughter and sense tiny something dancing around in the air. At the same time, the skirt of her vestments billowed, and she rushed to push it down with one hand. The laughter, if she wasn't imagining it, turned into something rich and joyous.

"Well, I for one am rather heavy. If the yoke of the land's power were not lightened up on my neck, it might well break me." Priestess didn't really follow, but Lizard Priest gave a great swing of his arms and took a step forward. "I know where my Dragontooth Warrior is, so no worries. Someone must be the first to cross the fishes…!" No sooner had he spoken than he gave a great screech and jumped into the school of sand mantas. Despite his huge size, he floated down onto a sand manta's back with remarkable lightness, then he kicked off the scales on its back with his clawed feet, lunging again.

"Argh! If I had a thousand lives, it wouldn't be enough! …No fair! Wait for me!" High Elf Archer went leaping after him. With the grace of a leaf on the wind, with the enthusiasm of a bouncing ball, she got smaller and smaller in the distance. Perhaps for a high elf like her, walking across a school of sand mantas was no different from walking across a river.

"Bah, hold up— If yeh get too far from me, the spell won't hold!" Dwarf Shaman scrambled to follow them, jumping into the air. He moved from the back of one fish to the next like an overfilled balloon; it looked a bit dangerous. One wrong move could have seen him plummet to the ground, yet oddly, he never appeared to be in any real

danger of falling. Maybe he was just used to this. But if anyone would
have said so, he probably would have just laughed it off.

"What do you want to do? Will you go next?" This was Goblin
Slayer, standing guard at the rear as everyone else went ahead of him.
This question seemed like a gesture of consideration for Priestess and
Female Merchant. Though his expression was hidden behind his
visor, as ever, and they couldn't be sure.

"...No. It's all right." Priestess looked at Female Merchant, still
in her arms. It took her a second, but she nodded firmly. "We'll go
together."

"...Will you?"

"We certainly will."

"I see," Goblin Slayer said with a nod. "Very well."

He put his sword (when had he picked up a new one?) in its sheath,
then kicked off the wall and leaped into space. Now it was just Priestess and Female Merchant. There was the roar of the storm, inducing
a continual creaking and swaying in the tower. It wouldn't be long
before the place came down on their heads. There was no time to lose,
no room for failure. And yet somehow, Priestess was calm. Her heart
was undisturbed, even warm. It felt like it was already floating, like it
beat in time with the world around it.

"...Shall we?" she asked.

"Yes!" Female Merchant nodded and clasped Priestess's hand extra
tightly. "Let's go!"

And so, hand in hand, they walked to the edge of the tall tower.
They shared a look, then they both took a deep breath.

"Here we..."

"...go!"

And then the girls jumped, trusting themselves to the sky, to the
adventure.

The air rushed past them, blowing their hair about wildly. Priestess
simply pressed her cap to her head with the same hand that held her
sounding staff. And then they could see it through the whipping sand,
the fast-approaching back of a giant fish.

"Yaaahhh!"

They both kicked off the creature, and to their amazement found themselves hurtling through the air again. It was like they were passing through the night and to the source of day. The sun gleamed ahead of them, the rose-tinted world spread out below. The young women looked at each other. They started laughing. Somehow, they couldn't help it.

"Ah, ah-ha-ha-ha...ha-ha-ha!"

"Hee-hee...!"

They stepped lightly as if clicking together the heels of a pair of silver slippers—or perhaps ruby.

§

If only that had been the end of it.

"GOOROOGBB!!!"

When the roaring came from overhead, one goblin started running like his life depended on it. A size bigger than the others, he had long ago abandoned his chain. Now he wore a horned helmet and an overcoat along with some armor, and he carried a halberd he didn't know how to use. He owed it all to having been the first to rush into the opulent room and start stealing everything he could find. He had no intention of sharing any of it with the ones who came after him looking for leftovers. Then he had taken a glance outside and promptly decided to run.

He wasn't like those other fools—the ones who would fight a soldier, enjoy tormenting them, and then be cut down by another guard while they were having their way with the first one. All those others were riffraff and trash; of course they would die. Not him. Indeed, he hardly believed he *could* die.

The others had never helped him. Not once; in fact, they had laughed at him and mocked him. Let them die. Perhaps that's what he was thinking.

Whatever the case, he raced down into the dungeons, with their protective layer of thick bedrock, faster than the stronghold above him could collapse. He was still enraged at the thought of the people who had forced him down into this filthy hole. But now wasn't the time. He had a goal, and he would reach it before any of those other idiots overtook him.

He clutched a single piece of paper so hard it was practically destroyed in his grip: a single piece of paper. He had just so happened to pick it up the same time he had acquired his beloved helmet; it looked like a picture, a diagram. Probably one of those "maps." He grinned at his own intelligence. He was smart; that's how he knew what it was.

This here was the underground tunnels. And deep within them, there was some kind of mark. He just had to go there. There was treasure there, he was sure. Maybe women. Possibly food. Whatever it was, it would be good.

That was all that filled his head, just those good things and how he was going to get them. He never wondered why the humans had forced the goblins down here and filled the place with traps. It would be a true fool who expected any kind of serious reflection from goblins. They simply went for what was in front of them, stole it, used it until it no longer interested them, and then moved on to the next thing.

That's how goblins are.

§

Thankfully, the sand ship didn't capsize when the adventuring party came tumbling down onto the deck from above. Although it rocked noticeably along the sandline.

This truly was a military-grade vessel: Even with the entire party aboard, along with the former captives and the Dragontooth Warrior, it ran light and easy over the sand.

"I swear, I can't believe this!" On board, High Elf Archer looked just as excited and just as angry as ever. She glared fiercely at the metal helmet, fixing it with a long, slim finger. "First the water, *splash!*, then the flour, *bash!*, and now an entire stronghold, *crash!* Unreal!"

"I believe I've done more than that."

"Not what I mean!"

The others watched the exchange with evident relief. There must have been a sense that it was finally over. They knew perfectly well that High Elf Archer's anger was itself a sort of game.

Dwarf Shaman captained the ship, the sails billowing as he pointed the craft toward the ruins and off it went along the sand. Priestess finally let go of Female Merchant's hand and went to tend to the rescued women, offering them first aid and protection from the sun. She cleansed their bodies again, daubed antibacterial ointments on their wounds, and bandaged them as best she could. The Dragontooth Warrior, to her surprise, creaked over to help her, which she found oddly heartening.

"It's best not to act in haste at a time like this," Lizard Priest said lightly, sitting himself down and looking around in every direction. Appearing quite comfortable, he produced a lump of cheese from his bag of provisions. Come to think of it, it was morning already. They had worked all night, and Priestess placed a hand on her belly. She discovered she was quite hungry.

"Or else it might appear that we're fleeing the scene," Lizard Priest added, taking a bite out of his cheese. Priestess, eager for a meal of her own, rifled through her bag.

The fish and drink that I had at the tavern were so tasty.

She thought she could have eaten quite a bit more of it had there been time. For now, though, she pulled out the baked goods, breaking them up with a strike of a wooden mallet. Otherwise it was difficult to share the hard-baked provisions.

"When the circle of our pursuers widens enough, we can either drive deeper inside..."

"...Or punch through a thin part of the circle and get back to our home."

"Just so, just so," Lizard Priest said with a nod of his long neck. As he declared his food to be sweet nectar, Priestess took a bite of her own. The baked goods were sitting on a handkerchief; she shared some with Female Merchant, who also took a bite. Or more specifically, who took delicate nibbles befitting a woman of refinement or possibly a squirrel. It was cute. When Priestess couldn't help a giggle, Female Merchant said, "What?" and looked at her in puzzlement.

"Oh nothing," Priestess replied and took another bite. It was wonderful sustenance for her tired body. She noticed that Goblin Slayer had likewise taken some of his dried meat from his item pouch and was nonchalantly stuffing it into his helmet. High Elf Archer was munching on some dried fruits, and Dwarf Shaman was having a swig of his wine. Everything felt relaxed, almost lazy on board the ship. Priestess had learned over the course of these two years that the hours after an adventure were often deliberately thus.

Most of the stories end with the heroes finishing the fight and getting the treasure.

But if you were an adventurer, then after it was all over, you had to get home. You had to figure out how to carry your mountain of loot, and sometimes you were tired or even sleepy. Come to think of it, Priestess had never even seen "loot" to speak of so far...

"Heeey, gonna reach the ruins shortly," Dwarf Shaman called out. "Might be easier to get a rest once we disembark."

"You're not piloting drunk, are you? I don't want to end up beached just because you were too soused to remember how to steer," High Elf Archer chided the dwarf before adding, "Steer—that is what you do with a ship, right?" She didn't really know.

"We won't, and I'm not," Dwarf Shaman shot back. As they argued, the sand ship arrived alongside the ruins with a spray of dust. Yes, they would certainly be able to make a landing here. As they got off the ship, they found the ground remarkably solid underfoot. "Mm...," High Elf Archer sniffed at the air. "I smell grass."

"It is sometimes postulated that the desert was once a land of great abundance," Lizard Priest said, hopping heavily off the ship, only swaying a little as he landed.

The area was ringed by a number of round pillars; it did indeed look like a place that might have been a temple many ages ago. Now it was buried in rock and rubble, offering only hints of its former glory.

Goblin Slayer quickly surveyed the area and said, "It'll serve to keep us out of the sun while we take a few hours' rest." He sounded relieved.

One thing was true: They had been at work since last night. None of them would say it, but they were all clearly spent. Thankfully, there was water flowing nearby. They could drink some fresh water, wash themselves, and rest until evening. Then they could go back to the capital city or some other town. Their adventure was over. They could just rest and—

"Hey," High Elf Archer said sharply, interrupting Priestess's intended relaxation. "Do you smell something weird?"

"...?" Priestess raised her head, sniffing. "I'm not sure..."

"Sure it ain't the grass and flowers y'mentioned?" Dwarf Shaman asked.

"No, I'm sure of it," she replied. "We've smelled it before, remember? The first time the three of us adventured together!"

Priestess didn't know what that meant exactly, but Dwarf Shaman and Lizard Priest seemed to understand. Their expressions tightened, and Lizard Priest made sure he had a catalyst—a dragon's tooth—in his hand.

"Sulfur again? Ugh, don't tell me it's more demons?! I've had just about enough...!" Dwarf Shaman cried, then took a swig of wine and wiped the droplets out of his beard. It might have looked like a touch of desperation, but maybe it was just what he needed to fire himself up.

"Demons?" Goblin Slayer said. He didn't seem more certain about what was going on than Priestess felt, but his sword was already in his hand. Taking her cue from him, she got up and clutched her sounding staff, brushing the crumbs of the baked goods off her knees with her hand.

Demons...

She had faced one before, down in the depths of that most terrible dungeon. She would never forget it. "You mean...another of those things that's just an arm?"

"We once battled a lesser demon, back before we met your two honored selves. And once or twice more after that." Lizard Priest had bared his fangs; he looked downright eager. "This one hasn't even diamond eyes. Ha-ha-ha, a straight fight...!"

"And you sound happy about this why? I'd be just as happy never to fight another demon in my life, you know!" High Elf Archer seemed exasperated, but she jumped up to the top of one of the stone pillars with the same lightness as if she were running across a branch. If they were going to need her arrows, a high vantage point would be to their benefit.

"Hmm, now," Lizard Priest said, watching her and shaking his head. "Strange— Demons don't typically come out while the sun is high in the sky. And demons are not the only things that might smell of sulfur."

"Then what do you think—?" Priestess started to ask, but then a massive earthquake assaulted the ruins, and the open area (perhaps once an altar) began to crumble away beneath them.

The first thing they saw from the resulting gaping hole was a flash of gold. Something came flying out, almost as if overflowing: enough gold and silver and equipment to dazzle the eye. And sitting upon the mountain of treasure was a creature like something out of a bad joke. Its outspread wings darkened the sky. Its scales were harder than steel. Its claws and fangs were sharper and deadlier than many a famous blade carried by many a storied knight. Its breath, a sulfurous miasma, seemed to scorch the sky, and its intelligence made even the elves seem like children.

"GOOROGGOBOG!!"

Poised triumphantly on its back was a hideous goblin—the weakest monster in the world bestriding a massive, deep-red body. Anyone who had words in the Four-Cornered World, even the youngest child, would have recognized it.

Ask what was the strongest person or beast in the world, and the answer would be immediate:

"A red dragon!"

As if in response, there came a great roar that rent the air from the dungeon up to the sky.

No Hit No Run

How did this happen?!

The captain groaned to himself, racing through the stronghold even as it was swallowed up by the storm of Chaos. Things might not have been going perfectly, but he had thought they were going well enough. Breed the goblins, domesticate them, use them for soldiers: When the idea had struck him, it had seemed so inspired he thought it might be a revelation. Slaves or kidnappees could serve as a nice, cheap source of both food and procreation. He would have an endless source of disposable troops. An infinite army. They could even win a war with these forces.

The captain remembered the withering look of disdain the prime minister had given him when he had suggested the idea. When the prime minister had brought her to parade before the troops, the princess didn't even look at him. As the goblins grew more numerous, the soldiers also began to give him dirty looks. It was humiliating. Why didn't they share his devotion to this country, his willingness to do anything, even something underhanded, for its sake?

"Hey, out of my way, you dogs!" The captain brandished his saber; there was a gibbering cry and a spray of blood. He ignored it. The wailing soldiers and the goblins were all alike: merely in his way.

Now that the prime minister held the power in this country, that made the prime minister's second-in-command the next most powerful person—and that was him. One day he would take that despicable minister out of the picture, force the princess to marry him, and then *he* would stand at the top. He had the knowledge and the intelligence. He had been educated in the singing of ballads and the ways of etiquette and culture. And as for combat ability, he was displaying it now.

So why doesn't anyone see me for the jewel that I am?! The captain charged through the stronghold, looking around with bloodshot eyes, saliva frothing at the corner of his mouth. He had been informed of the goblin attack just as he had been preparing to entertain the foreign merchant woman. He had been on his best behavior. He would whisper a welcoming word or two into her ear so that when the time came she might aid him. He'd even had something special up his sleeve to make sure it would happen. Everything had been going according to plan.

And then the goblins rebelled.

He was sure the foreign woman had started it somehow. Another country instigating rebellion in his ranks. That was as good as a declaration of war.

"It's war!" he shouted. "Do you blaggards understand that? We have a war on our hands!" But though he shouted orders, no one listened to him. That only made him angrier.

Can't even count on my own soldiers anymore!

If he wanted this job done right, he would have to do it himself. He'd come this far. He knew he could trust only his own genius.

They would subdue the goblins eventually. The monsters had caught them by surprise, but the soldiers were stronger than they were. The problem was what came after that. It would be war. There was no question in the captain's mind. He had to be prepared. He would have to use that something special. After all, it wouldn't be special if he never used it.

He hadn't lost yet. He just needed to win. Achieve victory, and everything would be his. All the country's treasures, all the power, the women. Even that birdfolk dancer he'd heard so much about, the one who was supposed be the most sublimely talented in all the world, even she would come to serve him.

The captain kicked open the door to the living quarters and flew inside. "Where is it?! My map—I need my map…!"

He turned desk drawers inside out, pulled everything off the shelves. He didn't even care when a wine jar crashed to the ground and shattered open on the thick carpet he took so much pride in. A truly great man would not be distracted by such trivial things. No, never. The captain was sure.

"Yo, Excellency. You have a minute? I've got a message for you."

The voice came from behind him, interrupting his desperate search. The captain already had one hand on the sword at his hip as he turned around. "What the hell is it?! And who the hell are you?! Don't waste my time with worthless reports. Help me find—"

His widened eyes were filled with the sight of a flying pellet of steel.

"Die, you rat."

§

There was a *thwack* and the force of the bullet penetrating his eyeball spun the guard captain around, then he finally ended up flat on his back.

The spy replaced the smoking cylinder across his back, letting out a sigh as he grabbed the captain's helmet. "See? I told you these things were made for killing enemies from close range in a single shot. Armor or no armor."

"You aimed at his head. I would be surprised if it didn't turn out this way." Beside him, a red-haired girl gave a sour smile and tried to get the helmet to sit comfortably. She was a changeling, but her ears were longer than those of an ordinary human. Maybe the helmet didn't fit quite right. She finally gave up, pulling off the helmet and rubbing her ears. "More important business," she said by way of keeping the spy focused. "We aren't doing things the usual way today. We have to hurry. Could be some trouble getting out of here, eh?"

"Gee, sorry," piped up a third person. It was a guard with a delicate build—the young woman who served the God of Knowledge. She was smiling. "Didn't mean to horn in on your racket."

"...It's fine, and you know it." The red-haired elf frowned and looked away. The cleric of the God of Knowledge chuckled. "I'll pretend the helmet did that."

"I said, it's fine," the red-haired elf said with a snort. "Just do your job."

"Sure, and you keep your eyes open for any problems." The red-haired elf was her comrade, a fellow woman, and a friend, and the cleric had no special desire to upset her. She jumped over the captain's corpse. As she went, she spotted something that seemed to have been torn from around the man's neck: a sigil of a single eye. The cleric frowned.

Truthfully, she had some misgivings about this herself. She would normally just leave everything to the two front-rowers.

Everyone's got their part to play, right? Nothing special about that. She very rarely came out to the scene of the action like this. She had to get in a little banter or she wouldn't be able to stand it.

"Sorry," the spy said, his crossbow always at the ready. "Afraid we can't read the writing around here."

"You both need to study more," the cleric replied, reaching down for the papers at her feet. There were quite a few of them, many of the pages all but bursting with writing. It would take some time to find what she was looking for.

Which means you're up, God.

"*Watchman of the Candle, out of this googol of beams of light, show me that illumination I seek.*" The cleric grasped the holy symbol hanging underneath her guard's tunic, invoking the Search miracle.

In an instant, her mind was full of the contents of all the texts in front of her, until she felt light settle on one place in particular. "Ah, here it is." She knelt down on a carpet saturated with wine and brains, and grabbed a few pages that had fallen in an inconspicuous corner. They had something to do with some kind of national secret, information about the castle in the capital. It looked like a floor plan—a very recent one. Escape routes and everything… Unless this was all just the prime minister's plotting.

Personally, I'd love to read everything here, the cleric of the God of Knowledge thought, almost quivering with a catlike curiosity. But it was all need-to-know, so to speak. If she didn't need it for the run, best not to know it. The cleric gathered up her haul, tucking the pages into a cylinder and sealing it shut.

Need to know or not, a little chatter wouldn't hurt. The cleric allowed a thin smile to creep onto her face. "Wonder who the johnson was who wanted this guy killed."

"Who knows? Maybe the family of one of the slaves he bought. Or maybe one of the people he kidnapped was nobility or something…" The spy offered the cleric some mild congratulations on completing her job, and she nodded in return.

"You make enough enemies, this is how you end up," the red-haired girl remarked. It was an uncommonly cold thing to say, for her.

The spy just shrugged, but as for the cleric, she could think of a few possible motivations. Changelings were few and far between— valuable. And this one could use magic. There were some out there who wouldn't hesitate to kidnap her. To do terrible things to her friends to get her. The world was divided into three categories: those who took, those who were taken from, and those who survived.

Ahh stop, stop.

It was all just idle speculation on her part. No evidence, no proof, and the only answers were locked up in her friend's heart. One could imagine endless reasons a person might engage in shadowy work like this. There was the spy, who had replaced lost body parts with forbidden magic. The driver, who had taken on the debt of a woman it seemed he barely knew. The fixer, forever laughing, and the mage who supported the group without ever showing what they looked like for whatever reason.

But who needed reasons? They all got along well. It was a good party, she thought.

For that matter, it was something of a riddle why the cleric had thrown herself into this world of shadows. She didn't tell anyone her reasons, and they were polite enough not to ask. She would respect their silence in return.

"All right, I'm done here."

"Got it," the red-haired elf said. Then she whispered, "*Umbra fac simile.* Make me darkness, as you are…," and touched her own shadow.

In obedience to the whispered true words, the shadow swelled and took on volume, assuming the shape of a stretcher. Most convenient. Especially when there was a limit to how much you could carry with you. "Charisma's still in effect, so let's do this while we can."

"On it." The spy nodded, and with his strength enhanced by that spell, he was easily able to heft the dead captain and drop him on the stretcher. He tore down the nearest curtain he could find and draped it over the body. "One wounded hero, ready for service."

Now they could march right out the front gate and get away in the waiting carriage. It was precisely in these chaotic, "crude" situations that one needed to be most technical.

"I'll hold the other end," the red-haired elf said, going around to the back of the stretcher.

"Thanks," came the spy's response. He held up his end of the stretcher with one hand, keeping his crossbow ready in the other. "Just pretend you're holding it up. It's fine."

Guess he doesn't need our help with that strength.

The cleric didn't want to get in the way. The thought brought an amused smile to her face. There were other objects in the room, like a halberd and a helmet, that looked like they could fetch a pretty price—but so it went.

"We're transporting the wounded! Everyone out of the way!"

The three of them flew through the halls with the corpse on the stretcher. They shoved soldiers out of the way, keeping the crossbow focused ever forward, occasionally loosing a killing bolt against a goblin...

"Hey," the red-haired elf said as they passed a motley party going the other direction. She seemed to be looking at a petite female cleric—a servant of the Earth Mother, it looked like.

"Everything okay?" the spy asked.

"Yeah, no problem," the elf said with a motion of her head. But the spy, like the cleric, would have picked up on the quiet prayer for success she then offered. Neither of them said anything, though. If there was someone in there she actually wished to pray for, then good.

Suddenly, the hallway—no, the entire fortress—gave a great shake. "Yikes..." The spy caught the elf and kept her from falling even as he prepared to react with his crossbow; the cleric closed her eyes and, just for a second, sent her consciousness into the void.

"Wow...," she marveled, more or less without meaning to. It was unreal—downright impressive, even. "Those adventurers summoned the sand mantas somehow. The mantas! Can you believe it?"

"It's a glitch!" the spy shouted. "Dammit, these people have no manners."

"Let's keep moving, or we'll be going down with this place," the red-haired elf said. Then she chuckled to herself. There was something to be said for panache.

"We just have to deliver these papers, right?" the cleric mumbled, without much interest. She wanted to get them off her hands before she was tempted to read them. "Do you know where we're going?"

"Yeah." The spy smiled. The red-haired elf caught his eye and smiled, too. Another mystery. Admittedly, one it would be rather nosy to try to solve.

"Here's what happens: We go, we give them the thing, we come back, we get our money, we go home."

Whatever happened to the rest of the soldiers in this stronghold, or whatever happened to this country, was no concern of theirs. They were just villains who killed for money, assassins who ran through the shadows. They weren't champions of justice, and they weren't out to set the world to rights: They were rogues. In the end it was just them in the dark, with nothing but their skills to rely on, "no hit no run," no one to collect their corpses if they died.

Let the adventurers and the heroes handle the dragons.

CHAPTER 6

NEVER EVER CUT A DEAL WITH A DRAGON

Dragon.

What can be said about the creatures that bear that name that hasn't already been said? The earth-shaking, sky-shattering roar. The shining red scales. The hot breath reeking with sulfurous miasma. The impossibly sharp claws, fangs, and tail. Creatures with enough treasure to fund an entire nation, intelligence that outstrips the greatest sages, and eternal life.

And one of them, among the most powerful life-forms in the Four-Cornered World, was standing before the adventurers now.

"GROOGB! GOORGGBBB!!" And on its back rode a gloating, cackling goblin.

"…This is like some bad joke," Goblin Slayer said, almost in spite of himself, and who could blame him?

Then the aggrieved red dragon struck out with its long, coiled neck, catching the pillars around the party in the blow. The adventurers had jumped backward almost before the dragon moved, so they were unharmed, but rubble and gold coins flew around like projectiles.

"GGOOGRGGBB!!" Seeing the adventurers raise their shields or crouch down to avoid the flying debris, the goblin rider gibbered irritably. He pulled the reins in every direction, and each time he did so, the dragon would twitch with evident anger.

High Elf Archer, who had jumped to another pillar, sounded

©Noboru Kannatuki

uncharacteristically bitter for a high elf as she exclaimed: "How does a dragon let itself get harnessed by a goblin?!"

"Oh, I think that goblin only *believes* he is in control," Lizard Priest said, far more at ease—perhaps even excited—than the situation would seem to warrant as he slapped the ground with his tail. "The dragon, in my estimation, is paying him no mind."

"You think Communicate could get us out of this, Scaly?!"

"Ha-ha-ha, this poor beast has just woken up and has no interest in conversing with anyone. My humble prayer would hardly make a difference."

"But we can't fight a dragon...!" The words escaped Priestess without her really meaning them to. Regardless, they weren't an expression of defeatism. Merely a recognition of the reality of the situation.

Dragon Slayer! Dragon Buster! Dragon Valor! These were names given only to the greatest heroes of legend. Many adventurers had challenged these monsters, and only a handful had emerged victorious. It was a strenuous test. The party had just finished an entire adventure in this desert land; in their exhausted state, it would be suicide to challenge this beast. Adventures always entailed some measure of danger, but there was no call to foolishness or recklessness.

"Half-hearted attacks aren't going to get us anywhere," Goblin Slayer said, quickly appraising the situation in the hopes of seizing the initiative. "I believe a quick strike is our only option, but what do you think?"

"I very much agree," Lizard Priest replied immediately. "Battle has been rather constant for us. We are much spent."

"And we haven't got many resources left—magically, I mean. I think we do this in the first shot, or not at all...though I don't like it." Dwarf Shaman was frowning; he had a catalyst from his bag in his hand and was summoning the last of his strength. "Stone Blast won't even scratch it."

"In that case..."

Lightning. Priestess said the word without speaking it. Female Merchant's face became a mask of anxiety and terror and determination, but she nodded. "I'll...I'll give it my best shot!"

They didn't have long for this little strategy session with the enemy right in front of them, and now the adventurers went decisively into action.

"Y-yaaaahhh!" Female Merchant cried. To repeat, adventuring is always dangerous, but simple foolishness or recklessness is no adventure. Yet, when Female Merchant summoned all her courage and launched herself forward, none could deny her valor. How many would have had the nerve to do as she did when confronted with a dragon?

"I'll cover you!" High Elf Archer shouted and went hopping through the ruins, firing a series of arrows to draw the enemy's attention. Needless to say, although containment may have been her only goal, her aim was unerring. She hit the dragon in the eye and landed a shot on the goblin rider. But the armor class of those scales was too high.

At the same time, Female Merchant interlaced her fingers, focusing on an image of lightning. She bit her lip, concentrating as hard as she could on her spell, staring down the dragon even though she was pale with fear.

Or was she staring at the goblin on the dragon's back?

"*Tonitrus...oriens...iacta!* Rise and fall, thunder!" She formed the sigil of the spell and thrust her hands forward, and a white bolt of electricity came howling forth.

There was an instant between when the crackling snake left her fingers and when it reached the dragon, and Goblin Slayer didn't miss it.

"Hraaah...!" He spun the sword in his hand into a reverse grip, then took one step, two steps, three, and flung it as hard as he could. All but invisible against the great white flash, the weapon hurtled through the air toward the goblin.

But then the lightning ricocheted away. Perhaps the magical power in the dragon's scales, or in its eyes, was simply too much. The creature gave a lazy flap of its wings, as if swatting away a fly, and Goblin Slayer's sword was smacked down and broken. "Wha...?!"

"Eek?!"

And then the red dragon roared.

The rumble of it wiped out the crack of thunder from a moment earlier, shaking the air around them. If one were to hack away at a stringed instrument while wearing thick leather gloves, perhaps one could catch the faintest echo of this sound.

The pressure of the sound wave easily cost Female Merchant her balance, and she went tumbling to the ground.

"Hrm...!" Goblin Slayer, for his part, was already moving. Perhaps it was the grit of a Silver-ranked adventurer at work. Or maybe he was just putting into practice his master's old advice: *"Anyway, keep moving!"*

Whichever it was, he was in time. He swept Female Merchant up while she was still squeaking and shaking and dove into the shadows of a pile of loot.

"Eep?!" Female Merchant exclaimed, but he ignored her, putting her in front of him and shielding her from the rush of wind with his back. There was a whirlwind as the dragon took in a breath so deep it seemed it might use all the air around, its throat and chest expanding dramatically.

"...?!" Even Priestess could tell what this meant. She clutched her sounding staff, almost stumbling forward as she brought the words of her prayer to mind. But...

I'm not going to make it...!

This was the reality: One small human girl was going to find it very difficult to seize the initiative.

The dragon's jaws opened. She could even see the blinding light hovering behind its fangs. The light that would mean death itself if she couldn't avoid it. Search as one might, one would find nothing in any of the four corners of the world that could stop it. It would scorch a hero's armor, blacken the white walls of a castle—indeed, if it didn't simply melt them away.

Sweat beaded on Priestess's forehead. Her hands shook. Even here in front of a dragon, she tried to weave together the words of a prayer...

"O Dilophosaur, though it be false, grant to my breath the miasma that proceeds from your organs!"

Before she could get the words out, though, a massive form leaped in front of her with animal agility. Lizard Priest sucked in the biggest breath of air he could, then released it with all his strength. "Kaaaaaahhh!"

The dragon's breath collided with Lizard Priest's own burning exhalation.

The blinding, searing cloud expanded through the ruins faster than the Wind of the Red Death. Lizard Priest met it head on, but even he was at a disadvantage here. He was pushed slowly, ever so slowly, backward, scales melting and falling away with the poison. "Nrrrgh...!"

"No, stop...!" This time, Priestess was not too late. She rushed toward the lacerating heat, placed a hand on Lizard Priest's back, ignoring the way it burned the flesh of her palm, and prayed. *"O Earth Mother, abounding in mercy, lay your revered hand upon this child's wounds!"*

Let the blessings of the Earth Mother be upon him!

Using Protection might well have cost her her life. She was thinking in part of the dancing girl's performance. But what power was more fitting than that of the Earth Mother to resist a dragon's poison befouling the land? In response to this faithful disciple's prayer, a divine miracle protected and healed the lizardman's huge body. The skin that looked like it had been about to melt off the bone regained its power immediately, and Lizard Priest steadied himself on the ground.

"Ha-ha! Compared with the Fusion Blast of my forebears, this is nothing!"

When the smoke from the dragon's breath cleared, Lizard Priest was still standing proud, ready for more. The girl who had fought so hard to save his life, and all his other companions, were at his back. Defeat—death that does not bring forth life—was the shame of a lizardman. Nor was it proper to use weapons and equipment against such a powerful enemy as this. Lizard Priest flourished his claws and fangs and tail as he prepared to face the dragon, howling out: *"O proud and strange brontosaurus, grant me the strength of ten thousand!"*

Then he flew at the enemy with a shriek, his limbs lashing out, colliding with the claws of the red dragon.

But even this could be only for so long. His forefathers' strength would not last forever. The creature in front of them might have been young, but it was still a dragon. Even a lizardman could not resist it.

Priestess, determined not to waste the time that he bought, tried to breathe evenly as she worked her way backward. Maybe that last miracle had taken a lot out of her, or maybe it had something to do with the dragon's breath, but her vision seemed dim; everything around looked so dark. She couldn't quite seem to get breath into her lungs. Her arms and legs felt numb, and she stumbled the last few steps.

"GOOROOGGBBB!!" The way the goblin cackled even though he probably hardly understood what was going on irritated her immensely. Clutching her staff, her eyes brimming with tears, Priestess still managed to fix the monster with a glare. She wasn't weeping from fear. It was simply the way her body responded as she battled the pain.

How could it be from fear? I'm not afraid.

"You all right?!" High Elf Archer shouted to Priestess, jumping down from one of the pillars and running over to Goblin Slayer and Female Merchant. She kept shooting as she went to buy them time to get on their feet and to help back up Lizard Priest. But the bud-tipped bolts bounced off the dragon's scales, and the rare shot that did stick surely did the monster no harm at all. She could try to aim at the goblin instead, but each time the dragon flapped its mighty wings, her arrows went spiraling away. The goblin was convinced it was his tugging on the reins that was causing this and was looking quite pleased with himself…

High Elf Archer ground her perfect teeth and turned to Dwarf Shaman. "Don't you have some kind of dwarf magic that can do something about this thing?!"

"Stupor, Sleep… It's too big for anything I've got!" Dwarf Shaman replied, a dispiritingly rational answer. He had one hand in his bag of catalysts, but he didn't unleash Stone Blast, just coldly surveyed the scene of battle. He understood that if Lightning couldn't stop this thing, his own spells weren't likely to break through its defenses.

How he chose to use his few remaining spells could determine the party's destiny. One who simply intoned whatever came to mind without considering the consequences would not survive very long.

"Might get the goblin to fall asleep, but when the dragon moves, he'll wake up again. Not going to knock them both out, I'm afraid."

"Can you do just the dragon, then?!"

"Then the goblin would give the dragon a whack and wake *it* up!"

What to do, then?

Goblin Slayer groaned from the burning on his back but slowly rose up. The Dragon might have just woken up, but apparently it wasn't upset enough to incinerate its own hoard; Goblin Slayer didn't appear to have any injuries to his limbs. Pain meant one was alive, that one could move. There was no problem.

"Are you all right?"

"I-I'm sorry…," Female Merchant said in a small, trembling voice. She was still curling into herself, her body tense. Her short-cut hair, her excellent clothing, and the rapier at her hip all showed no sign of scorching. His master had told him that having something between it and an explosion or fire did a lot for the human body, and it seemed he had been right. Privately thanking his master from the bottom of his heart, Goblin Slayer took Female Merchant's arm and pulled her to her feet.

They were fighting a dragon, and they still hadn't suffered any losses. He thought that was a pretty good job for someone as witless as he was. Not, of course, that he had done it all on his own.

"But there is no room for error…" He shook his helmeted head, forcing himself to focus, and then he took stock of the situation. Lizard Priest had the red dragon in check, but the next round of its breath would likely overwhelm him. Goblin Slayer suspected the only reason any of them were still alive was because the dragon was still shaking off sleep.

The dragon is not protecting that goblin, he concluded. No dragon could be controlled by the likes of a goblin. At least not so long as there were no goblins with dragon blood in their veins, but such a ridiculous thing could not exist. That left one explanation. *It's trying to knock the goblin off.*

Yes, that was it. The dragon had awoken, bad mood and all, when a goblin had jumped on its back. But that didn't mean they could leave well enough alone or try to simply run away. Once the dragon got its wits about it, it would smash the goblin, kill all the adventurers, and give one of its great roars. And the next meal it would find would be the women who had been saved from the goblin breeding ground.

In other words, as ever, goblins are at the root of all my problems.

"If I take out the goblin, do you think you can get the dragon back to sleep?"

"I can at least give it a try!" Dwarf Shaman pounded himself on the chest.

"Good enough."

Goblin Slayer nodded. Their collective stamina was much reduced. They had few spells left. He had lost his weapon. He had comrades. Former captives were behind him. His enemy was a goblin. The situation was grim.

But what about it?

He almost thought he could hear the sound of dice rolling in the heavens. He groaned softly. He didn't care about them.

Now it's only a matter of do or do not.

He pulled a stamina potion from the item pouch at his hip, popped the stopper and poured it through his visor in one gulp. It was better than no relief at all. He tossed the bottle aside, then took his item pouch clear off his belt.

"You know how to use this, right?"

"Huh? Oh…!"

He tossed the pouch to Priestess, who scrambled in surprise but managed to catch it.

His equipment: He was entrusting it to her. She found that gave her strength.

"…Yes, sir!"

"Take care of it, then."

Priestess nodded energetically; Goblin Slayer simply placed a rough, gloved hand firmly on Female Merchant's shoulder. She stiffened. The young woman looked upset—was it from anxiety? Fear, maybe? Her eyes appeared to be wavering, but Goblin Slayer looked right into them from within his helmet.

"I'm going to kill all the goblins. That hasn't changed."

Female Merchant swallowed. She clenched her fist to still the trembling of her hands. Then she nodded. "Right. I understand."

"Good."

All was well, then. What he had to do next was clear. He would kill the goblin. All he had to do was focus on that. Goblin Slayer looked at Lizard Priest fighting the dragon and then at the rest of his party. "I'm going to do it now. Back me up."

"Against a dragon! All right, this just got interesting!"

Goblin Slayer and High Elf Archer started moving at almost the same instant, kicking up gold coins from the ground as they went. But the high elf quickly overtook the human, jumping from one pillar to the next, finding her aim.

She took three arrows from her quiver. Then she loosed them in a literal rain. They flew faster than the speed of sound, rocketing toward the dragon's eye, its throat, and the goblin on its back. But none of them could penetrate the dragon's defenses. For a red dragon, the puny arrows and the obnoxious goblin were both only as annoying as flies. The creature shifted irritably, and the arrows bounced off it scales with a dry *clack-clack-clack*.

What I wouldn't give for a dwarf-forged wind lance and some black arrows right now...! High Elf Archer thought, a very frustrating thing for an elf to have to think. She compensated by shouting, "What are you doing down there, dwarf?!"

"Pipe down, I've got my own way of handling things!" Dwarf Shaman replied with rather familiar conversation. But sweat was beading on his forehead, and his concentration was worn down to the nub.

He was going to try to cast a spell on a dragon. It was an all-or-nothing gamble. If he didn't use everything he had at this moment, when would he? They had nothing to spare. Well, the adventurers didn't. The same couldn't be said of the dragon.

Whoosh. Sand particles jumped up from the ground as the air went rushing by, and High Elf Archer's ears flicked.

"Hnrr...rrrgh...ghhh!" The Partial Dragon miracle was still in effect, but blood was pouring from Lizard Priest's body. Even so, he laughed aloud as if he was truly enjoying this, the crazy thing; he faced down his adversary, but it couldn't last long. The red dragon opened its jaws wide, sucking air into its lungs once again.

Dragon breath!

If they got hit with another one of those monstrous exhalations, neither Lizard Priest nor any of them would walk away. The flesh would rot off their bones in the heat and poison, and they would die where they stood. In this, the high elf—the descendant of fae who had lived for virtually eternity—was no different from any of them. She felt the fear of encroaching death just as they did. Yet, she didn't run but nocked another arrow into her bow and pulled back the string. She had to aim. Take aim at the—

"The jaws!" Lizard Priest howled. "We bite with great force, but the muscles that keep our jaws open are much weaker!"

"That's it! Here...goes...nothing!" High Elf Archer looked up at the heavens, then loosed the arrow with all the strength she had.

The instant the arrow was away, she started running, rushing through the wind, toward the blinding light in the dragon's jaws—she was heading just underneath it. Even as she slid and twisted, the next arrow was already in her hand. "Take *this*!" she shouted, firing the bolt straight upward. Just as she had planned, it lodged in the dragon's lower jaw.

Suddenly, the arrowhead was not a bud but a flower and then a seed. At the exact same instant, the arrow she had fired from above came rushing down like shooting stars, slamming into the dragon's upper jaw.

The jaws met with a *slam*, and an explosion began inside the creature's mouth.

"GOORGBB?!" the goblin on the dragon's back screeched as it was licked by the flames coming out of the creature's mouth. The goblin gave a hard pull on the reins.

As for the dragon, it could by no means be killed by its own flames; even the poisons in its breath would not be fatal. But the goblin on the dragon's back, so confident that no one could touch him? He was a different matter.

"GOROGBB?! GOOROOGBB?!?!"

Goblin Slayer saw it all as he ran straight toward the monster. He stayed low, dodging the flying debris and treasure that the flailing dragon kicked up. He suddenly found himself remembering the story of a legendary king that his sister had once told him.

His helmet was suffocating, his shield too heavy—wasn't that it?

That king had challenged, not a dragon, but a transformed god. Goblin Slayer wished he had even one ten-thousandth of that courage.

He grasped his shield and, without hesitation, threw it aside. What he needed was speed and mobility. He would not take off his helmet, though. However much it might restrict his vision, he couldn't afford to risk being hit in the eyes at a moment like this.

He had only one goal. To kill the goblin. And how could he do that? In his proverbial pocket, he had everything he needed.

Goblin Slayer grabbed a sword out of the pile of loot, an enchanted blade whose name he didn't know. Answering the warrior who had taken it up after all its many years of sleep, the blade glowed a golden color.

"Now...!"

The girls sprang into action. They had been watching the battle, biding their time, and if they didn't move with utmost speed, they certainly acted with precision.

Female Merchant leaped forward in front of the dragon, whipping her hands into a sigil. Long, long ago, great braves had used this spell to defeat evil sorcerers and send demons back to the hell from whence they came. It *had* to work on a dragon, she told herself, focusing on her enemy through a haze of fear and vision blurred by tears.

"Together now!" she called out as Priestess arrived beside her. The bag was in her hands. The gear she had received from the master she respected so much. She knew what she had to get out of it. The same thing that had once saved their own lives.

"Right!" Priestess nodded firmly to her. Then they counted, one, two...!

"Tonitrus! Oriens! Iacta!"

"Yaaaaahhh!!"

As purple electricity shot from Female Merchant's hands, Priestess flung the bottle. The lightning went everywhere. The bottle crashed against the dragon's face and shattered open to release a dark, viscous liquid. The dragon roared. No sooner had it landed than it ignited into flame. The stuff went by many names: Medea's Oil, petroleum, Iranistan's fire. In short...

"Burning water!"

Even a great red dragon couldn't abide getting fire in its eyes and being struck directly by lightning. With a roar like the crazed strumming of a stringed instrument, it flailed its massive neck. It was, of course, paying no attention to whatever might be on its back.

Goblin Slayer didn't miss his chance. "Hrrrah!"

He had practiced this. His footing was sure. His aim was true. He could feel the weight of the sword in his hand. Now all he had to do was throw.

The adventurer called Goblin Slayer took the nameless, enchanted blade and flung it as hard as he could. We cannot know who forged this weapon, but they would surely have been pleased to hear of its fate. After wasting away in a dragon's treasure hoard for so long, it would finally know battle again, casting aside any lingering dissatisfaction with its existence.

Whether it be wielded against a red dragon or a mere goblin, to faithfully serve its master is a weapon's pride.

There was a golden flash like daybreak, as if the sun were rising here and now. The enchanted blade became a single ray of light, piercing the goblin's neck like a hungering fang, tearing through his throat. Even at the very last instant, the goblin rider did not realize he was dead.

His decapitated head still jabbered as it tumbled down off the blade, which had lodged itself in one of the stone pillars.

"An awfully grand death for a goblin," Goblin Slayer spat as the rest of the rider's corpse slid off the dragon's back. What happened next was out of Goblin Slayer's hands. But he had faith.

"Sandman, Sandman, rasp of breath, kin to th' endless sleep of death. A song we offer, so take your sand and on our dreams now place your hand."

He was confident that the most capable spell caster he knew would not slip up at a moment like this.

When Dwarf Shaman tore up a piece of paper and scattered it about, the sand around them began to swirl up once more. It formed a gigantic corkscrew, and amazingly, immediately swallowed up the red dragon. The creature's massive body listed to one side.

Claws had not scratched it, arrows had not pierced it, lightning had not hurt it, fire had hardly burned it. But now, it wobbled like a great tree in a storm—and then fell over, almost as if it were being sucked back down into the hole from which it had emerged. There was a

©Noboru Kannatuki

crash from deep underground, a literal earthquake, as if to prove it was gone.

The red dragon was defeated. The adventurers had been pushed to the limits of their endurance and had put the creature to its slumber at last.

§

"……"

They stood all but doubled over, their breath coming hard. They were still trying to take in the situation. They couldn't see the dragon anymore, and they heard the gentle rumble of its snoring, but somehow it still didn't quite seem real.

Even as they acknowledged the fact of their achievement, they still felt no triumph or joy. All of them were smeared with soot and dark smoke. The stench of sulfur and miasma clung to them, and their heads hurt. Their skin was preternaturally dry from exposure to the great heat, and their eyes and throats burned. Some of them wanted nothing more than to jump into a river right about now. Others would have given anything for a drink of wine.

As for Goblin Slayer, he just wanted to go home. Go home and eat some stew and sleep.

Or perhaps he was dreaming now. He could hardly believe such a thing had actually happened to him. It was like the silly imagining of some child.

"Ah…"

Then it came to him. He had felt lost before this battle, a feeling that vanished entirely during the fight. He picked up a single red scale that had been torn off during the battle, but when he moved to put it by his hip, he was reminded that he didn't have his pouch.

"…Here you go." Priestess jogged up to him and handed him the pouch with an exhausted smile.

"Thank you," Goblin Slayer said and took it, then tucked the scale carefully inside.

"What are you going to do with that?"

"A gift," he said.

He had no interest in taking any of the dragon's treasure. It was said that if you took even a single gold coin from a dragon's hoard, it would chase you to the grave to get it back. There was even a story of a land where the vassals of a certain councilor had stolen a cup and been burned up by a dragon, which the aged king had then destroyed all by himself.

What was more, though—Goblin Slayer had no desire to obtain treasure. He was already satisfied. He knew from experience that giving her money only seemed to make her angry.

"She had one particular request—but as for anything more, I couldn't decide what to do."

That was all it took. Those words cut the tension among the party, and suddenly everyone relaxed. The first to let out a sharp breath and toss herself backward into the sand was High Elf Archer. "Are we alive? We *are* alive, aren't we? I kinda can't believe it."

"Yes, we are alive. 'By the skin of our teeth,' I believe the expression is." Lizard Priest sounded downright easygoing—and the nod he gave was truly satisfied. The strength of his forefathers had already fled his body, and blood seemed to be pouring out of him. But he looked almost pleased about this, making a strange hands-together gesture of thanks to his forebears. "I did not imagine that one so small and weak as myself might be blessed with the chance to confront a dragon!" Still grinning, he began to intone prayers of healing.

High Elf Archer remarked that "Oh yeah, he'd had one miracle left, hadn't he?"

"...You think this makes us dragon slayers?" she asked after a moment.

"More like dragon sleepers," Dwarf Shaman said, sitting down heavily. "Not quite as, uh, cool." He sounded distinctly sour about it. "As if we were ever going to beat a dragon fighting like that," he spat out. He turned his flask upside down over his mouth, licking out the last drops of wine. "Not to mention when we get home, I'll have to make up a song about this adventure. Gods, it makes my head hurt..."

He continued to complain: This was why he hated relying on the Sandman.

"Want some help?" High Elf Archer offered, but he snorted, "Don't need it."

In the blink of an eye, they had gone from this simple disagreement to a full-fledged, classic argument. Priestess, finding the familiar sound oddly sleep-inducing, let out a little yawn.

"I'm…tired," said Female Merchant, sitting down as if her legs had failed her. She probably didn't have the strength to get up. *Exhaustion* had never seemed a better descriptor of what they were feeling. Priestess, feeling much sympathy with Female Merchant, sat down beside her. Her whole body felt heavy; she let out another yawn. "Me too."

"Let's stay at least a day in town," Female Merchant said, after murmuring to herself. "Yes, that's a good idea. We can take a bath. I *will* take a bath."

Priestess chuckled and nodded at her. As they sat there side by side, their heads bumped into each other. They couldn't even sit up straight anymore. They leaned against each other for support, and Female Merchant's warmth made Priestess even sleepier.

Maybe the Sandman is…still here…

A third yawn accompanied the thought. As she rubbed her eyes, she heard Lizard Priest laughing. "After goblins, a dragon. Whoever the enemy commander may have been, they chose a poor way of doing things."

"…?" Priestess, not understanding, opened her mouth in an effort to ask what he meant.

"It's a warning from the Age of the Gods." The answer came from Goblin Slayer, busy emptying the contents of a canteen into his visor. "My master mentioned it to me once."

It is said, one must not cast the good "pawns" after the bad.

"It means that when you've been defeated, you shouldn't be so set on using up your trump card."

That made sense. Priestess nodded. She didn't understand it completely, but it made a certain kind of sense. Her thinking didn't quite seem steady; thoughts with no context bubbled up and then faded away.

Someday, a dragon.

She remembered the red-haired wizard saying something like that. Not the elf. Someone more familiar—just the once.

The boy with a sword. The girl with black hair. They hadn't all had time to get to know one another, yet still the words had been said. They had been a sort of promise, a sort of wish, a sort of hope.

"Warnings? I know one, too."

Someday. Someday, certainly. But for now...

"Never make a deal with a dragon."

For now, it was a bit too soon for dragon slaying.

CHAPTER 7

ONE JUMP AHEAD

"And that's how I think the adventure would go!" Guild Girl said, holding up an index finger and smiling.

"Hmmm…" Cow Girl tilted her head, not quite sure how to respond.

It was just before noon at the Adventurers Guild—the people who had gone out weren't back yet, and the people who hadn't were still sleeping. The formerly crowded front desk was devoid of people now, and Guild Girl had time to spare. And so she engaged Cow Girl, who was afraid she might be intruding, in idle chatter over tea.

Flying carpets, spirits in lamps, burning water, star-sand…

The desert country, which Cow Girl had heard of but never seen, seemed fantastical, full of so many impossible things that a thousand and one nights wouldn't have been time enough to tell them all. She decided that when he got home, she would probably ask him about it. She had all kinds of questions—and perhaps he would have things he wanted to talk about as well.

This was what she had wanted to do once, long, long ago.

"Well, in any case…as long as everyone gets home safely, that's what matters." She smiled with a hint of difficulty. New lands meant unknown dangers and monsters.

This was an adventure unlike his others, in a place unlike any he had ever been. Sometimes adventurers left in high spirits and with high expectations and never came back. Adventuring was always dangerous. If it was completely safe, if you could be totally sure you'd come home, then it couldn't be called an adventure.

"They're all seasoned veterans now, and I'm sure they know what they're doing. But…" Even so, it was hard to be the one who had to wait and worry. Guild Girl played with the quill pen she was holding, looking despondent.

Cow Girl understood those feelings very well. She didn't know much about this occupation called adventuring. She saw adventurers from time to time when she stopped off at the Guild to deliver provisions. There was the one who carried the huge sword on his back and the one who was never far from his spear. Then there was the witch with the wide-brimmed hat. Cow Girl herself had relied on them before, and she had every reason to hope they would come home safely. And if Guild Girl shared those same feelings, then…

"I think he's just fine," Cow Girl informed her with a smile.

"Hmm?" Guild Girl said, blinking. "How's that again?"

"Yesterday. A lumpy donkey arrived, supposedly sent by him."

In other words, that was the reason for Cow Girl's good mood. He had remembered the simple conversation they'd shared before he left. And at least until the moment he had requested that thing, he had been safe.

…Would it have killed him to include a letter or something, though?

He did have his own strange sense of how to be considerate: He had included a manual detailing the care and feeding of the creature.

"Oh, a…*camel*, was it?"

"Camel?"

Ah, that's right, camel, Cow Girl remembered now. She thought it was such a strange name. The "lumpy donkey" was a camel. Something she had always thought belonged only to fairy tales, which she had now seen with her own eyes. When he got home, she would tell him what she had named it—although she thought he might know.

Could that "camel" possibly be his idea of a souvenir?

Well…with him, it's hard to say. She giggled at the thought, waving a hand when Guild Girl gave her a strange look. "Anyway…," Cow Girl said, keen to change the subject, "…is it okay that we got so caught up in our little chat?"

"No, it isn't," Guild Girl replied with a smile. "I'm on the clock."

Cow Girl strived to keep her expression ambiguous so as not to draw attention to herself. She was thinking about her surprise to discover this side of this young woman.

I thought she was supposed to be a pampered young noble. And yet here Guild Girl was, having a pleasant conversation with her. Several years ago, she would never have imagined it of herself.

"Here I'd planned to do some paperwork today," Guild Girl lamented. "Our little secret, okay? Hee-hee." Then she discreetly showed Cow Girl some of the papers. Cow Girl couldn't help looking even as she asked herself whether this was really all right, and on the sheet she saw a familiar name. It was the cleric girl who worked with him.

"This is…what do you call it? For a promotion interview, right?"

She knew he had undergone several of those himself, such that he was now Silver-ranked. But she had never seen the paperwork before, and all she could do was exclaim in astonishment at it.

"She herself may not really realize it yet, but she has more than enough experience and ability…" Guild Girl straightened the papers with a quick rap on the desk and put them back in their place. "The realization will come naturally, as she works."

"True enough. It can be hard to really know what you can do or how well." Maybe people wouldn't fret so much about it if they could write out all their skills and abilities and qualities like labels on a product. Cow Girl briefly considered what her "stats" would be if she could quantify them and laughed aloud at how meaningless they would be. "I wonder if she's out there, sweating whether she'll be promoted or not."

"I doubt it. She's probably got her hands full with her adventure."

Maybe. Then again, maybe not.

I wonder what expression this woman will have on her face as she welcomes that girl home.

First, no doubt, she'd congratulate the group on its efforts. Then she would ask about the adventure. It would all be about goblins, no doubt. And then...then, she would certainly take great pleasure in changing the subject of the conversation to the promotion interview. The girl would flinch, then looked panicked, worried, and nervous one by one.

Ah...I see it.

Even Cow Girl was starting to get excited just imagining it. So much so that any anxiety all but disappeared.

"Is that how you survive the wait?" Cow Girl asked.

"Hmm," Guild Girl muttered, putting a finger to her lips thoughtfully. Then she nodded. "Yes...I suppose this is how I get through it."

Trusting they'll come home. Preparing the paperwork for when they do. Getting ready.

"Huh," Cow Girl said softly. She agreed completely. "Then... maybe I'll do the same thing."

She rose slowly from her chair. It would be lunchtime soon, and there would be more adventurers around.

She didn't know if it would be tonight, or tomorrow. So—well, she felt bad for Uncle, but...

"Oh, leaving already?"

"Yeah. Got to get dinner ready, you know?"

...tonight she would make plenty of stew and wait.

A NEW HOPE

When I opened my eyes, I was in a simple bed, the twin moons high in the sky, proving that it was late at night. My frail body shivered against the cold, and I curled into myself, hugging my slim shoulders. I had been given only a thin blanket and a one-piece garment with a hole for my head. And the indifferent starlight wasn't going to keep me warm.

The weight and chill of the collar and chains reminded me unpleasantly of where I was. It was pathetic enough to make a person want to cry—but it could have been worse.

True. For a moment there I wasn't sure I was going to survive.

Almost immediately after parting with the rogues, we were picked up by kidnappers, sold at a cheap price...

But I made it... If you can call winding up as a slave on a farm making it.

We could just count ourselves lucky that the farmers weren't too cruel. I clutched the golden charm that glimmered at my neck, grateful they hadn't taken it from me. Across the room, the rhea girl was snoring loudly, as if she hadn't a care in the world. We'd been friends a long time, and I had always found her impudent streak admirable and aggravating in equal measure.

I'm glad we at least wound up with personable masters. A corpulent, good-natured one, and a young man who seemed to be his nephew. The two of them treated us like slaves, yes, but quite well for all that.

They spoke to us almost the way one might to a friend or at least a servant. If it hadn't been for the mission with which I had been entrusted, I might have been more than happy to stay here for decades.

Although the young master does seem a bit reckless at times.

I couldn't resist a bit of a smile there in my freezing bed. Earlier today, I'd seen the young man get a scolding for starting a fight at the bar or something. Why were human youngsters always so eager to rush ahead with no thought for what might happen?

I must say, it makes little sense to me.

Born as an elf of the desert and nobility at that, I had long served as a lady-in-waiting to the royal family of this land, for generations, no less. And yet even now I didn't understand humans. Come to think of it, I had been the perpetual companion of the princess. I had never met such a straightforward young human.

As for my snoozing rhea friend…maybe she knew differently. Still unable to sleep, I looked out the window, up at the stars, but then finally shook my head.

Ugh, forget the stars. I should be thinking about the princess…

How could I help her? Should I break out of here? I didn't really want to make life that difficult for my new masters, but…

"…?!"

Suddenly there was a soft noise outside my room. I flicked my long ears and pulled up my bedsheets. Nobody could deceive the ears of an elf on a night as silent as this one.

As I expected, it was the young man standing in the doorway. I went still as a board in the bed, watching him with only my eyes.

"I-i-is something the m-matter, young sir…?" I privately chided myself for letting my voice tremble. But the young man didn't seem to notice. It appeared that his uncle, the owner of this place, had gone out in the middle of the night, and he wondered if we might know something. The uncle had claimed he would be back by morning, but something about him had seemed strange.

"It's true," I said, bracing myself against the bed under the covers and pushing myself up. "The master did go out. That much I know."

As I said, no one can sneak past an elf. Of course I noticed when the master left.

"Come to think of it… Someone did come to visit the master in the evening." I had been so busy with my work that I didn't even have the leeway to look up and see who it was, but I knew someone had been there. The master had accepted a message cylinder from them, checked the contents, and gone pale. "Perhaps that's connected somehow."

The young man looked very disturbed by this. He told me to wait a moment, then left the room, but he soon returned. In his hand was an old, but still truly brilliant, scabbard in which resided an elegant curved blade. It looked heavy, perhaps because the scabbard was made of lead. Now that I thought about it, I seemed to recall the young man had the same sword with him when he had gone to the tavern this afternoon.

"What manner of sword is that, sir…?"

He informed me that it was an heirloom passed down through his family. Many generations ago, one of his forebears had traveled to this place in order to seal away this sword. Privately, I thought that all seemed like a bit much work for one measly blade. Humans always had to be so dramatic about everything they did.

But I thought again when, with a look of absolute determination, the young man drew the sword from its sheath. At that instant, the charm at my neck began to jangle violently, producing an earsplitting screech. The sword glowed bluish-white and emitted a low thrum. It seemed absolutely imbued with magical power—and a fearsome aura of death.

"M-Master… That s-sword…" Now my voice was really shaking. Even my friend, who I had thought was asleep, sat up and looked wide-eyed at the blade. She whistled, impressed, and I didn't have the wherewithal to admonish her for it.

Gulp. The sound seemed so loud— Was that me swallowing?

Before I knew what I was doing, I had thrown myself at the feet of the young man, pressing my forehead to the ground. I couldn't even bring myself to hide anything anymore.

"Help!" I exclaimed. "Please, you must help her…!"

The princess—she was imprisoned in the castle. Her life was in danger! Tears started to pour from my eyes, so overwhelmed was I with emotion. The young man listened to me silently and finally responded with just a few quiet words:

He was a knight. Like his father before him.

§

Thus the young man, with the shimmering sword still shining in his hand, left with us, his servants, in tow. He was heading into the wild desert, where fearsome Chaos and evil plots were swirling. But the young man had no strength, no knowledge. Only courage.

Only the dice of Fate and Chance knew how the boy's adventure would turn out. Truth, Illusion, and all the many gods around their table could not imagine it. They did not know where his next step would take him nor where he would finally arrive. All of that would be determined by the boy's own will, swayed by the force of his own spirit.

But one thing, and one thing only, was sure. Like the adventure before his, his quest would become one known to all in song. Even a long time hence, in places far, far beyond the Four-Cornered World.

It is the tale of a new hope.

AFTERWORD

Hullo! Kumo Kagyu here! How did you like Volume 11 of *Goblin Slayer*? In this story, goblins appeared in the country of sand, so Goblin Slayer had to slay them.

I poured my heart and soul into writing it, so I would be thrilled if you enjoyed it.

When you do a job long enough, you find yourself having to do more than just your so-called job. Like say all you want to do is slay goblins, but somehow other things seem to keep coming up, too. Like maybe you were supposed to be slaying goblins, and suddenly something totally unexpected happens.

Like a surprise dragon.

So suppose you stay alert at all times so as not to run into any dragons. You take every precaution, prepare for every possibility, and are always careful not to have anything to do with them. But then one morning, you wake up, and for some reason you're in the morgue, with no memories, and your brain feels like an explosion!

…And then you find out it was a dragon pulling the strings all along that's left you like this, and all you can do is put your head in your hands.

A world where you can just bump into a wandering dragon is a pretty scary place, huh? No time for whining then. It's do or do not, kill or be killed.

However, it turns out dragon slaying isn't that easy!

But maybe you work really hard at it, and as a result, you find yourself involved in all sorts of things. Wouldn't that be nice? Heh!

Over the last several years, to my amazement and gratitude, I've received invitations to go to Taiwan, the United States, Germany, and Switzerland. The novels I wrote have been turned into manga then anime; they've been translated, and I have overseas fans now… It's like the ripple effect, or, you know, that thing about a butterfly flapping its wings. It's amazing to experience.

I'm utterly grateful for all of it, and none of it would have been possible without the support of everyone who has known and encouraged me. Thank you all so much.

I'm happy to report that we have another side story in addition to *Year One*, called *Dai Katana*. Again with your collective support, I hope this one will likewise be translated and introduced to readers overseas. Call it another "butterfly effect." It's really something.

Oops, I went on too long, and now I don't have room for all my usual thank-yous. Believe me, they're still there in my heart. Thank you to all my creative friends and gaming buddies. Thank you for the efforts of the aggregator blog admins.

Immense appreciation to Kannatuki for another volume's worth of fantastic illustrations. Thank you to everyone who was involved in editing, publishing, distributing, and marketing this book. And finally, profound thanks to all the readers who have encouraged me. I'm considering a short-story collection for the next volume, but rest assured that goblins will appear and have to be slain.

See you in Volume 12!